*B*ALTIMORE WAS SPObusier closer to O'Donnell Square and the restaurants. But since her dad lived a few streets over, there wouldn't be many people on the streets until the bars closed at two.

"His car's not there," her father said as they got closer.

"No. But he said he was going in the back, maybe he drove there?" Cassie headed around. She'd attended this school as a child, had met Michelle there. She remembered it as a place of constant excitement and commotion. But without the kids and teachers to fill it up with noise, attitude, and hopefully even some learning, the school was just an empty, desolate building.

They followed the alley to the back of the school. "Isn't that his car?" She peered into the dark. There was a car there, facing the back wall. She lifted her flashlight and aimed the beam at the car.

She dropped the flashlight. "Oh my God!"

TWO WRONGS DON'T MAKE A Write

Cathy Wiley

Dare to be Entertained.

Unique voices in fiction.

Books in the Cassandra Ellis series
Dead to Writes
Two Wrongs Don't Make a Write
Write of Passage (available in 2012)

More Zapstone Books
~~~~
Science Fiction/Action
T. M. Roy
*Convergence — Journey to Nyorfias*, Book 1
*Gravity — Journey to Nyorfias*, Book 2
*Stratagem — Journey to Nyorfias*, Book 3 (TBA)
~~~~
T.M. Roy and Sara V. Olds
Casualties of Treachery — The Ukasir's Own, Unit One
(check website for details)
~~~~
Sff-Romance
T.M. Roy
*Discovery — A Far Out Romance*
~~~~
Middle Reader/Historical
Sara V. Olds
Anna — A Farewell to Juarez
~~~~

Visit
www.zapstone.com
for the latest releases, updates, sneak previews, and more!

To contact, please email:
publisher@zapstone.com

Please write with any comments, concerns, or questions

TWO WRONGS DON'T MAKE A *Write*

A Cassandra Ellis Mystery

Cathy Wiley

A Zapstone Production

This novel is a work of fiction. Names, characters, places, and incidents are the products of the author's imagination or are used fictitiously. Any resemblance to actual persons, living or dead, or events, incidents, or organizations is entirely coincidental.

Copyright 2011 Cathy M. Wiley
All rights reserved.

Cover Design/Illustrations Copyright 2011 T.M. Roy www.TERyvisions.com

This book is protected under the copyright laws of the United States of America.
Any reproduction or other unauthorized use of the text or artwork contained herein for any reason is prohibited without the express written permission of Zapstone Productions LLC.

ISBN-10: 0-9826419-5-8
ISBN-13: 978-0-9826419-5-8

Trade Paperback Edition
Published by Zapstone Productions LLC

Library of Congress Catalog Number (LCCN): 2011944117

To Joshua Brayden and Josephine Marie, who, like this book, made their debut into the world this year.

Acknowledgements

For their advice and suggestions, I want to thank Aleta B., James C., Bryan E., Rachael G., Arlene J., Emily S., and Colin W.

Thanks to my friends and family for all of their support, especially my mother, Sharon, Tina, and Jenn.

I appreciate all the assistance from the members of my critique group, especially Mary N. for her edits and support.

And thank you especially to Terry, who once again, takes the words I write and makes them much, much better.

Cathy Wiley

TWO WRONGS DON'T MAKE A WRITE

A Cassandra Ellis Mystery

chapter 1

*N*OT AGAIN.

Not another murder.

She knew she should move, she should take immediate action—but all she could do was stare in shock and dismay at the lifeless form.

She thought she understood devastation the day she'd found her best friend's body. The day she'd arrived too late to prevent a senseless death.

But it was almost worse to see this kid, this young man barely out of high school, lying on the stained rug. All that youth, innocence, and opportunity wasted.

She reached in her purse for her cell phone and called 9-1-1. At the same time, she visually searched the room to see if she was right as to what caused this boy's death. By the time the emergency operator answered the call, she'd found the evidence.

"What is the nature of your emergency?"

"Another murder," she answered, staring at the cluttered kitchen table and the lonely bottle of Merlot surrounded by a jumble of empty beer cans. "I thought I was going to find the killer, but I think I just found another victim."

"I'm sorry, ma'am, can you explain? First, please state your name and location."

She quickly gave the necessary information, then took a deep breath. "You have to call the Homicide Department. I know that this isn't a regular death, it's murder. Someone poisoned—"

"Who's dead this time, Cassie?"

Cassie blinked away tears and struggled to focus as the voice interrupted her train of thought. She finally noticed the homicide detective standing next to her. "What makes you think someone's dead?"

"Your facial expression," James Whittaker answered.

Then he smiled, revealing the dimples that made her weak.

She decided the story she'd been working on could wait. She pushed the computer away and swiveled around. "What kind of facial expression?"

"You get this look on your face when you're writing a murder scene in a story. Typically though, it's fierce. This one was more sad." Leaning down, Whittaker kissed her lightly and smoothed a hand down her hair.

She could have told him that was a waste of time. These muggy Septembers in Baltimore wreaked havoc on her curls.

"Really? Well, it was a sad scene." Cassie hit save before she stood up from the table and walked across her kitchen, pausing to stop at the crockpot. She opened the lid and stirred the contents, breathing in the chili's spicy aroma. "It's usually a fierce look? I'm not sure what that says about me." After taking a bottle of water from the refrigerator, she turned and leaned against the counter. "I know what it says about you. It says you're trained at reading facial expressions and a good detective."

And a good-looking one, she thought, drinking in the sight of him as she drank in the cool water. Chiseled features, intense gray eyes, and thick dark hair.

"Damn right, I'm a good detective. A good cop. Unlike some." He stalked over to her refrigerator, deftly avoiding the cat that flopped on the floor in front of him.

She was surprised to see him pull out a beer, one of the few she kept for potential guests. He didn't drink at home very often. Her concern grew as he wrenched the cap off with such force it flew across the room. Her cat dashed after it.

"Hard day today?"

Whittaker shook his head as he took the bottle top from her cat, Donner, and placed it in the trash can. "Frustrating one. But I haven't seen you in almost a week. I didn't come over to talk about work. "

"Why not? You know I love to hear about it." She waved her hand at his automatic frown. "Yeah, yeah, I know, you're not supposed to give information to a civilian." She deliberately put a sneer into the last word and was rewarded when he grinned.

"How about a little later? Let me ease into it. Talking about easing into it—" Putting down the beer, he pulled her close and kissed her again, this time long and deep.

As the kiss intensified, Cassie realized he was trying to distract her—and boy, was he succeeding. Whenever he put this much effort into a kiss, it was hard for her to remember her own name, let alone what they were talking about.

Her only thought was happy relief that there were no longer any roadblocks to their relationship. When they'd met, Whittaker was investigating multiple homicides in which she was a potential suspect. Since he'd never seriously considered her guilty, she hadn't thought it was a big deal. He'd been worried that it would look improper, though, and had fought his attraction to her, while she fought to get him to relax his rules a little.

Now they were no longer fighting. In fact, it was quite the opposite.

After a few moments, he broke off the kiss and took a few steps back. Cassie was pleased that he seemed as breathless as she was.

He took a couple of deep breaths, picked up his drink, and took a swallow. "I hope it's okay I used my key to get in; you didn't answer when I knocked." Since he'd volunteered to cat-sit Donner while she was away on book tours, she'd given him a key.

She shrugged. "I don't mind at all. I tend to get totally wrapped up when I'm really in the writing groove."

He eased out of his black suit jacket and folded it carefully over the banister before sitting down at the kitchen table. He nodded at the laptop. "So, I assume you were working on *Merlot Murders*. What was with the tears? I thought you got them all out when you killed Elaine. I still can't believe you killed off a main character."

"Yeah, I can't either. Maybe I shouldn't have done that. It's really darkened the whole tone of the story. Of the series."

"Maybe you can change that."

"James! I'm three-quarters of the way through the book."

"At least you've got the option to hit delete and bring a victim back to life. I never get that option."

When he sighed, she wondered if that was what had him so moody this evening. No, he'd looked more angry than sad. She got up and sat on his lap. This way he couldn't escape when she pursued their earlier conversation. She knew he was trying to pay attention to her, but she could also tell he was distracted. "So, is it later enough that we can talk about your day?"

"Cassie—" He sighed.

"I know, I'm a pain. But first of all, I'm curious. Second of all, and more importantly, I'm worried about you. Does this have to do with a murder case?"

"No. No one is dead, unfortunately." He shook his head. "I shouldn't say that. I hate the son of a bitch, but I'm not going to wish him dead." He gently set her aside, stood up, and started pacing.

She had to smile. First of all, he was too tall to effectively pace in her cozy kitchen. Second, while pacing was one of her traits, it wasn't one of his. Did people in relationships pick up each other's quirks that quickly? After only two months—okay, one month and twenty days?

"To which son of a bitch are we referring?"

Even after only two months, she already knew him well enough to recognize that this degree of agitation was unusual for him. She ran through her list of suspects. He got along with his sergeant and all five detectives in his squad; they didn't usually receive such harsh descriptions. Detective Freeman, his preferred partner, teased him often, but the older man's ribbing had never garnered death wishes. There were some other long-time friends who might tease Whittaker, especially now that he was in a relationship, but as far as she knew, they didn't normally fight.

He stopped during one of his paces and faced her. "Detective Michael O'Reilly."

"A cop?"

He sneered. "In name only. He's a dirty cop."

"Really?" Cassie perked up at that; dirty cops could make for really interesting characters. Then she sobered. She forgot, sometimes, that Whittaker dealt with situations and people on a daily basis that were not fictional. "I mean, how do you know he's dirty?"

"Everyone knows he's dirty. IID knows it, too, they just can't prove it." He rolled his eyes in disgust.

From her interactions with police officers, even before she started dating Whittaker, she knew that was a typical reaction to any mention of the Internal Investigations Division, the section of the Baltimore City Police that monitored internal departmental concerns. She could understand their attitude, but as a civilian, she was glad there was a department to watch over police officers who might misuse their authority or commit crimes themselves.

"And while O'Reilly has gotten off mostly scot-free, he's the one who told IID, or IAB, since they were still the Internal Affairs Bureau then, that my father had been stealing money from evidence," Whittaker blurted. He finished his beer with a couple of quick swigs. "So today, I see him in the elevator and he makes some comment about asking me to say hello to my father. With some detectives from IID in the damn elevator with us."

"Oh," she said, realizing that this was the reason for his edginess. His hackles always went up if anyone mentioned his father. They were mostly estranged, even though his father lived only thirty minutes away, in Perry Hall. She also knew the basis for that estrangement: the elder Whittaker had left the police force under a cloud of shame.

She took a deep breath, deciding to take the plunge. "James, what did your father actually do? You've never told me the full story."

He sighed again, then went over to the fridge for another beer. She'd never seen him drink more than one beer in an evening, and he was about to drink two in an hour.

"You shouldn't drink alone," she said and grabbed one for herself. She also took a glass from the cabinet; her grandmother would have killed her for drinking beer straight from the bottle.

She followed him into the living room and sat next to him on the couch. Donner jumped up and burrowed between them, a furry chaperone.

They both took their first sips before he said anything. "I don't know the full story either, honestly. I'm not sure anyone knows the full story, other than my father, of course. Basically, the entire Drug Unit was having a problem. A huge problem that kept coming up at almost every drug trial. When an officer would testify about the amount of money confiscated from the dealer, the dealer would swear that it should have been more, that he'd been carrying more cash than that. The police department finally realized whenever the cash and other items were confiscated, someone was taking part of the money before delivering it to the Property Room."

"Wait, I remember this. The *Baltimore Dispatch* called it the Drug and Dollar Scandal." She curled her legs under her.

"Right. This came to the attention of the higher ups and they started to pull in some of the officers in the Drug Unit for interview. O'Reilly was one of them. He told them that my dad had been flashing money around, maybe they should check him out. When they did, they found some bank accounts he couldn't—and wouldn't—explain."

She rubbed a hand on his knee in comfort. "But I thought they didn't get enough evidence to prosecute."

He leaned his head back and stared at the ceiling. "They didn't; all they could do was suspend him while they investigated. But the media didn't respect that the investigation wasn't complete. Someone leaked Dad's name, and they broadcast his link to the scandal all over the news that night. Mom heard about it and freaked, since she'd wondered about these other bank accounts, too. She grabbed my sister and they moved out that night. By the time I got over there, she was gone."

"What did your Dad say?"

He shook his head and stared at his beer. "Nothing. Not a word. We just stared at each other. Then I left to go back to the Academy. Dad ended up quitting the next day or so, I think."

"Your father couldn't have been the only one."

"He wasn't. A few others did resign, but no proof was ever found to implicate anyone. It caused a huge shake-up in the police department. They pretty much transferred everyone out of the Drug Unit and into other positions, hoping that would clear up the mess. It seemed to work for a while, but then other issues cropped up. In yet another useless effort to clean things up, they brought in an entirely new administration to head up the internal investigations."

"That's right. About five years ago, I think?" She could remember that more clearly. That was about the time she'd started paying a lot more attention to police and their politics. "They brought in some big shot from another city, right?"

"Yes. Major Bianchi, out of Chicago." He rolled his eyes again. "Not that he gets Baltimore. At its heart, this is really just a big town, not a city."

Cassie smiled. She'd heard that said about Baltimore before and tended to agree with the sentiment. "And that's when they changed the name from Internal Affairs Bureau to Internal Investigations Division, right?

"Yes, although I have no idea what they thought that would accomplish. They're still rats. And still not terribly effective, really."

Cassie kept quiet. Even as an author, she knew there were times when words didn't help. She rested her head on his shoulder, snuggling closer when he wrapped his arms around her. For a few minutes, she enjoyed holding and being held.

Finally, he sighed and kissed the top of her head. "Anyway, enough with that story. You promised me food. It smells good, what is it?"

"Chili. I made it in the crockpot this morning so I wouldn't forget to cook something once I started writing. Sour cream and cheese is in the fridge."

He stood, offering a hand to help her up before he headed to the kitchen. "Is it meat chili or turkey chili?"

She rolled her eyes. "It's turkey chili, and turkey *is* a meat."

He shrugged, went to the cabinet, and got down the bowls. "Close down your computer, Cassie," he said as he doled out the chili.

She walked over and started to shut down her laptop, but couldn't resist logging into Amazon. "Darn."

He glanced from the fridge where he was pulling out the sour cream and cheddar. "What's wrong?"

"I still don't have any more reviews on *Mailbox Murders*." She knew that she was downright obsessed about checking reviews, but she had a reason. The book was selling well—she knew that from her sales ranking—but that was mostly due to the unfortunate fame she'd developed from being a suspect in two murders. She'd prefer that her book sold because people liked them and enjoyed her writing.

"They'll come. You know that people like the book."

"I know they like buying a book from a suspected murderer."

"Cassie, honey, you know you were innocent. That's what's important."

"Maybe." She stared at the site for a few moments more, then powered down.

He waited until she sat down before beginning to eat. "This is good. You can barely tell it's not meat."

She glared at him as she scooped out sour cream. "Next time, I'm making tofu chili."

He smiled at her, and this time the smile reached his eyes. "So, do you have any more book tours to go on?"

"Just a few local ones," she replied. Originally, her publisher had only planned on having her do local appearances. They splurged on national book tours for the big-names, not for first-time authors. But when the first-time author ended up on television for being connected to real-life murders, they had expanded her tours to go nationwide. Today was her first full day back home in a week.

It was good to be home. When Donner rubbed against her calf, she figured he was expressing the same sentiment. Or he wanted some chili.

They ate for a while in contented silence. Cassie's mind, however, was racing. First, because she made a mental note to add more cumin next time she made chili, but mostly she was trying to figure out the best way to approach a sensitive subject.

Cassie had met Whittaker's mother and sister and got along very well with both of them.

She'd thought that Patti Whittaker was a lovely woman and strong for doing what she believed was right by removing her daughter from a negative environment. Cassie had immediately bonded with Chloe, James' younger sister, who was deaf. This was mostly due to the fact that Cassie was able to communicate with her in American Sign Language. Chloe was delighted that Cassie knew how to sign and had laughed when Cassie explained she'd only learned it because she and Michelle, her best friend, had wanted another way to "talk."

Cassie had enjoyed meeting his family; they were nice and kind. But there was more that she wanted to know, and she didn't know how to approach it. She could be clever, or she could be direct.

"Why don't you ask already?"

She looked up, surprised out of her thoughts.

Whittaker was sitting there, an indulgent smile on his face as he watched her. "Cassie, I'm good at reading facial expressions. I can see that you're sitting there, clearly trying to figure out how to say something. I can recognize that expression as much as I can recognize your killing look."

"If you're so clever then, what do I want to ask you?"

"You're looking mighty uncomfortable. And we've just been talking about my father. I suspect that you want to ask something about him."

"Are you okay with that?"

He shrugged and went to the counter to get seconds. "I'm not sure that okay is the correct word, but I don't mind if you ask. Doesn't mean I'll answer, but you can ask."

She bit her bottom lip, then blurted it out. "I want to meet him."

"You want to meet him?" He raised his eyebrows as he sat back down. "Why?"

"I've met your mom. And Chloe. And, well, he's your dad. A big influence on your life." At his emphatic headshake, she pressed on. "He's why you wanted to be a cop, and he's why you're the type of cop you are. That's a pretty big influence."

"I suppose you're getting to know me, too, aren't you?" He put down the spoon and laid his hands on the old oak table. "You really want to meet him?" At her nod, he took a deep breath. "I do see him occasionally. Honestly, I'm not supposed to, since he's definitely of questionable character."

"Because he's a disgraced cop or because he's a bar owner?" Cassie asked.

He smiled. "I'm still amazed at how well you know those General Orders. It's both, really. Since he's family, I'm allowed some discretion. But I still limit the contact."

Relieved that he wasn't mad, she smiled back at him. And decided to be clever after all. "As it turns out, if we head up to Perry Hall to visit, his bar is near a dance studio."

Obviously confused by this turn in the conversation, he furrowed his brow. "What does that have to do with anything?"

"My next victim is a dance instructor. And you know how I am about research."

He rolled his eyes and twirled his finger around, pointing at the cluttered first floor of her rowhouse.

She had to laugh. She was surrounded by research tools, especially books. Books on varied topics such as gunshot wounds, police procedures, poisons, true crime stories. She even had some weapons lying around.

She smothered another laugh when she saw Whittaker glaring at a wine opener. He had a bad relationship with that particular opener.

"Anyway," she said, "tomorrow is an instructional class. I figure we can go visit your father and then have a ready-made excuse to leave when we have to go to the class. We can learn how to dance and I can do my research."

"You want to learn how to dance, Cassie? I really don't dance." He looked pained.

"It's research. I don't want to go by myself; it would look odd."

He leaned back and stared at the ceiling. "Dance class it is. But you'll owe me."

chapter 2

C ASSIE WAS DEFINITELY GOING to owe him, Whittaker thought as he drove toward Perry Hall. Not for the dance classes. He'd go along with any reason to spend time with her, but he was very reluctant to visit his father.

He wasn't comfortable spending time with his father on his own, let alone with his girlfriend. Introducing Cassie to his mom and sister had been a lot easier, since he regularly visited them. It had been as simple as bringing her over for dinner.

His mom had raised her eyebrows, but he figured she was thrilled to see him in a serious relationship. Still, dinner had been a relaxed affair and no one made a big deal about it, other than Chloe signing various taunts to him behind Cassie's back. He'd actually learned some signs he hadn't known before.

He wondered where Chloe had learned words like that. It had better be from a theoretical basis rather than from actual real-time practice.

"What are you frowning over?"

"What? Oh, the sun's reflecting off the wet pavement." He lowered the shade.

"Are you worried about me meeting your dad?"

"Yes, but that's not what I was frowning about just now. I was thinking about Chloe, actually. She's growing up too quickly."

"She's twenty, James, she's a big girl now."

"That's what I'm worried about." When she laughed, he elaborated. "Look, it's hard being ten years older. She'll always be my baby sister. Since our dad hasn't been around, I've played that father role."

"So what, you want to meet all her boyfriends and interrogate them? While cleaning your gun?"

He liked that idea. "Can I do that?"

Laughing, she shoved at his shoulder. "No, Detective Whittaker, you can *not* do that. No fair intimidating the poor boys. But if you do, it should be in full uniform. Hmm... speaking of that, I'd like to see you in your uniform."

"And out of my uniform?" Whittaker asked, unsurprised when she blushed in response. He liked to tease her, even though they hadn't gotten to that point in their relationship—not due to a lack of desire, more due to a lack of time. He'd thought his schedule would have been the issue with their relationship, but instead she'd been just as busy with her writing and book tours.

It was good to have time with her, especially when she looked as sexy as she did now. She wore her red hair down tonight, something she seldom did. And she was wearing a dress—even more rare. Usually she dressed more informally, which was fine with him. He'd dated high maintenance women before. Less fussy definitely suited him better.

But, he admitted to himself, that purple and black halter dress revealed a lot of leg. The smart black heels displayed those long, intriguing curves at their best. He was a leg man, so the short dress made any request of hers very appealing.

But he had his limits. She'd tried to get him to wear a matching outfit, but no way in hell was he wearing purple. The closest he would come was to wear a black shirt and slacks.

"How long has he owned the bar?" Cassie asked out of nowhere.

"About five years. I didn't think it was a good idea at first, since he's a recovering alcoholic."

"Oh," she said. "While he was—"

"No, he wasn't an alcoholic while he was a cop. I mean, he's always enjoyed his drink, but he didn't have a problem with it until...well, until everything collapsed and he left the force. But he seemed to turn his life around about five years ago. I was worried when he opened the bar, but it hasn't set him back. I wouldn't call the place a success, but he's done what he could with it."

He parked the car and stared at the dark brick building, shaking his head. As usual, the lighted sign listing "Rick's Café" had several blown-out lights.

Cassie smiled hesitantly at him. "Ick's Afe. Cute name." At his sigh, she patted his arm. "Are you ready?"

"As I'll ever be."

She carefully picked her way through the puddles in the muddy parking lot. Despite a steady rain for the past two days, thanks to the remnants of a hurricane, the temperature hadn't cooled down a degree. She was very thankful she hadn't worn pantyhose that evening but was regretting leaving her hair down. Humidity always did bad things to her curls. In vain, she tried to smooth it down.

"Don't worry, you look great." Whittaker squeezed her other hand.

"The humidity always wreaks havoc on my hair."

"I like it curly."

She smiled up at him. "I like it curly as well. But now it's more kinky."

He waggled his eyebrows at her. "I like kinky, too."

She wanted to smack him for making her blush right before she met his father. "So what did he say when you called?"

"I didn't."

She stopped in her tracks. "You didn't call him?"

"Nope." He opened the door, revealing a dark interior.

"James," she chided and stepped inside.

Despite the fact that it was after five and the bar was presumably open, no one was there yet. Cassie assumed—hoped—it got busier later.

It was a small, dimly lit room, with several tables and chairs facing a miniscule stage. The air reeked of stale beer and smoke, although Maryland had passed a no-smoking law years ago. Perhaps when the building had more smoke-free years than smoky, it would smell a little better. Seeing the tall man standing behind the bar, she easily recognized Richard Whittaker. His son greatly resembled him: same broad shoulders, proud posture, and thick hair, although Richard's was going gray.

He was wiping the counter, his back to the door. This surprised Cassie, since as far as she knew, no cop—even a former cop—would stand that way, completely unguarded. Out of the corner of her eye, she saw this bothered Whittaker as well.

"I know you're there, James. I saw your car on the security camera." Whittaker's father turned around slowly. "And noticed you brought a passenger."

Whittaker took her hand and approached the bar. "You had me worried there. I forgot about the security cameras."

As she stepped up to the counter, she could see the television under the bar. The picture was a little grainy, but she recognized the parking lot as it flipped through various views of the bar and the outside. She was glad that Whittaker's father took his security seriously.

She waited a few seconds for someone to say something, then nudged Whittaker. "So, are you going to introduce me?"

"Sorry, I was looking at the cameras. Dad, this is Cassie Ellis. Cassie, this is Richard Whittaker."

The older man appeared delighted as he reached over the bar to shake her hand. "It's very nice to meet you, Cassie. Please call me Rick."

Cassie was instantly charmed, especially since Rick, like his son, had dimples when he smiled. They had morphed more into deep creases, but the effect was still incredibly attractive.

"It's good to meet you as well, Rick. You have a nice bar."

Grinning, he turned to his son. "She's not a very good liar, is she?"

Whittaker snorted. "No, not particularly. Sorry for the surprise visit, but Cassie and I were in the neighborhood. I figured we could stop by."

"In the neighborhood? You just happened to be in Perry Hall? What can I get you to drink, Cassie?"

She pulled out a bar stool and took a seat. "Oh, just water. We're taking ballroom dance lessons at six-thirty at Charm City Dance Studio. It's right down Bel Air Road." She took the ice water he offered her.

"I can tell you're a Baltimore native," Rick said.

"Close enough," she agreed. Like most Baltimoreans, she usually pronounced "Bel Air" with one syllable and more like "Blair."

"And dance lessons?" Rick set a soda water in front of Whittaker. "Here I thought the fact that he brought you here to meet me was evidence that he was serious about you. Taking dance lessons is concrete proof."

Whittaker scowled into his glass, then shrugged. "I can't offer any contrary evidence, so I'll just keep my mouth shut."

"So, what do you do, Cassie? Besides convince James here to go places he doesn't want to." Rick leaned on the counter.

She enjoyed having this chance to meet Rick. It was a way for her to see how Whittaker would look in twenty or thirty years. Or, in his case, probably thirty or forty years. She knew his dad was only about fifty-five, but the years had been hard ones. She wondered if it had been the years on the force or the years in disgrace that had engraved the lines on his face and faded his hair to gray.

She smiled at him. "Do you want the boring answer or the fun answer?"

He raised his eyebrows, deepening the worry lines in his forehead. "Both."

"The boring answer is that I'm an English professor, teaching Technical and Creative Writing online. The more interesting answer is that I'm a murder mystery author."

"I can't believe a pretty thing like you writes murder myst—"

"Cut it out, Dad." Whittaker interrupted. "I know you know who she is. She was only on the news all of July, both for the murders and for her first book coming out."

Rick tilted his head in admission. "True, I did know about her book…and the murders. I'll admit I followed the story. I had a vested interest in those cases, since my son was investigating the murders."

Whittaker waved that away. "Not only me. Freeman was also investigating." He slanted a glance toward Cassie. "So was she, despite my warnings."

She rolled her eyes. "I was fine, wasn't I? I was careful."

"You've got a different definition of careful than I do." Whittaker shook his head and laughed. "Running toward a—"

When he cut off, she followed his gaze to the television screen. Not the one for the bar's security system, but an ancient television mounted in the upper corner of the room. Turning toward the screen, she watched also.

It was easy for her to recognize both men on the screen since they were on television often. The first was WBAL's prime time news anchor, the other was the Baltimore City Police Commissioner. The latter was solemnly looking out of the television with a mixture of concern, competence, and firmness. Personally, she'd always suspected that they had chosen Commissioner Spaulding solely for that facial expression. She figured he must practice it at night.

"What is Commissioner Spaulding so worried about now?" she asked, since the sound was muted.

"They just released a report from the Internal Investigations Division regarding statistics about Baltimore City Police. Data on how many times police officers discharged their weapons last year, which police officers did so, reports of excessive force, things like that," Whittaker answered. He nodded at the screen. "That's why Bianchi, the IID major, is there, in case there's any question Spaulding can't answer."

There were three people standing behind the Police Commissioner. She knew the dark-skinned female was Baltimore's Deputy Mayor for Public Safety. The other two people were wearing police uniforms and Cassie quickly dubbed them Bland and Blander. Both were about average height, average weight, and were neither attractive nor unattractive. Both had the pale skin that came from sitting in an office the entire day. The only difference between them was that one had hair—dark brown and worn close to his head—and the other balding, with a rather desperate combover.

"Which one is Bianchi?"

"The one behind Spaulding," Whittaker answered. "Caucasian, brown and brown."

Rick shook his head at the screen. "Maybe if they spent more time searching out dirty cops rather than conducting asinine surveys, they'd manage to clean up the department."

She bit her tongue to prevent herself from saying something in response and hoped that Whittaker would keep his mouth shut, too.

No such luck. He leaned across the bar into his dad's face. "I'm surprised that you, of all people, would think that, Dad."

The older man slammed down his hand. "You'd be surprised at a lot of things, James."

Cassie was struck as she saw two sets of similar gray eyes mirroring each other with their angry, stormy expressions.

"Umm, I hate to interrupt, but we actually need to get going to the class." She didn't want to end the meeting on such an angry note, but the class was starting in fifteen minutes.

Whittaker pulled out his wallet.

"Oh, put that away, James. I don't want your money." Rick spread his hand over his forehead and rubbed. "I'm sorry about that, Cassie. And James, I'm sorry. Look, believe it or not, I still love this city. Don't know why sometimes. So yes, I'd prefer for the cops who guard it to be honest."

At her nudge, Whittaker spoke up. "I'm...I'm sorry, too."

Rick turned as the front door opened with a scrape and two people entered. "I guess you guys should get going. Cassie, it was a real pleasure meeting you. I hope I see you again soon." He held out a hand, shook hers, then turned and shook his son's hand. "Have a good time dancing."

The humidity hit as soon as they stepped out of the bar. When they reached the car, Whittaker opened the passenger door for her. "That wasn't too bad."

She waited for him to get in. "That wasn't bad? What do you consider bad?"

He shrugged. "My dad and I always get in fights. Hell, even before they discovered he...before he had to resign from the force, we'd fight. My mom always said we were just too much alike, especially our tempers."

"You look incredibly alike, too." She took one last glance at the bar as Whittaker reversed out of the parking spot.

"Yes, but the temper and looks are where the similarities end. I'm not like my dad in any other ways," he growled as he pulled into traffic. "Not at all."

She let that go; there was nothing she could say that wouldn't cause the two of them to get into a fight. She wanted to dance, not spend the night apologizing.

* * * * *

CASSIE DID SPEND THE evening apologizing, but that was due to her lack of coordination.

She had to give Whittaker credit. He'd picked up the tango immediately, while she seemed to be dancing more on his feet than her own.

Both Whittaker and the dance instructor were incredibly patient with her.

"Miss Cassie," the instructor said as he strode over, his lithe body completely encased in black. "That is not the proper position. You need to place your right hand on his shoulder. That will let you feel his lead better." He tried to lift her hand up from Whittaker's back.

She winced. "I can't lift it that high. I was shot recently."

The instructor blinked at her in shock and shook his head, sending his blond ponytail flying. "Oh, okay then. I suppose you'll have to modify things a bit." He scurried away.

"Couldn't you have told him that you were injured? Did you have to say you were shot?" Whittaker asked, taking her back into his arms as the music began to pulse.

"What fun is that? I like shocking people. I have to get some enjoyment out of getting shot."

He shook his head. "Cassandra, please don't find any fun in getting shot, okay? I think I can only stand watching you run at a loaded weapon once."

She laughed, then stepped on his foot. "Oops. I'm sorry, I'm not any good at sports."

"That's not true. You can bike and you can shoot."

"Those aren't really sports," she complained, humming along with the sexy Latin song.

"Are too. You obviously have the coordination. You just need to relax. Listen to the music." He smiled down at her. "And stop trying to lead."

She needed to stop focusing so much on her proximity to Whittaker. This close, she could smell the spicy aftershave he used and feel his body temperature rising as they continued to tango. Unlike her, he could dance. In fact, he seemed naturally gifted. It made her wonder if he moved that well in bed. He probably did. And with the amount of control he exerted in all aspects of his life, she bet he could also—

"Ow."

Noticing his wince, she realized she must have put her full weight on his foot this time. "Sorry, James. I was... distracted."

"Oh? Fantasizing?"

"What?" she choked, feeling her cheeks start to flame.

He chuckled. "I meant about the story you're writing. You know, the one that required you to come here and research dance instructors."

"Right. That."

He lowered his voice to a deeper pitch. "Or were you fantasizing about something else? I'd be happy to hear about that later tonight." He leaned down to kiss her, then grimaced. "That one was my fault for distracting you."

"No, no, no." The instructor stalked back over to them, a pretty brunette in tow. "There's supposed to be more distance between you. Let's switch partners. Now remember, Miss Cassie, you need to follow the *man's* lead."

Whittaker snorted. "That's what I keep trying to tell her. In all areas of life, not only dancing."

She stuck her tongue out at him as she got into her modified position with the instructor.

"Cue the music," he called out. "Now Miss Cassie, for you it's right, left, right, side side. Right, left, right, side side. Right, left, right, side—ow."

* * * * *

CASSIE HUMMED A TANGO melody as they pulled up to the curb. So maybe she wasn't the next dancing reality-show star. But by the end of the lesson, she'd finally gotten the hang of it. Mostly.

"So, that was for research, was it?" Whittaker asked as they stepped up to her door.

She stopped humming. "What? Oh, yes, of course. Absolutely." She ignored the cat twining between her legs. "Don't even start, Donner. You have an automatic feeder now. Which this nice man gave to you. You're not hungry."

Whittaker followed her into the house, pausing to give the Russian Blue cat a quick scratch. "So where's your notebook?"

"Notebook?"

His grin widened as he leaned against her door. "Yes, your notebook. Your ever-present one that you have next to you whenever you do actual research."

She struggled for a look of innocence and batted her blue eyes at him. "Would you believe I left it here?"

"No."

She gave up. "Fine, I tricked you into going dancing. But you enjoyed it, didn't you?"

"I enjoy any excuse to press my body against you. In fact…"

He pulled her closer. Cassie thought he was going to kiss her, but instead, he swept her into his arms and started dancing. This time, however, he eliminated the space between their bodies that the instructor had recommended.

He hummed a sultry song as he led her through the moves they had learned that night, adding his own flair to them.

Spinning her around, he drew her close, then dipped her back. Far back. She was about to protest that she was going to fall when he deliberately threw them both off balance.

They landed on the couch, him on top. Now he did kiss her.

There was no quiet build-up, not that she minded. The entire time they were dancing, being so close to him was like one long hour of foreplay. She responded passionately.

"Why don't we take this upstairs?" Standing up, he offered a hand to her. Then cursed.

As his cell phone's ringtone became audible, she joined in the cursing.

"Sorry, honey." He pulled the phone from its carrier on his belt. "Whittaker here. Really? Positively ID'ed? Great! Yeah, I'll be there." He turned apologetic eyes toward her. "Yeah, fifteen minutes." He closed the phone.

"Work?"

"Yeah, that was Garcia. He got confirmation that a suspect we've been after is finally back in town. I, um, I've got to go. I'm sorry." He kissed her hard. "Really sorry."

"Yeah, me too. Go get the bad guy."

She watched him get into his car. Then she went to the kitchen, turned on the police scanner, and brewed some herbal tea. She needed something to calm her down.

chapter 3

CASSIE WAS STILL WORKED up the next day, but not because of the kissing. It was the situation with Whittaker and his father that bothered her.

She scratched her cat behind the ears, sending Donner into ecstasy. His contented purring soothed her as she analyzed her opinion of Rick.

She liked him. If she hadn't been told of his history, she would never have believed he was on the take. He seemed as honest, honorable, and trustworthy as his son. And Cassie trusted her first impressions. She was a good judge of character—although not psychic like her friend and fellow author Linda Kowalski.

Cassie jumped as the cat nudged her, upset that she'd stopped petting him. Her need for contemplation was no excuse not to pet the cat. She worked at doing both.

Rick Whittaker simply didn't match her image of a bad cop. Perhaps it had been a one-time thing. Maybe he took the money for an altruistic reason. Maybe it was the drinking, although from what she understood, he'd started drinking to excess only after he quit the force. Whatever the reason, it was a mystery to her. And in her world, mysteries were meant to be solved, preferably with a happy ending.

But after watching the altercation that had taken place between Whittaker and his father, she wasn't certain a happy ending was possible. It was sad to see the two of them at odds. It was obvious that Rick was proud of his son, and just as obvious that Whittaker cared deeply for his father and his well-being.

There was only one person who was best suited to talk to her about family.

* * * * *

THE FEELING OF COMFORT trickled into her as she trotted up the stoop to the Canton rowhouse. When her father opened the door and hugged her, the trickle became a flood.

It's probably different for a father and son than a father and daughter, she thought, surrounded by her father's love. She wished Whittaker and his dad could be even half as close as she and her father were.

He held her out at arm's length and gave her the once-over. "So, how's my favorite daughter?"

"I'm your *only* daughter, Daddy."

Raising his eyebrows, he cocked his head. "Daddy? Uh-oh, someone's feeling sentimental. Since high school, you normally call me Dad."

Rather than being annoyed that he knew her so well, today she took comfort in that knowledge. "I suppose *sentimental* is the word for it." She wandered into the homey kitchen, soaking up the cheerful yellow walls and kitschy knickknacks. Although she loved her own rowhouse, this would always be home.

She stopped her perusal of the paintings—they'd hung in the same places on the fridge since she was six—and sat at a bar stool at the island.

"It's not sentimental as much as sad."

Cassie smiled when her father poured a glass of orange juice for each of them. She knew that he believed there wasn't anything that couldn't be fixed with a glass of orange juice.

"It's James, actually." She had to laugh as her father furrowed his brow and frowned. "Don't worry, Dad, this isn't anything that you have to go and kill him for. It's actually about his father."

"His father?" He took a sip of orange juice. "I thought he didn't have much contact with his father."

"He doesn't. But I wanted to meet him. I'd already met his sister and mother. And James had already met you."

"I had to find out his intentions, didn't I? Anyway, did you get to meet him?"

She got up to pace. She had too many thoughts going in her head to sit still. "I met him. James and I stopped by his bar before some dance lessons."

"Dance lessons?"

She smiled at his shock. "Yes, dance lessons. I tricked him into them."

That drew a deep chuckle from her father. "How does one trick someone into dance lessons?"

"First of all, one had previously noticed the proximity of Rick's bar and the dance studio. Then one tells one's boyfriend that she's got a character that is a dance instructor. And he goes with you to visit since he knows how much you like to research things."

The chuckle turned into a full-fledged laugh. "That's perfect. I love that he fell for that."

"Well, he didn't, really. I forgot to bring along my notebook, so he figured I'd just used that as an excuse."

"Oh, that boy already knows you, doesn't he? Very cute idea on your part. So, what happened when you went to meet Mr. Whittaker?"

"It was depressing. First of all, his bar isn't in the nicest area, nor is it the nicest bar I've seen. Kind of decrepit, lights out on the neon sign type of decrepit. When we got there, it was completely empty, but then of course, it was only five-thirty. Rick was really glad to meet me, I could tell that. I think he was rather honored, actually. Happy that his son felt he was important enough to introduce me to, if that makes sense." At her father's nod, she took a deep breath and continued. "And he's completely proud of his son, you can tell that, too."

"That's not surprising. Most parents are proud of their children. I know I am." He toasted her with his orange juice.

"Thanks, Dad." She returned to the island and picked up her own glass. The bright taste of the orange juice was soothing. "Anyway, for a while, it was fine. He poured us something to drink, we chatted a bit. James did get a bit annoyed at the fact that Rick was pretending he didn't know who I was, but that was okay. But then the Baltimore Police Commissioner was on TV, and we started talking about it. That's when it got bad."

"Ah, not surprising things got ugly then. I'm sure that James' father doesn't want to think about the Baltimore Police."

"Which made his comment somewhat surprising. Rick said that he wished that they'd catch dirty cops. Then James reacted badly to that." She sighed. "It makes me sad. I know it has to kill James, to love someone as much he loves his father, but not respect him."

"It has to be hard on the family when something like that happens, Cassie. I'm sure Rick is consumed by guilt, and James had it hard when his father fell off the pedestal."

"What do you mean, fell off the pedestal?"

"I suspect that James is the type of person that idolizes those on the police force, right? Takes his vow to protect and serve more seriously than anyone I know. I'm sure he idolized his father: for the work he was doing on the force, working to get drug dealers off the street, as well as just for being his father. You know," he said, nudging her and flashing a devilish grin. "Like you worship me?"

She smiled. "That I do, Dad."

"And how would you feel if I fell off that pedestal? And not just in a normal, small way, when you realize that your father isn't perfect. But in a big way when all of a sudden not only is he not perfect, but it's now been publicly announced to the entire world that he's not perfect."

She nodded and took another drink. "I think the public aspect is a big part of James' discomfort, too. He's a very private person and hates to think that others are looking at him and thinking he's like his father. I keep trying to teach him that it doesn't matter what others are thinking of him, but—well, he's James."

"And you want to fix things for him." He took her hand in both of his. "You can't, Cassandra. Even as a child, you always wanted to make things right for others. You were so good to me when your mother died, even while you were grieving."

"I did want to take care of you, Daddy." She got up, hugged him, and leaned her head on his shoulder, sighing when he stroked her hair. "I wish I could take care of this problem with James and his father."

He took her by her shoulders and held her out at arm's length. "James has to fix it, sweetie, not you. He has to determine if he can get past his father's indiscretion. Whether he can just let it go and get past it."

Her father's advice was even better then the orange juice for fixing what ailed her. She went to refill their glasses. In her life, it truly was "Father knows best."

"I'm not sure he can, that's the problem. He's so damned proud. So is his father. I don't know if it's something he'll ever be able to resolve. Especially since I doubt they've ever talked about it. Accused, argued, and angered, but never talked."

Charles shrugged. "That would probably be a good first step for them, but again, Cassie-girl, it's *their* first step to take. If it's not the right time right now, and if you forced the issue, you might make it worse."

Okay, sometimes it was annoying when father knew best. That was exactly what she'd been planning on doing. She held out the orange juice to him, then took it back at the last second. "Do you have to be right all the time?"

He laughed. "That's what your mother used to say." When she stared at him, he laughed again. "Okay, maybe not. I can't say I was always right with Helen. I think it's virtually impossible in any relationship to be always right."

"I like being right," she said as she drank her juice. Her next thought almost made her swallow the wrong way. She liked being right, but it was almost an obsession for Whittaker. What would happen when they disagreed? Especially if it was over something important—like his father?

* * * * *

SHE WAS IN THE middle of grading when she was interrupted by loud music. She blinked for a few minutes as she tried to figure out the cause, then had to remember where she'd left her cell phone.

She smiled when she saw the readout. "Hello, James."

"Cassie, are you doing anything right now?"

She was surprised to hear the urgency in his voice. Whittaker was always cool and in control.

"Umm, not anything that can't be interrupted. Why? Is everything okay?"

"Yes, but I need you. Freeman and I are trying to track a suspect and it's taking off in too many directions."

"Oh, the one you were after last night with Garcia?"

"No," he said and took a breath. "That one is closed. This is a different perp."

She could hear street noises in the background, so Whittaker must have been driving as he called her. "Are you primary for the murder I heard mentioned this morning?" She quickly saved and shut down her computer before running toward her shoes. She didn't know what he needed her for, but she wanted to be ready. That proved difficult as she tried to balance herself, shove on shoes with one hand, and hold the phone with the other. She sat on the floor and put the phone on speaker to hear his voice.

"Ummm, yes, that case. I keep forgetting you listen to that scanner all day. Anyway, we have figured out that he's in one of two places. Freeman is headed off to one, and I'm going to head off to the other. But if I go alone, it's going to look incredibly obvious. Can I come pick you up?"

She felt a thrill as she realized he was going to take her on a stakeout. Whittaker barely even told her about his cases. This was definitely an important step in their relationship.

"Yes, of course." She sprang up, ran for her purse, then ran back since she'd forgotten the phone. She was surprised to hear the beep from the street. "Is that you?"

"Yes, hurry out."

Cassie took a quick glance at what she was wearing. She assumed it was acceptable wear for a stakeout. Faded jeans, dark green T-shirt, and sneakers. She tried to remember if she'd showered before going to her father's. Yes. For vanity's sake, she grabbed an Orioles cap from the peg on her way out the door.

As she ran down her steps, Whittaker stepped out of his car to open the door for her. She had to smile. Only he would insist upon such etiquette even when time was of the utmost essence. She was surprised to see him in jeans and an Orioles T-shirt. He usually wore suits when he was working. He must keep some regular clothes at work for going undercover.

She sat down, belted in, and turned to him when he slid back inside. "Where are we going?"

"Loch Raven. We got word from a witness that the perp had a cabin in the woods there. We're going to go and pretend to have a picnic while staking it out."

"Oh. Do you have any picnic stuff?"

He shrugged. "I have a blanket. Hopefully, since we're going as a couple, it won't look too suspicious."

She nodded and watched the traffic stream by as he drove up the Jones Falls Expressway. "Sounds great."

"Don't sound so excited, Cassie." His reprimand made her turn back to him. "Stakeouts are often dull. You'll be bored out of your mind soon enough. And I'd never take you on one that I thought had even a chance of being dangerous. We're only going to watch, not do anything. Got it?"

Rolling her eyes, she nodded. "Got it. Watch only, no action. It makes me feel like a voyeur when I say it that way."

He laughed, then gunned the motor.

Cassie watched in admiration as he threaded his way around the slower drivers. She wished she had the freedom to do the same without worrying about speeding tickets.

"Where's Freeman headed to?"

"What? Oh, he's heading toward Columbia. Evidently the suspect has a part time job at a grocery store there."

"Why are you going separately then? Won't it be bad if he finds the guy there without you?"

"He took along another officer. We think there's a higher chance we'll catch him there than at the cabin."

"That's why you're taking me to the safer location."

He squeezed her hand. "I'd never risk you, honey."

For some good luck, she raised her legs each time they went over train tracks as they neared Loch Raven. She didn't want Whittaker to make fun of her for believing in that superstition, one she had held since she was a little girl. So she did it discreetly as she admired the forest around Loch Raven.

It always amazed Cassie to see such vast wilderness so close to Baltimore. She was a city girl, had always been a city girl—to her southern grandmother's dismay—but she did enjoy occasionally getting out to nature.

The trees provided a natural canopy, and the sunlight streaming through the leaves created a dappled pattern over the roadway.

"Okay, we walk from here." He got out of the car, opened the trunk, and withdrew a blanket.

"Why don't you drive further? Aren't you authorized?" She pointed out the AUTHORIZED ACCESS ONLY sign.

He tucked the blanket under one arm and started on one of the small paths that led from the parking lot. "Too obvious. Like I said, the point is to look casual."

They walked for about five minutes, long enough for Cassie to feel grateful she'd worn sneakers, but sorry that she'd worn her brand-new white ones.

Whittaker stopped. Using hand gestures, he pointed to a cabin and mimed to her to keep quiet.

She rolled her eyes. Then she lifted her hands and signed to him. *"I know American Sign Language, goofy."*

He shook his head, then signed back. *"Right, I forget sometimes."*

She grinned at him. *"Yes, like when you signed to Chloe to stop talking about sex and I was still in the room."*

He colored slightly. Cassie loved when he did that; it was so thrilling to see the proper Whittaker get all embarrassed.

"Anyway," he signed. *"The cabin is there. Let's put the blanket down by the lake. Then we can sit there and watch."*

"Can we make out?" she signed. *"Look more natural."* She grinned when, once again, he blushed.

He leaned in to whisper in her ear, his hot breath stirring up a lot more than her hair. "That would be distracting."

He nudged her forward, pointing toward a rather picturesque spot, perfect for the picnic blanket. She helped him spread it out and then sat down to watch.

And watch.

Cassie tried to act as if there wasn't a care in the world, like the two of them were just enjoying the midday sun. She *was* enjoying it, since it was at least ten degrees cooler out of the city.

She kept a constant watch at the wooden building, hoping someone would come outside. It took her all of five minutes to get bored. It took ten minutes before she was squirming in frustration at doing nothing.

Whittaker was having more fun watching Cassie than the cabin. He knew his woman and knew it wouldn't take much for her to get bored. "This is what police work is usually like, Cassie," he said quietly.

She frowned at him before whispering back. "I know that."

He patted her knee. "We're sticking out right now, doing nothing. I've got an idea. I need to run back to the car." He got up before she could protest and headed toward the car at a light jog.

He reached the car in under three minutes and opened the trunk. He grinned as he pulled out the rest of the supplies, gripping everything in one hand as he closed the trunk. Running back, he fought back a laugh when Cassie caught sight of him and narrowed her eyes.

"Fishing gear?"

He smiled as he handed her a rod and the tackle box. "Yes, fishing gear. It looks more normal for us to be out here fishing than just sitting down."

"I suggested making out. *That* would look normal."

Laughing, he leaned down and kissed her nose. "Yes, but we wouldn't be able to pay attention to anything else then, would we? I can barely remember my own name sometimes when I'm with you." He wandered around the area, looking for two perfect sticks.

Glancing back, he saw her frowning at the conglomeration of things he'd brought from the car. In addition to the rod and tackle box, he brought two other fishing rods, a net, a covered bucket, and a cooler.

She opened the cooler. "Beer? You brought beer? You don't drink on duty, right?"

"Of course not," he said and took one out of the cooler. Opening it, he took a deep swallow. It was a struggle to hold back the laugh when she narrowed her eyes even more.

"Detective Whittaker," she said through gritted teeth. "Are you working today?"

"Nope, it's my day off." Which was why he'd hoped to spend last night with Cassie until he got the blasted call from Garcia. At least they managed to capture the guy.

"So this *isn't* a stakeout?"

"Of course not. Do you *really* think I would have taken you on a stakeout? Even if rules didn't prevent me?"

She pouted, which set off his libido immediately. "You tricked me."

He curved his lips into an innocent smile. "What do you mean? You mean like how you tricked me into, oh, I don't know, ballroom dancing by pretending it was research?"

She grabbed the fishing rod from him and shrugged. "Fine, you got me."

He took the bait container from the cooler. When he opened the lid, he again had to fight back a laugh at Cassie's expression. She was staring at the squirming worms with the disgust most people used while looking at dead bodies.

"Why are they red?"

"They're bloodworms."

"Oh, gross." She turned her head away and looked toward the water.

Now he had to laugh. He took out a penknife and dug a hole in the ground for the pronged sticks, just like his dad had always taught him. He frowned and wondered where that thought had come from.

He turned to look at her. She sat there, once again staring in disgust at the bloodworms.

"You crack me up, Cassie. Here you are, writing about murder with guns and knives and poisons, but you're freaked out by worms?"

"Hey, I'm not actually out there using those guns and knives and poisons and everything. I just write about it. And worms are gross."

He laughed again. "You're being such a girl. Anyway, we need to keep quiet," he said as he impaled a worm on his hook. He did the same for hers.

She glanced over at the shack. "Why, is there really supposed to be someone over in that building?"

"No, that was all made up. It's because you'll scare off the fish. Now here, take this."

She gingerly took the rod from him. "Now what?"

"What, you've never fished before?"

"Never. Why the hell would I have fished?"

Cocking his arm back, he casted smoothly. He nodded in satisfaction when the bobber landed in the absolutely perfect spot. He set the rod in the forked stick and straightened. "You're Southern. Southerners love to fish. Haven't you listened to any country songs?"

"Okay, first of all, I was born in the South, but have been in Baltimore all my life that I can remember. The only fishing most people do there is from the pier in Canton, and I'll pass on eating anything that swims in the Inner Harbor."

"It's gotten cleaner," he said philosophically. Taking Cassie's rod from her, he cast to another spot on the lake, far enough away from his to make sure their lines wouldn't tangle. He placed it in the other holder, then sat down on the blanket.

"Second of all, I don't listen to country songs. That's your bad habit, not mine."

"I listen to many different types of music. Anyway, come sit down." He patted the blanket.

Cassie reluctantly joined him. "So, we're fishing?"

Nodding, he dug a beer out of the cooler for her and another for himself. "Yes, we're fishing."

"Wait! Don't you need a license to go fishing, Mr. Follow the Rules?"

She sighed when he pulled out his license and a day license for her.

Although Whittaker managed to catch two fish rather quickly, her line just sat there, doing nothing. She started to feel insulted that the fish preferred Whittaker's worms to hers.

When still nothing happened, she started plotting. Not about her current book, but on how to get back at Whittaker for tricking her into going fishing—never mind that this was him getting back at her.

She took a quick peek at him. He hadn't managed to catch another fish, but that didn't seem to bother him. In fact, this was the most relaxed she'd ever seen him. He was just watching his bobber and occasionally taking a drink from his beer. Funny, she would never have thought that he was a fisherman. *The things you learn.*

She glanced at her own bobber. It was just sitting there, doing nothing. She supposed doing nothing was part of fishing. Too bad she was horrible at doing nothing.

She took out her smartphone, but she didn't have enough signal to go online and check her reviews. She shouldn't have been surprised, they were far from civilization out here. In fact, they were pretty isolated.

It would be a perfect place for a murder. Maybe her next book could be the *Minnow Murders*.

```
It was the perfect day to skip school,
Skyler thought as she and her boyfriend ducked
under a low-hanging tree branch.
    The sky was the fresh, bright blue of
spring, the sun was reflecting off the surface
of the lake in bright pinpricks of light, and
the dark red blood was dripping off the trees.
    Blood?
    Skyler looked up in the tree and screamed.
    A man had been tied up there, using what
looked like fishing line. His throat had been
slashed and—
```

"Cassie!" Whittaker shouted.

By the time Cassie was aware of the real world again, she could do nothing but watch as he lunged toward the water for her rod. It was too late. She watched as her fishing rod was dragged into the lake. *Strong fish*, she had a chance to think before it disappeared into the inky depths.

"That wasn't supposed to happen, was it?" she asked, smiling at him.

He stared at her before bursting into laughter. "No, you're supposed to be paying a bit more attention to the fish, and less to your stories." He waded out into the water a bit, then shook his head. "That was a good rod, too."

Laughing again, he picked up his own rod, where a fish was evidently pulling the bobber down in the water. He started to reel it in but was stopped by the insistent ringing of his cell phone. He passed the rod to Cassie, who had no idea what to do with it.

She yanked a bit on the rod, surprised to feel the resistance. Must be a strong fish, she thought again as she looked over at Whittaker, who had the cell phone to his ear. He mimed reeling in the line, so she let go of the rod with one hand, almost lost control, then took the handle-thing and started cranking. Whittaker's shocked exclamation stopped her cold.

"What? When the hell did that happen?"

He listened intently for a few moments and closed his eyes. "They pulled him in? Oh, God. Why? All right, I'll be there in about thirty minutes."

Cassie knew the situation was critical when Whittaker pulled a penknife from his pocket and simply cut the line, letting another fish get away.

Then he reached for the gear, shoving items under his arms and into his grip at random. When it all tumbled back to the ground, he gritted his teeth in frustration.

"James." She touched his shoulder. "What happened?"

He looked at her, dismay clouding his eyes. "That was Freeman. Evidently O'Reilly's body was found about three hours ago. He'd been shot." He picked up the bucket and poured the few fish they—well, he—had caught into the water. Evidently, letting her know what had happened had calmed him down; this time, he started picking up the gear in a methodical order.

Cassie stared at him. "Do they know who did it?"

"No, but they have a suspect they've pulled in to interview."

She started to fold up the blanket, needing to help somehow. "Who?"

"My father."

> Day off.
> Payback: Go on "stakeout" with Cassie.
> Bring worms.
>
> **MONDAY 4 SEPTEMBER**   09:34:14

chapter 4

WHITTAKER MADE A MENTAL note to thank Cassie later for not pestering him with questions on the drive down to the Baltimore Police Headquarters. The silence let him concentrate on getting down there quickly.

Of course, it also gave him plenty of time to worry.

Perhaps he shouldn't be so quick to head down to the station and check up on his father. It might make him look bad in the Department if he interfered. Part of him also thought it might be best not to associate with his father.

The other part of him clung to a loyalty and love for his dad that wouldn't quit, even with everything that had happened. The shame and disgrace when his father was caught and forced to resign, his subsequent abuse of alcohol, even the divorce couldn't completely erase his good memories of the man who had raised him.

He knew that his father would never kill someone. He took a deep breath as he realized he wouldn't have thought his father could have been a bad cop, either.

He pulled into the garage, drove to his space, and parked. Bracing for Cassie's reaction, he turned to her. "Honey, I need you to—"

"Stay in the car," she finished for him.

He drew in another deep breath, this time in relief, reminding himself again that he'd need to thank her. "Yes. I don't know what it's going to be like in there, but I doubt it'll be pretty. Let me go up, check out the situation, then I'll come back down and see what we should do next. Ten minutes at the most. I'll leave the A/C running for you." It was hot and humid now that they were back in the city.

"Okay, I'll stay," she said, then leaned in for a quick kiss. "Tell your dad I believe in him."

"I will," Whittaker said, wishing he felt as confident.

As soon as he got off the elevator, Whittaker could tell things were hopping in the homicide department. Generally, the detectives liked it dark in the room, but not when they had a hot case to investigate. Then the overhead lights would be blazing, as they were now.

Normally, his blood would start pumping when he saw those lights, and he'd gear up to start his shift. This time, knowing they were for the murder of a cop, and a murder for which his father was a suspect—his stomach clenched in worry and fear.

He hadn't gone more than five steps into the room before he felt it. Other than the one time when John Rocker, a notoriously unpleasant baseball pitcher, had stepped onto the field at Camden Yards, he'd never felt such group anger before. He could remember being at the Orioles game, feeling the dark rage circulating through the air, filling the crowd with something of a mob mentality.

He felt it here, too, in the cops milling about. O'Reilly might have been a bad cop, but he was still a cop. Nothing enraged them more than the murder of a police officer. The violence throbbed through the air, especially as he got closer to the back right corner and the interview rooms. He knew his father was back there in one of the stark rooms, empty but for two chairs, a skinny table, and some homicide detectives who were trying to get him to break down and confess his crimes.

But his father hadn't killed anyone. No way.

When his fellow officers turned toward him, recognized him, and added up his connection to their suspect, he realized he might be the only one in the room who believed that.

He recognized a number of the officers in the room, and not just his fellow homicide detectives. There were plenty of people from O'Reilly's patrol squad, some union representatives, and many officers from the Internal Investigations Division, including Major Bianchi.

Again, his stomach clenched. He knew IID always came out when an officer was killed, mainly so they could make certain that the rest of the police force behaved themselves. Occasionally, that swirling anger he sensed would get the better of the investigating cops, and the suspect would be tried, convicted, and punished by the cops in the interview room. All without benefit of due process.

So he knew IID was there to prevent that from happening, and not just because his father was on the premises.

Still, he slipped behind some of the other detectives in an attempt to keep out of their sight. He'd done his best to avoid any contact with the Internal Investigations Division, to abide by all the General Orders, and to do nothing that would make anyone compare him to his father.

He sighed in relief when he finally saw a friendly face. Perhaps *friendly* was an exaggeration; no one was going to be friendly in this atmosphere. But Detective Arthur

Freeman, one of his squadmates and his preferred partner in investigations, approached him.

It had been Freeman who'd contacted him after hearing about the murder and subsequent investigation from one of his many sources. Freeman had been a cop for over twenty years and had contacts in every department. Whatever news the other detective had learned couldn't have been good, as there was a pallor underneath his dark skin.

"Thanks for calling, Freeman," he said as his partner pulled him aside and toward their cubicles.

"No problem." Freeman leaned against his desk. "I knew you'd want to be notified."

"How'd O'Reilly die? You said he was shot?"

"Three gunshot wounds, all to the chest. Initial evidence, namely cartridges left at the scene, indicates he was shot by a 9 mil weapon. And since his service piece was missing, that might've been what did it."

"Shot by his own weapon?" Whittaker shook his head. Not a way he'd want to buy it. "When?"

"Looks like late last night or early this morning. The body was in an alley outside the Black Raven Pub—a favorite hangout of O'Reilly's—so he wasn't found until this afternoon by a homeless man who was looking for a place to take a leak."

Whittaker relaxed his shoulders in relief. "Then it can't have been my father, he wouldn't have had the opportunity. He was working in the bar last night. Cassie and I saw him."

Freeman raised an eyebrow at that. "When?"

"Right when he opened." When Freeman's other eyebrow joined the first, he gave more details. "Cassie wanted to meet him. So we visited quickly before—going to do something else in Perry Hall."

"That might be the case, but you won't be able to alibi him. I'm told he closed up early, around twenty-one hundred hours."

Whittaker tensed again. "I'm sure he had a reason. Probably better than any idiotic reason anyone has for bringing him in for questioning on this murder. What's the connection? I don't think Dad's seen O'Reilly in years. Not since—" He just couldn't say it.

"Right. Not since the D&D Scandal. Which, of course, would be the motive, since O'Reilly is the one who gave up your father's name to the investigators."

"Okay, I get that. But why the hell would he have waited nine years to strike back?"

Freeman shrugged. "Can't answer that. But the reason he was pulled in is that when the investigating detectives— Newmann and Dirruzo, by the way—went to O'Reilly's apartment, he evidently had a freaking scrapbook about the D&D scandal, and had plenty of articles about the fallout, including ones about your father and the other police officers that resigned. They've brought in a number of former Drug Unit detectives, not just your father." He nodded toward a woman sitting apart from everyone. "That's former Detective Harding waiting for her turn next. Ever meet her?"

Whittaker clenched his jaw.

"Sorry, stupid question. This all went down while you were in Academy. She's this Amazonian blond number. Known for using her charm—which she has in spades— and her body to get information, promotions, whatever. Used her former contacts to stay out of the holding room and just wait out here. Oh hell, she's coming over here."

The statuesque woman sauntered over to them. It didn't seem to bother her that every cop in the place was watching her, suspecting her.

"Hello, Freeman. Long time no see." Her voice fit Freeman's description. Soft, sexy, seductive.

"Guess so," Freeman said stiffly.

She ignored Freeman's coldness and turned a brilliant smile to Whittaker. Even expecting it, it was hard for him to resist that pull.

"I don't even need Officer Friendly here to introduce me. You have to be Rick's son. You look like a younger version of him." She stuck out a hand.

He wanted to ignore it, but his upbringing wouldn't allow it. He shook her hand, noticing it was warm and dry. No nerves on her part, obviously.

"How are Jordan and Jada doing, Freeman? I'm sure Jada's a lovely young woman now."

Whittaker could see Freeman warming up, however reluctantly. He loved talking about his family.

"They're both great. Jada's eleven now and smart as a whip. This is last year's school photo. She's grown so much already." He pulled out his wallet and showed Leslie the picture.

"Oh, she's beautiful. Of course she would be with her parents."

"I thought you'd moved home to Illinois," Freeman said.

"I did, to be closer to my children. But my youngest just graduated from Northwestern, so my husband and I moved back here this summer. I've always had a fondness for Baltimore. Charm City, you know."

"Husband?" Freeman asked.

"Yes, a new one. I met him at the college. Anyway, I better get back. I'm sure they'll want to talk to me about this murder. I'm not sure why anyone is surprised. O'Reilly had it coming. Nice meeting you, Detective Whittaker."

Whittaker watched her stroll back. "I see what you mean about charming."

"Oh yeah. I wonder how old her current husband—number three, I believe—is."

"I guess it depends if it was a professor or student she met at the college. She's another that resigned under a cloud of suspicion, right?"

"Yes, a few days after your father. The other detective that resigned, Detective Simmons, moved to Arizona after the scandal. He was admitted to the hospital two days ago, so they aren't looking at him."

"Are they seriously looking at my father?"

Freeman glanced toward the interview room. "They're looking."

* * * * *

CASSIE CHECKED THE TIME.

She sighed when she saw it was only three minutes from the last time she checked. When was he going to come back downstairs? He'd probably only been gone for fifteen minutes, but it felt like an hour.

It didn't help that she didn't have anything to entertain herself in the plain garage. Not only were the cement walls and cement floors uninteresting and unattractive, but they also blocked reception so she couldn't use her smartphone.

Every few minutes, she could hear nearby sirens as police left the area. She wondered what those officers were headed toward. Drug busts? Muggings? Murder?

Of course, murder made her think about Whittaker and his father. And worry about both of them.

She took a deep breath to sigh again and immediately regretted it. What *was* that smell? She sniffed again, then gingerly sniffed her hands.

Dirt. Worms. And fish.

"Oh God, I need to wash my hands," she said aloud. But that meant going to a bathroom and—

Great, now she had to pee.

Checking the clock again, she saw that two more minutes had passed. She stared across the parking garage and willed the door to open. She really wanted Whittaker to come out and let her know what was going on.

And to escort her to the bathroom.

She squirmed in her seat.

After what felt like days, but was really only a few more minutes, she decided that she needed to take matters into her own hands. Her own fishy-smelling hands.

He would understand that she had to go to the bathroom, right? Of course, the only place in the police station where she knew the location of the bathroom was the fifth floor and the homicide department.

She gave him two more minutes. When he didn't come out, she scooted over, turned off the engine, and took the keys from the ignition. She pressed what she hoped was the lock button on the keychain, thankful when it didn't let out some type of special police alarm. She scurried across the parking garage and into the building. Hopefully, no one would accost her for being unescorted. It was an emergency.

It really was an emergency by the time the pokey elevator made its way to the fifth floor. She ran across to the bathroom and into a stall, then immediately went back out and washed her hands *before* she did her business.

Afterward, feeling much relief, she washed her hands again and started out the door. She headed toward the elevator, pushed the button, then worried that she and Whittaker might have crossed paths. Perhaps he was downstairs in the garage now, wondering where the hell she was.

She should check. She'd visited him once or twice since they had started dating, so she knew where his cubicle was located.

After hesitating for a moment at the entrance, she pushed open the door and went in. She almost stopped again as soon as she got past the rows of file cabinets. The anger of the police officers in the room was almost palpable. She could hear it in the low murmuring and muttering going on all around her.

Finally, she saw Whittaker at his cubicle, talking to Freeman. Her relief was short-lived. By his expression, he was obviously not happy to see her.

"Cassandra," he hissed. "I told you to stay in the car."

"I had to go—" She stopped when she noticed Whittaker looking over her shoulder. He went pale and stood up straight. Cassie turned around and realized what had caused his reaction.

Major Bianchi was walking toward them, followed by the man with the thinning hair that she'd seen on television. She straightened up herself when she realized the major's beady brown eyes were focused on her.

"Are we allowing civilians in the Homicide Department now, Detective Whittaker?" the major said, sneering at her.

"Actually, I just came up—"

Whittaker interrupted her explanation. "She was just leaving, sir."

"Good. Control your woman," the major said, then turned around and headed back toward the interview rooms.

"Did he really just say that?" Cassie asked, glaring in disbelief and disapproval at the man's back. "Control your—"

She turned her glare on Whittaker as he clamped a steely hand on her wrist and steered her toward the door. Freeman followed behind.

They had almost made it out when the muttering grew louder. Whittaker paused and spun around, although he never released his grip on her.

She heard his quiet but fervent "Thank God" when his father emerged from the wall of angry cops. Rick was alone and obviously not in custody.

He spotted them and raised an eyebrow, reminding Cassie yet again of his son. Whittaker had inherited so many of his traits. Not just handsome features and sexy dimples, but also pride. Even now, with everyone staring at him, Rick strolled toward them, confidence in each step.

"Since I don't feel like taking advantage of the nice officers who drove me here, I don't suppose I could ask one of you for a ride?" Rick said when he reached them. He glanced over his shoulder with a shrug. "I don't think anyone else here is feeling terribly accommodating toward me right now."

"Let's go," Whittaker said, releasing Cassie's arm to open the door for his father. He ushered them all out.

Cassie took one last glance at the mob of cops and exchanged a pointed glare with Major Bianchi.

Freeman cleared his throat, dragging her attention back to him. "Don't taunt the rats, Cassie. You're not supposed to look them directly in the eye."

"Let's go, Cassie," Whittaker repeated.

Dropping the eye contact, she strode out as he held the door.

No one spoke in the elevator. She followed Rick and James as they headed to the cars.

"I better go, let you all be alone. Take care, Rick. Cassie." Freeman gave her a quick hug, then whispered in her ear. "Take care of them both." He gave a nod toward Whittaker as he slid into his car. "See you tomorrow, Whittaker."

"Uh huh," Whittaker said as he patted his pockets and frowned at his vehicle.

She handed him his keys. "Here they are."

Now he turned the frown toward her. "Why the hell did you come in the building anyway? I told you to—"

She put her hands on her hips and faced him down. "I had to use the bathroom—badly. And you said ten minutes and it had already been twenty."

"Why the hell didn't you say that then?"

She rolled her eyes and tried to defer the passenger seat to Rick.

"Absolutely not. Ladies first." When Rick held the door open for her, she had to hold back a smile. Again, something else Rick and Whittaker had in common. She slid inside.

Whittaker quickly maneuvered out of the garage and down Gay Street.

None of them spoke as he drove away from the station. Cassie thought about saying something, anything, to break the tension. After a quick glance at Whittaker's clenched jaw and tightly gripped hands, she decided to keep quiet.

When they reached the Fells Point area, he drove up the cobblestone roads, parallel parked, and swiveled around. "Okay, Dad, spill it."

A writer should write with his eyes and a painter paint with his ears. — Gertrude Stein

3 SUNDAY
SEPTEMBER

Meet Whittaker's Dad - 5pm
Dance class 6:30pm

My idea of a writer: someone interested in everything. — Susan Sontag

4 MONDAY
SEPTEMBER

~~Grading~~
Visit Dad - then grade.
~~Starbucks~~ Fishing?
BCPD HQ.

chapter 5

Cassie turned around in time to see Rick's eyes cloud with annoyance.

"There's nothing to spill. O'Reilly's dead, which I won't even bother saying I'm sorry to hear. But I had nothing to do with his murder."

"Then why did the detectives pull you in for interview?" Whittaker demanded.

"I've already spent the last two hours being interrogated. I'm sure as hell not going to sit here and have my son accuse me of things. Again." He reached for the door handle.

Whittaker reached over the seat and grabbed his hand. "I'm not accusing you of anything, Dad. I'm asking."

Rick closed his eyes and took a few breaths. When he opened up them up again, he looked less angry. And about ten years older. "It appears that O'Reilly was a bit…obsessed. He had an entire photo album full of articles from the Drug and Dollar Scandal—God, I can't believe I'm calling it that— from the cases where monetary evidence was going missing. Evidently, he'd been reviewing it recently, since it was open and on his dining table."

"They showed you the scrapbook?" Cassie asked.

"They did. Wanted me to explain it. Not that I could, I hadn't talked to O'Reilly in years. Not since he kindly offered my name to the Rat Squad."

Cassie pushed down the memory of her dad's warning about pressing the issues between father and son. At this point, she was involved anyway.

"So, the D&D scandal case." She watched as the same pained expression passed over the faces of both men. "Mr. Whittaker, can I ask a question?"

"It's Rick, and yes, of course."

"Were you actually taking the money from the dealers?"

Rick slumped back in his seat. "You asked. Finally, someone actually asked." He glared at Whittaker. "Everyone just assumed it was true. You, your mother, my co-workers. You never said a damn word. Never questioned it."

He turned back to Cassie and answered her question. "No. I never took any money from the dealers. I knew other cops were doing it, found some evidence showing it, but I couldn't prove who it was. I suspected Detectives Anderson, O'Reilly, Harding, and a few others. I kept watching, but I figure the others weren't stupid enough to do anything around me."

She waited for Whittaker to say something, but he was just staring at his father. So she asked the questions. "Then where did the extra money come from? You had some hidden accounts, right?"

Rick closed his eyes again. "I was getting money from the Feds. FBI agents had approached me a year before my resignation, since they had gotten wind of what was going on with the Drug Unit. They wanted an 'in.' I was supposed to find out what I could and report back to them. Each time

I did, they gave me cash. So I started flashing it around at work, hoping to draw someone out."

He turned to address Whittaker. "I'd been ordered by the Feds not to tell anyone what was going on. And, of course, if I was ever caught, they'd deny any involvement. But after I was brought in for questioning, I decided I'd at least tell your mother, you, and Chloe. I never got the chance. I got home that night, and it was already all over the news. About the scandal, about me. Patti was already packed when I drove up. Then you came, didn't bother to ask either. You left, and I was alone. So I started drinking. I figured you were all better off without me anyway. I still think that sometimes." He opened the door and got out.

Cassie wanted to panic. Whittaker sat there, not saying a word while his father strode away. Just when she was about to burst, he took the keys out of the ignition.

"I'll be back," he said as he opened up his door. "Can you entertain yourself around here for a while?"

"Yes, just call me when you're ready. Go after him."

As Whittaker trotted after his father, she said a short prayer that he could remedy their relationship.

Checking the time, she realized that her best friend, who lived only a few blocks away, was probably home from work.

While walking toward Michelle's house, she kept thinking of what Rick had said. She could imagine the entire dramatic scene.

```
        Rick watched, without a word, as Patti
    slammed the trunk of car, hurried his
    daughter into the car, and gave him one
    last disappointed look before pulling away.
    Whatever happened to "for better or for
    worse"? Perhaps she hadn't realized how bad
    the worse could be.
        But she was supposed to know he would never
    do anything to dishonor his duties to the
```

police department. How could she believe that of him?

When a car pulled up into the driveway, it took him a moment to recognize his son. He wasn't supposed to be here. He was supposed to be at the Academy. Rick felt mixed emotions seeing his son in a police uniform. There was pride, but this was also the uniform that he'd been accused of disgracing.

Here was someone who would believe in him. After all, he'd raised his son to honor his responsibilities, to protect and serve, to abide by a strong moral code. His son would understand he could never have done such a thing.

But when James got out of the car, it was obvious his son also believed what he'd heard on the news. Rick had thought the disappointment in Patti's eyes was heart-wrenching, but the expression in his son's eyes was worse. The fall of a hero.

James didn't say a word as he brushed by him. He went inside, must have seen that Patti and Chloe had left…and headed back to his car.

Rick took a step toward him, ready to protest his innocence.

No! This was his family. They should have known he was innocent. So he refused to say a word.

He watched the car until he could no longer see it, and then headed inside to take comfort in a beer. Then another. Then something a bit stronger. At least the whiskey didn't stare at him with disappointed eyes.

Cassie shook her head as she climbed up Michelle's steps. She had to respect Rick for eventually beating his addiction to alcohol. But why the hell hadn't the man told his family the truth? "Pride goeth before the fall" was definitely true in this case.

"Hey, Cassie. What are you doing here?" Michelle asked.

It was easy to see that Michelle had been home long enough to change out of her work clothes, switching from human resources manager to girl next door. She was wearing jeans and a Ravens shirt and had pulled her long brown hair into a ponytail.

"Long story," Cassie replied. She sat on Michelle's leather recliner and proceeded to tell her everything, although she kept to what she'd been told, leaving out her imagined scenes.

Michelle, always sensitive to others' problems, was nearly in tears by the end of the story. "So then Rick lost everything? His career, his wife, his son and daughter?"

"He did. For no reason, either. I mean, neither the FBI nor the police department ever managed to catch anyone who had actually committed the crimes." Leaning her head back on the sofa, Cassie huffed out a breath, watching as it sent a few curls tumbling over her eyes. "And now things have gotten worse. One of the other detectives in the Drug Unit, the one, in fact, that made the initial claims against Rick, was killed last night. And he had a lovely scrapbook full of articles about the D&D Scandal. Evidently Rick's name was mentioned in some of the articles, so the police pulled him and a few others in to interview."

"I vaguely remember that scandal. We were at college, weren't we?"

"Yeah, we were. Can I borrow your computer to look up the articles?"

"You mean you're actually without your laptop?" Her friend pretended to be shocked. "Hell must have frozen over."

"Ha ha, Chelle. Now come on, let's go." Cassie ran up the stairs to Michelle's office and booted up the desktop. "Have you changed your password yet?"

"Of course not. It's the same as always."

"Like no one is going to think to put in your favorite band, Michelle."

She shrugged. "It's my home computer. I'm not stupid enough to use that at work where I have sensitive information."

"I suppose that's a comfort." Cassie clicked on the icon to open the browser. She glanced over at Michelle. Since her friend was paging through her bills, Cassie quickly logged on to Amazon to check for new reviews. When she saw her review count had increased by one, she felt a quick flutter in her stomach.

"That's not the *Baltimore Dispatch* site," Michelle complained. She leaned over Cassie's shoulder. "But hey, you've got a new review, cool. What did they say?"

Cassie pushed Michelle aside so she couldn't read it first. Her stomach fluttered again, this time in distress and not nerves as she read it. "Damn it."

"What? It's a five star review, how can it be bad?"

"He said he loved the book, that it was well-written and well-researched. But then he ended it with 'It's obvious that the author has done her research on guns, body trauma, and murder. Then again, that's not surprising since she had hands-on research when she was involved in two real-life murders.' Wonderful," Cassie said bitterly.

Michelle put a comforting hand on her shoulder and squeezed.

"This is bullshit, Michelle. Up until last month, the only dead body I'd seen was at my mother's viewing." She put a hand up on Michelle's when her friend squeezed her shoulder again. "I'd written the books years ago. It's not like I planned the murders as research." She shook her head to try to erase the image of the second victim, one she'd discovered and one she'd known for years.

"Why don't we look up the articles now, Cassie?" Michelle whispered.

Cassie nodded and navigated to the *Baltimore Dispatch* website. She put Rick's name into the search bar, figuring that was the fastest route. She clicked on the first article that appeared.

"Scoot over." Michelle shoved her over to share the computer chair with her.

Cassie hadn't even gotten halfway through the article when Michelle started talking. "That's a dumb—"

"Wait, I'm not done yet," Cassie complained. "Let me finish this." She quickly scanned the rest of the text. "Okay. Now, what were you saying?"

"I said the fact that O'Reilly had articles that mentioned Rick Whittaker seems like a dumb reason to bring him in for interview. There are all sorts of names here, including Rick Whittaker. But there are also mentions of other detectives that resigned, Leslie Harding and Paul Simmons, and then some officers who had been questioned, including Michael O'Reilly himself. I hope they're pulling everyone in the articles in for interview or they're really stupid. No offense to your homicide department."

"They aren't my homicide department," Cassie protested. "Just one of the detectives is mine."

"You got the hottest one," her friend said. "And since he didn't think you were guilty of murder, he must be one of the smartest, too."

"I think so," she said. Hopefully, he was also being smart with dealing with his father.

> Day off.
> Payback: Go on "stakeout" with Cassie.
> Bring worms.
>
> MONDAY 4 SEPTEMBER   09:34:14

chapter 6

When Whittaker caught up, his father crossed the street to the other side. He did the same. After a few more turns and a ten-minute game of follow-the-leader, Whittaker lost patience. He lengthened his stride and stepped in front of his father.

"I'm just as stubborn as you are, Dad, so why don't we just stop screwing around and talk?"

Rick glared at him. Anger had obviously replaced the sadness he'd shown in the car. "So, now you want to talk, do you?"

"I'm sorry."

Those two words seemed to take the fight out of his father. "I'm sorry, too."

As Whittaker stared at his father, he thought back to that time nine years ago, when neither of them had said a word, when both held back so much that should have been said.

He refused to make that mistake again. But before opening his mouth, he glanced around to get his bearings. When he realized they'd stopped right outside the Recreation Pier Building, where the television show *Homicide: Life on The Streets* had set the Baltimore Police Headquarters, he snorted. It seemed neither of them could manage to get away from the police world.

Placing a hand on his father's arm, he turned him around and led him over to The Daily Grind coffee shop. "Come on, Dad. Let me buy you a coffee."

The Daily Grind was busy as always. Whittaker was about to pull out his badge to clear a table—the three teens in the corner would probably bolt if he combined the badge with a hard-nosed glower. Luckily, a young first-date couple got up from a table in the opposite corner. Whittaker pointed it out to his father and headed to the counter.

"Can I have two coffees, black?"

"What size?"

"The largest, please."

"Would you like flavored syrups? Soy milk?"

"No. No. Just black."

"Whipped cream?"

"Just black."

He counted to ten while the checkout person explained to the barista that really, it was just two plain coffees. Pulling several bills from his wallet, he ground out, "Keep the change," and carried the two cups back to their table. Setting one cup in front of his father, he sat down. He sipped the hot beverage, savoring the aroma as well as the taste, before taking a deep breath.

"So," he began, then wasn't sure what he should say next.

"So."

That went well, Whittaker thought. He took another drink of coffee. Maybe he and his father were more alike than he preferred to think. Both of them were too stubborn and proud to take that first step.

But one of them needed to take it, so he'd just have to suck it up.

"James—"

"Dad—" Both spoke at the same time.

"No, let me go first," they insisted in unison.

Rick set down his cup. "Okay, kid, I'm pulling rank on you, both as a sergeant and as your father. I was stupid before, I'm not going to be stupid again."

Whittaker was ready to agree with him, but then realized he'd be calling his dad stupid. So he kept quiet and let him continue.

"I've had nine years to realize the things I did wrong. And boy, did I ever do things wrong. From trusting the Feds to not trusting my wife enough to tell her what I was doing before I did it. If I'd just given your mom a heads-up that I was working for the FBI, she wouldn't have left. I wouldn't have lost out on watching Chloe grow into a lovely young woman, or missed watching my son grow up to be a fine young man. I wouldn't have lost Patti."

Whittaker sighed. "Okay, Dad, allow me to remind you of some wisdom that you've passed on to me. If you spend all your time regretting your mistakes, you'll never be able to build your future."

"I suppose it's flattering that you remember things I told you." The older man picked up his coffee again. "I must have done something right. But hey, I'm in the middle of a pity party, so don't try and throw my words back at me now."

"We all made mistakes, Dad. You, me, Mom—I won't include Chloe. She was too young, and honestly, she never thought you'd done it."

Rick paused mid-sip. He stared across the table, holding the cup to his open mouth for the space of a breath. Swallowing, he lowered the cup and closed his mouth. "Really? She didn't?"

Whittaker nodded, remembering the arguments he'd had with his sister about this. Anyone who didn't know a hearing-impaired person might not realize you could yell with sign language, but he knew better. The conversations could definitely grow heated. "She didn't, Dad. But then—" He looked away from his father. "Mom and I convinced her that if you were innocent, you would have told us."

Rick sighed loudly. "That would have been the normal reaction, I suppose. I was an idiot. And then I made it worse by being a bigger idiot."

It was time to kick his dad out of his pity party. "I can't disagree with you on that."

His father sat up very straight and scowled. "I beg your pardon?"

"You were an idiot." He laughed at the expression on his dad's face. "Hey, you should be glad I'm agreeing with you for a change. Although—"

"Although?"

"Although I have to disagree with one thing you said. You were wrong when you said we were better off without you."

"There you go, thinking you're so smart." Rick shook his head, but pride was plain to see in his eyes. "Yeah, I definitely did a good job."

"I'm a good cop, too, thanks to things you taught me," Whittaker told him, and then smiled fiercely. "I'm going to prove it, too, by finding out who the hell killed O'Reilly. I know you didn't."

"Thank you for that, James. But I don't want you to get in trouble. This isn't your case. It'll complicate things for you to look into it, even unofficially."

Whittaker noticed a group of students who'd just entered the coffee bar. He used his peripheral vision to observe that the glassy-eyed male had pegged them as cops in seconds. The boy's pat of his pockets probably meant that he was making sure no drug paraphernalia was showing. "So then I just won't get caught."

That drew a smile. "Now, I never thought I'd see the day when Detective James Alexander Whittaker would say something like that."

"Yeah, it's going to shock the hell out of Cassie, too. I've driven her crazy before with my utter adherence to every single rule. But—" he paused, unsure how to say what he wanted to say next.

"You didn't want anyone to compare you to me. I understand that, son. And I know you said I'm supposed to stop worrying about regrets, but I hate that what I did affected you so much. There were times I thought about trying to explain what had happened, but honestly, there was no way to prove I was working with the Feds without them backing me up."

"I can see that, Dad. But right now, we need to focus on O'Reilly. Did your interview with Homicide give you some clues to the focus of the investigation?" Whittaker and his father both knew that if you were clever, you could learn just as much from either side of the interview table. The questions they asked would give it away.

"Newmann and Dirruzo aren't idiots, so they were careful what they asked. Maybe they thought the scandal might be part of the motive for the murder, maybe it's just someone targeting known dirty cops. O'Reilly was mentioned a few times on the lovely list IID put out."

"Not surprising that he's had complaints lodged against him," Whittaker muttered.

"And not surprising that he slipped out of any kind of punishment. He's always been slick. Newmann and Dirruzo also asked if I'd gotten any threats."

Whittaker gripped his coffee cup. "Have you?"

"No. Why would I? I'm merely the owner of a small bar now, not a police officer. The biggest threat I got recently was from Rodney Howe when I dared to tell him that the Yankees weren't going to make the playoffs this year."

Whittaker snorted. "I'm glad to hear that, Dad, and hope you're right about the Yankees. But part of me wishes it was that easy, just someone going after the guys involved in the D&D scandal."

"I don't know. It still wouldn't be easy. I can give you a list of the ones I remember working in the Drug Unit then, and I can let you know who I thought was involved. But again, I hadn't managed to get enough information before O'Reilly made his allegations and took me out of the picture."

Whittaker took out his notebook and pen and signaled to the barista for two more coffees.

"I know, Dad. And honestly, I don't know how the scandal would lend itself to motive anyway. It wouldn't be revenge for someone whose life was ruined by the scandal. The only ones really affected negatively were—"

"Me," his father said.

"You were the most affected. But two other detectives resigned. And didn't they transfer almost everyone out of the department?"

Rick nodded. "Yes. Detective Leslie Harding and Detective Paul Simmons resigned. Detective Lawrence Anderson got knocked down to patrol again. Since they couldn't actually prove anyone's guilt, they just tried to start over with a fresh department. Of course, that was stupid, too, since you now had totally inexperienced people in one of the most important units in Baltimore."

Whittaker wanted to disagree. He believed Homicide was the most important division in a city with the fifth highest murder rate per capita. But many of the murders were drug-related, so he wasn't going to argue. "So, who do you remember?"

"I remember everything from that time, honestly. Hard to forget, even though I tried. It was a shock to see Detective Harding, though. They were bringing her in while I was walking out. Interview didn't seem to bother her though, since she just winked at me."

They went through the rest of the list. Whittaker wrote down the names and tried to fill in where the former Drug Unit officers ended up. He knew he could get Freeman to fill in any blanks.

When they were done, he leaned back and scanned the information they'd recorded. "By the way, did you tell the detectives that you were actually innocent of the accusations?"

"No."

"Dad! Damn it, they might be able to use that information to find the killer." The barista had been about to set down their new coffees, but flinched and jerked back at the outburst. He apologized and offered his nicest, most sincere smile and a generous tip in addition to his bill for the coffees. After she'd stepped away, he lowered his voice and hissed, "You should have told them."

Rick's face was set in stubborn lines again. "They didn't ask. I mean, they asked if I'd interacted with O'Reilly and whether we had committed any theft together, and I told them no. But they didn't ever ask if I'd really been on the take. Why would they?"

Whittaker was glad the coffee wasn't as bitter as his father's words. "No, they assumed that you wouldn't have left the force if you were innocent." He sighed and tried to handle this delicately. "And, just because I want to know, Dad, not because I need to know, why did you close the bar last night?"

Rick snorted. "Honestly? Because the men's room toilet clogged up, badly. It was nasty. I don't want to talk about what I got to clean up. I called the damned plumber, who promised to come out as soon as possible. Of course, that appears to be on the far side of never. In fact, when the uniforms showed up this afternoon, I was hoping it was the plumber."

"So I guess you've been dealing with a bunch of shit for a while then."

The snort became a laugh this time. "I suppose I have."

"What did you do last night while you waited?"

"Went upstairs and watched the O's lose. So no alibi for me, really. Other than the fact that I called the stupid plumber, but that was pretty early in the evening. I'm sorry you're getting dragged into this. Sorry to have interrupted your day today. Since you're in civilian clothes, I assume you weren't on the roll."

Whittaker drained the last of his coffee. "No, I was out with Cassie when Freeman called to let me know what had happened."

"Again, sorry to have interrupted." His father waggled his eyebrows. "I hope that it didn't interrupt anything important."

"We were out at Loch Raven, actually, trying our hand at some fishing."

"Fishing? Cassie fishes? I knew I liked that girl."

"No, she doesn't fish. She doesn't have anywhere near the patience for it. But I was getting back at her for tricking me into going dancing last night." At his dad's quizzical look, he explained. "She had claimed that she needed to research dance instructors for her next book."

Rick laughed. "Oh, that is too much. I definitely like that girl."

"So I told her that I needed help with a stakeout. You know that abandoned deer shack on the north shore of the loch? I said there was someone in there, and I needed a cover for doing surveillance on it."

When Rick laughed again, Whittaker realized that it was the most he'd heard his dad laugh in years.

"You're crazy about her, aren't you?"

"I thought you came to that conclusion when she managed to drag me out to see you and out dancing on the same day. But yes, I'm crazy about her. Although she drives me crazy, too. In fact, do me a favor. Don't let her know, don't even indicate in any way, that I'm investigating O'Reilly's murder. She'll try to get involved."

"What, she thinks because she writes murder mysteries, she should investigate murder mysteries?"

"Exactly. And although I'll give her the fact that she's very clever and thinks like a cop when it comes to her fictional cases, I don't want her getting into danger. I tell her to stay out of it, but she doesn't listen. She's stubborn." He watched as his father finished his coffee and tossed the cup into a nearby receptacle. Following his dad's example, he lobbed his cup in the trash with a clean throw. His father had done a darned good job of teaching him to play basketball, among many other things. They stood up and headed for the door.

"Sounds like a normal woman then. And perfect for you."

"Yeah, let me call my perfect woman and have her come meet us. It'll only take her a couple of minutes; I'll lay odds she's with her best friend who lives a few blocks from here." He hit speed dial, smiling as he thought about his dad's words. Cassie was perfect for him. She not only was willing to put up with his job and his duty to the badge, she appreciated it. She was smart, funny, and had a knack for storytelling. He'd really enjoyed reading her books: the one already published and the ones in the works.

She answered on the first ring. Whittaker felt certain that she'd been impatiently waiting for his call, anxious to know what had happened between him and his father. She was sweet, really, the way she wanted to help fix his relationship with his father. Definitely a fixer, his Cassie.

"Hi, James. Everything okay?" she asked breathlessly.

"As okay as it can be, honey. And how is Michelle doing?" At her silence, he smiled. He could just imagine her pouting because he'd guessed so easily what she'd been up to while he and his dad talked.

She huffed out a breath. "She's okay. And I hate that you figured out that's where I was."

"Basic deduction."

"Well, let me see if I can deduce now. I bet you're standing outside The Daily Grind, after having had some coffee with your father. You're probably leaning against the stop sign out front, about ten feet away from your dad, who is checking out something, possibly a drug deal."

Whittaker whipped his head around and spotted her a couple of blocks down with the phone at her ear. "Clever, Ms. Ellis. Maybe you're psychic. You should join the Psychic Consortium."

She laughed. "Yeah, yeah. I got tired of waiting. I spoke to Michelle for a while, then started walking toward Thames Street again."

He walked over to his father, who was, in fact, watching a drug deal going down. Rick was frowning, hands shoved deep in his pockets.

"I hate watching shit like that. I want to go over and bust them, then remember I can't." He shook his head violently. "Christ, all this rehashing of what happened is really bringing all that anger back to the surface."

Whittaker put his arm around his father's shoulders and they walked back to the car.

* * * * *

"How was the coffee?" Cassie asked brightly.

"Better than anything you can get at headquarters, I'll tell you that. Hell, to think I even miss that," Rick said, then slumped down in his seat.

She called upon on all of her chattering power to cover up the obvious sadness and exhaustion radiating from the two men. She told them some stories from her online English classes. By the time they reached Perry Hall, everyone was laughing at the Tales of Stupidity, as she and Michelle called them. The clear favorite was the student who tried to use the excuse that he was unable to complete his assignment due to having to celebrate a Jewish holiday. When Cassie had asked him why he hadn't prepared the assignment beforehand, he replied that he hadn't known he was Jewish before that week.

She had dozens of stories like that and rolled them out to boost the atmosphere in the car. All of the emotional heavy lifting had her exhausted by the time they pulled up at Rick's bar.

"Hey, Dad, can I use the bathroom before we head back? All that coffee got to me," Whittaker said with his hand on the door handle.

"Sure, but the one in the bar is still broken, since the police came at the same time the plumber finally showed up. Why don't you both come up to the apartment?"

Since Cassie hadn't had coffee, she wandered around the small apartment while she waited. Like the bar downstairs, it was a little old, a little dingy. It wasn't messy, no, everything in the apartment was in its proper place. Not that there were many things to put into their places. A beer crate that held a tiny television, another beer crate for a coffee table, a small brown sofa, and one green rocking chair in a horrible flowered pattern that was probably as old as she was.

It was empty and sparse, with just the necessary things, none of the little pretty things and comfy objects that make a house a home. She wondered if that was just because there wasn't a female around to provide a woman's touch, or if it was a sign of Rick's depression.

She was fairly certain it was due to unhappiness. He tried to hide his misery, but it was obvious to a trained observer. She might not be a cop, but as an author, she was constantly watching people and analyzing body language.

Watching Whittaker follow his dad's movements and seeing the concern on his face, Cassie knew there was no way she was going to stay out of this. She was involved.

She also caught Whittaker's expression when he turned to her and saw her observing him and his father. He knew what she was thinking, she could tell, and he wasn't happy about it. Bracing herself for another lecture about being careful, she said goodbye to Rick and headed down the stairs.

Once in the car, Cassie was surprised he didn't start immediately into lecture mode. She was even more surprised when he apologized instead.

"I'm sorry for manhandling you there in Homicide, Cassie." He reached over and gently squeezed her hand. "And sorry that I was longer than I thought I'd be. I didn't realize I'd been up there so long."

"You're forgiven, James. You didn't know I had to go to the bathroom. *I* didn't know I had to go the bathroom until about ten minutes after you left. And as for your Neanderthal behavior, I guess Major Bianchi's misogynist attitude affected you, too."

"Now wait, I hope I wasn't that bad! I hope I didn't bruise you either, I just wanted to get the hell away from Bianchi." He glanced over at her while they waited at a red light.

"No, you didn't squeeze that hard." When he lifted her arm and gently kissed a circle around her wrist, she melted completely.

"I suppose the Major's stupidity is contagious," Whittaker said. "He's an ass."

"Based on what I saw today, I won't argue. Oh, and talking about what I saw today, who's the man I saw with him?"

"When?" He sped up as they merged onto the Beltway.

"Today. And the other day on television. He's about five foot seven...oh, let me see if I can do it like the cops do. Wait, how do you do it for this guy? I know I'd describe you as brown and gray, and I would be red and blue," Cassie said, describing hair and then eye color. "But how do you do it when someone is a bald dude? Shiny? Invisible?"

Whittaker laughed. "We just say bald. And the bald dude is Officer Raymond Carter, the major's driver."

"Driver? Like what, a chauffer?"

"Very much like a chauffer. Also a general gofer type. Gets his dry cleaning, runs errands, that sort of thing."

Cassie contemplated this. "That's his *job*? The city pays for someone to get his dry cleaning?"

"They do. Don't start—next you'll start complaining about the homicide department's clothing allowance, and I don't want to hear it. Instead, tell me about your visit with Michelle."

"It was okay. Although I checked my reviews, got a *great* one," she said sarcastically.

"I'm sorry. Did you get a bad rating?"

"Yes and no." She told him about the five-star review with its comment about her having real-life experience.

He squeezed her hand again. "I know that bothers you, Cassie. But look at it this way: your research was so thorough that it looked like you had real-life experience."

"Before I did have real-life experience, you mean." She shook her head, not anxious to dwell on it. "We also looked up articles about the D&D scandal."

She watched him clench his jaw and prepared herself for a lecture about staying out of it. He didn't disappoint her.

"Cassie. I know you want to help. But please stay out of this."

"Okay, you know I like to help, right? Can we also establish that I care about you?" She was careful not to use the "L" word. She was determined not to say it until he did, and she suspected it would be a while before that happened. At his nod, she continued. "So, that means that things that happen to you, that affect you, also affect me. Agreed?"

He hesitated for a moment and nodded again.

"So, how can you really expect me to just sit there and not try to help?"

"I suppose I can't expect you to do nothing, Cassie. Can you at least be careful about what you do? I don't mind if you do research, maybe even make some phone calls. But no going to visit suspects in their homes."

She smiled coyly, fluttering her eyelashes. "How about if I visit them at work, then?"

She saw the sides of his mouth twitch as he shook his head.

"Okay, note to self, must find a neutral location to meet suspects. I'll be careful, James. I'll just do nice, safe research. I promise not to visit anyone, okay?"

"Thanks."

Cassie smiled at him and realized he hadn't said a word about having anyone visit her.

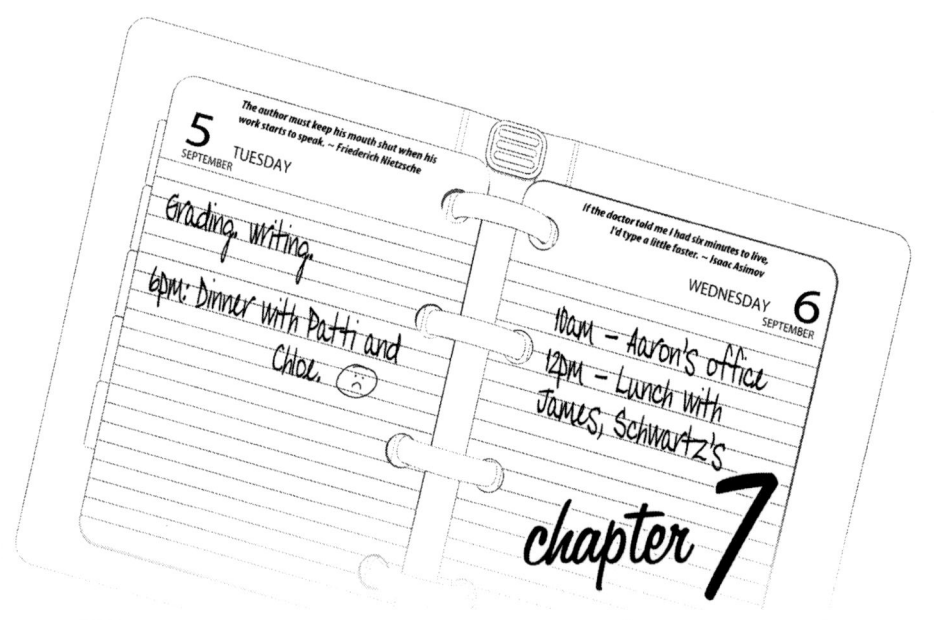

> **5** SEPTEMBER TUESDAY
> *The author must keep his mouth shut when his work starts to speak. ~ Friederich Nietzsche*
>
> Grading, writing.
> 6pm: Dinner with Patti and Chloe. ☹
>
> **6** WEDNESDAY SEPTEMBER
> *If the doctor told me I had six minutes to live, I'd type a little faster. ~ Isaac Asimov*
>
> 10am - Aaron's office
> 12pm - Lunch with James, Schwartz's

chapter 7

THE FOLLOWING MORNING, CASSIE was ready to get started on her now officially sanctioned research. But she had a few steps to take before she could begin.

First, she called Michelle.

"Good morning, Human Resources," Michelle said crisply.

Cassie often pretended she was calling HR for a job to mess with her best friend, but she had other priorities this morning. "I had a nightmare."

"Darn it, Cassie, now you're going to tell me all about it, aren't you?"

She leaned against the refrigerator. "I *have* to, you know that. If I don't, it'll come true."

"You and your superstitions," Michelle said. "But you sound upset, sweetie, so tell me about it."

"Well, I suppose it's actually too late this time, anyway, since this nightmare actually did come true."

"Cassie—" Her best friend's voice was full of sympathy.

"I think it's due to the reviews yesterday, talking about the murders." She relayed her nightmare, how she remembered finding the body, seeing all the blood and gore and knowing that this wasn't a murder in a book. This was her friend, dead because of her.

"Cassandra!" Michelle interrupted. "It is not due to you. *You* did not kill these people. You know who did, darn it. You are not to blame for some insane person's actions."

Cassie leaned her head back on the refrigerator and spoke quietly. "You're right. I know. But it bothers me that I'm benefitting from those same actions. I hate that people are buying my book not because I'm a fantastic author, but because of my connection to murder. I wanted to be famous, not infamous."

"I know. But you are a fantastic author, so take comfort in that, okay?"

"Okay," she whispered. "I'm also struggling with writing *Merlot Murders*. Every time I think of how Marty found Elaine's body, I think of how I found—"

"Cassie," Michelle interrupted. "Don't go there, sweetie. Stop thinking about it. Maybe you should change that part of the book."

"Maybe I should. It's been really hard to write this one. Anyway, I've taken enough of your time. You should get back to work." She worked to keep her voice light. "Do you have anything interesting lined up for today?"

"I do. I have to interrogate people regarding a sexual harassment case. Evidently one of my employees grabbed another employee's 'junk'—the victim's words—so I've got to see if anyone can corroborate that story."

Cassie smiled. Michelle always had the most fascinating stories, although she was careful to maintain confidentiality. "I don't know how you handle this job, Michelle."

"I don't know either, sometimes. One day at a time, I guess. Anyway, talk to you later."

Cassie closed her phone and thought of Michelle's last words. "One Day at a Time" . That particular motto of Alcoholics Anonymous made her think about Whittaker's father. It also made her think of the old television sitcom with Valerie Bertinelli. But mostly Rick Whittaker and how much she wanted to help him. First, though, she needed to accomplish some work.

She slipped the phone into her pocket and headed for the computer to grade assignments. Although her first book was selling well, she still wasn't making enough money to give up her online teaching.

The online format gave her the flexibility to choose her hours and conduct classes on her own time. Typically, that time was in the morning, before she got sucked into her own writing.

Not that she was at her best in the morning. It normally took her two cups of tea before she was able to really focus on the assignments. Occasionally, she wanted to add some liquor to those cups of tea when she read the really bad stories.

Today was one of those days. A few semesters ago, one of her worst students had been Plagiarizing Boy. Although she had to give him credit for being clever enough to plagiarize from a Japanese story, she sure as hell wasn't giving him credit for the creative writing course. He'd dropped out after she had threatened to have him kicked out of the college.

But this semester, there seemed to be his younger, stupider sister: Not Even Going To Try And Hide It Plagiarizing Girl. Cassie shook her head in disbelief at this assignment in "original writing" .

Glancing down at her cat, she complained. "Donner, does she think I'm not going to recognize *The Princess Bride*? Couldn't she at least have made a little effort to change it? Maybe not use 'As you wish.' Maybe, a more modern 'No problem.' Although I hate that; why can't people say 'You're welcome' any more?"

Donner glanced over at her momentarily before turning back to stare intently at his automatic feeder.

She checked the clock. "Donner, you have *four hours* before the magical food dish dispenses your food again."

Donner knocked the food dish a few times with his paw before plopping down next to the dispenser. She laughed at him, then went back to grading.

It took her nearly an hour to compose the email to Not Even Going To Try And Hide It Plagiarizing Girl. It should only have taken twenty minutes, but she started thinking of Cary Elwes' dreaminess and popped *The Princess Bride* into her DVD player to watch for a few minutes. When a few minutes turned into forty, she finally summoned up enough discipline to turn it off.

She phrased the letter carefully and made sure to send a copy to the dean of the college. Often, her attempts to correct plagiarizing behavior resulted in complaints by the students that she was harassing them.

Thankfully, the other stories only suffered from the minor problems of sloppy grammar and spelling. Cassie was very pleased with the progress displayed by Enthusiastic Guy, even if his four thousand word story had taken eight thousand words to complete. Since his previous story had been three times longer than the assigned word limit, she was happy he was improving. He even showed a real talent for writing.

It was after twelve before she was finally able to stop grading, so she decided to stop for lunch before starting her next project. As she munched on an apple, she researched online to check out the media reports about O'Reilly's murder. Rick's name wasn't mentioned, which was good news. The bad news was there was no other information to help her delve further. She decided to refresh herself further on the circumstances of the D&D scandal. Maybe she'd be able to ferret out a clue.

After forty minutes of reading, she took a break and called Whittaker. When he answered, she grinned; she loved his official voice.

"Homicide. Detective Whittaker."

"Hello, Detective Whittaker. This is no-longer-a-murder-suspect Cassie. Since I'm allowed to do research, as long as it's not dangerous, I've been reading up on the D&D scandal. Which sounds stupid, by the way. It sounds like it involved a bunch of role-players living in their parents' basements."

She was pleased when she heard him chuckle. When he was in work mode, he often didn't show any obvious reaction to her comments.

"Anyway, I can't believe they weren't able to catch anyone. It was a much bigger deal than I remembered. Estimates were that over two million dollars went missing, at least. But I wasn't able to find out more about O'Reilly's murder, other than what was in the *Baltimore Dispatch*. Is there anything more you can tell me about it?"

"Not while I'm at work, no."

"You can answer yes or no questions though, right?"

"Yes."

She laughed at his brevity. "Have they completed the autopsy and confirmed he was shot with his own weapon yet?"

"No."

"Have they brought in anyone else for questioning, other than your father?"

"Yes."

That threw off her rhythm. "Oh, who?"

When she was met with silence, she sighed. "Let's see. Were the other people that resigned at that time also called in?"

"Yes and no."

"James." She blew out a breath in frustration. "Do you have to be so annoying?"

"Yes."

He managed to still sound serious, but she laughed. "Okay, so only one was brought in." She pulled up the articles. "Was Harding brought in?"

"Yes."

"So then Simmons was *not* brought in."

"Correct."

She wrote everything down on her pad. "Thank you for varying your answers."

"You're welcome. I need to go soon, Cassie."

"Fine. One last question. I read he was found in an alley in Fells Point. Do we know which one and why he was there?"

He paused this time. "Maybe. But don't even think of going there and asking questions."

"That wasn't the deal we made, so I wasn't going to. I was just curious." She shook her head at his apparent lack of trust. Just because she'd done it once before didn't mean she was going to take risks again. "Anyway, are you coming over tonight? And yes, I know that's one more question. But you can tell me more then."

"I don't know much more. It's not my case. As for tonight, I was going to see if you'd come with me tonight to visit Mom and Chloe. I wanted to let them know the truth about Dad. Dad said it was okay if I tell them and a few others. I've told Freeman already."

"Oh, right." Cassie was glad that Whittaker wasn't able to see her wince. She'd blurted out the whole story to Michelle without first clearing it with Rick. She shook her head and hoped he didn't notice the guilt in her voice. He usually noticed everything. She was relieved when he continued talking, apparently oblivious this once.

"I'd thought about bringing Dad along tonight, but I think that it would be too much of a strain. It'll probably be a strained evening regardless, so I could definitely use a buffer with me."

"I'd be happy to be your buffer, James. Although I'm sure Michelle would say that sounds like a euphemism."

* * * * *

WHITTAKER HAD TO LAUGH. After a few more minutes of talking, he hung up and sighed.

"Cassie's investigating again," he said, then leaned his head down on the gray counter of his desk. "What have I agreed to?"

"What makes you think that?" Freeman asked. "I mean, other than the fact that she's Cassie, research guru extraordinaire."

"Isn't that enough?" he mumbled, then raised his head. "She's asking me all sorts of questions about the case. Why exactly did I tell her it was okay for her to do some research on this situation with O'Reilly?"

"Because you're stupid? Did you forget the last time she did some on-her-own investigating?"

Whittaker would never forget that. The images replayed in his mind—Cassie running at a loaded gun, his own powerlessness to save her, the deafening loudness of the gun. And the relief that her injuries weren't worse. "I'll always remember that. And hey, I told her to be careful, right?"

Freeman shook his head. "Like that'll mean anything. You just don't understand women, Whittaker."

"I think even if I did understand women, I wouldn't understand Cassie." He sighed. "But she did promise not to go out and interview someone regarding this case, anyway. I made her promise that, at least."

"I guess that's something. Honestly, it's probably better if she looks into this rather than you. Since you're not assigned to the case. You aren't going to look into it, are you, Whittaker?"

He applied himself to the unnecessary task of straightening up an already neat pile of papers on his desk.

"I know you've now found out that you aren't in any danger of becoming like your father, but that doesn't mean you should immediately start breaking rules, son."

Whittaker rolled his eyes. He hated it when Freeman called him "son". Considering there were only eleven years between them, it was a bit ridiculous and pretty much physically impossible. "I'm not going to go out and immediately start breaking rules, Dad. Besides, just because you and I know that my dad wasn't guilty, doesn't mean others know that and aren't continuing to judge me for the sins of my father."

"True, although I'll be happy as hell if you're able to at least partially remove that stick up your ass about following the rules. You've been slightly more relaxed since you've been dating Cassie. Regular sex has been good for you."

Whittaker wished that statement were true. Hell, he'd even take irregular sex. "I'm not even going to respond to that."

Freeman's white teeth flashed in a grin. "Are you going to respond to my other comment or are you going to straighten those papers some more?"

Whittaker stopped fiddling with the papers and instead drummed his fingers on the desk. "I don't think it's a good idea to answer that question, actually. If I were to be conducting any private investigation—which I'm not saying I am—but if I were, I'd be certain to cover my ass and I absolutely wouldn't drag someone else's ass into it."

"You have a point. Not that those you might drag into it wouldn't have years more experience than you at covering their ass."

"You do have a bigger ass to cover. Of course you'd gain more experience." Whittaker smiled when Freeman scowled at his retort. It was about time that he got the last word. He turned back to his desk and picked up the paperwork he'd been reading before Cassie's call.

The last case he and Freeman had worked had been fairly simple to solve, less easy to prove. It had become incredibly hard in Baltimore, especially in the poorer neighborhoods, to find people willing to be eyewitnesses. Since this last case was in the Roland Park neighborhood, a more upscale and quiet part of the city, he'd thought the people there would be more likely to come forward with information.

However, when the murder took place at three in the morning, the quietness of the neighborhood worked against it. Very few people were up and about in Roland Park that late at night—or early in the morning. Any way it was phrased, there were not many people around to witness death when the victim and killer had come home together from a late party at Towson University. A young lovers' spat turned into something much more deadly when the knife came out.

He could still picture the devastation on the face of the girl's father when they interviewed him. The father had wept as he explained that he'd gone outside to get his newspaper and found his daughter lying next to the mailbox—his Lorraine, whom he'd believed was tucked up safe and sound in her lush pink bedroom and not out with the boyfriend he'd forbidden her to see.

Whittaker shook his head as he thought about the young woman, how innocent she'd seemed.

Freeman had led the interview with the father, gently drawing out information about his daughter. The man had wiped away tears as he told them how he'd threatened to throw his sixteen-year-old daughter out of the house if she didn't stop hanging out with the much older man. She'd agreed to end the relationship—at least he thought she had agreed—and now she'd died disobeying him.

Whittaker, on the other hand, led the interview with Andre Prokopy, the forbidden boyfriend, after they had finally managed to track him down at Towson. Oddly enough, he'd been absent from all his classes that day. A bad stomachache, or so he'd first claimed. Whittaker had him spilling the truth in only thirty minutes.

He and Freeman hated having to tell Lorraine's father that she'd been murdered when she tried to break off the relationship. Unfortunately, Andre hadn't taken no for an answer and had turned to violence.

Whittaker sighed as he finished up his report.

Freeman looked up from his computer, sorrow evident in his deep brown eyes. "It sucks when it's someone so young, doesn't it? Not that it's ever easy, but I hated looking at that girl and thinking about my daughter. Especially since I'm not sure I would have reacted any differently than her father had. If Jada were sixteen, I'd forbid her from dating some twenty-one-year-old. And if some son of a bitch ever hurts her, let alone kills her, you better lock me up when you catch the bastard."

"I'd have to lock myself up, too, if anyone ever hurt Jada." Whittaker thought about Freeman's bright and energetic preteen daughter. She was a definite Daddy's girl, so God help anyone who hurt her. Then again, Freeman would have a hard time getting in line ahead of his fiery wife, Jordan. She'd wreak vengeance upon any idiot stupid enough to mess with her daughter.

"You know, Whittaker, I think I should be upset that you're grinning right now. But I'm fairly certain that's due to the fact that you're thinking about what Jordan would do to the bastard. I suspect there wouldn't be anything left for you or me to do once she was done."

"There wouldn't be any evidence either. Jordan has learned well, what with being married to a homicide detective."

Freeman snorted. "That woman scares me sometimes."

"Only sometimes? You're a braver man than me." He laughed, then thought about Lorraine again. That sobered him immediately. "We should turn Prokopy over to her. That would be justice."

"Amen to that." Freeman sighed, long and deep. "Anyway, on to other cases. I've been reviewing the Carranza case file, trying yet again to find something we might have missed. No luck on my part, but why don't you check out the file? I'm going to grab some lunch."

He tossed three folders onto Whittaker's desk. "The other two folders were mistakenly given to me by Karen in Filing. Somehow we ended up with some duped files, not sure how that happened." Standing up and stretching tall, Freeman started walking toward the door. He turned around and threw one last comment over his shoulder. "Take a look at those files, Whittaker."

Curious now, Whittaker moved the Carranza folder aside to reach the other two. Seeing the labels of O'Reilly (Homicide) and Drug Unit Monetary Evidence Shortage (IAB), his eyebrows rose. Casually, he dropped the files into his briefcase.

Then he groaned. Freeman got the last word after all.

chapter 8

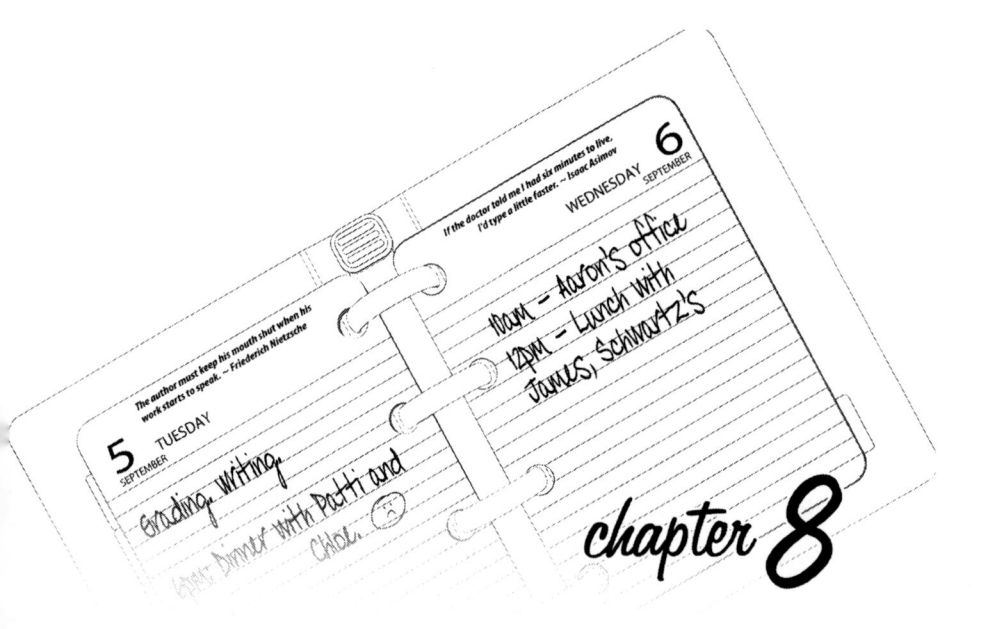

Cassie always wondered if her agent overscheduled on purpose. She'd never been to Aaron's office without having to wait for her appointments.

It was true that he was honestly busy now. His emailed newsletters were filled with names of new clients and new contracts. Now he said he had more exciting news to share with her. Of course, Aaron's idea of exciting might be different than hers. He thought it was wonderful to add more dates to her *Mailbox Murders* book tour.

She'd thought it was thrilling, too—at first—but the travel quickly lost its appeal. She missed her family, her friends, and her cat. Besides, every interview she gave inevitably morphed into a discussion of the Baltimore city murders and not the ones in her book.

Regardless of the topic of Aaron's news, it was bound to go better than last night, when Whittaker had revealed to his mother and sister that Rick was not actually guilty of any crime. That had been one of the most heart-wrenching experiences of her adult life.

She and Whittaker had left his mother's Annapolis house in silence. On the drive home, neither had said a word. She hoped she'd given him some comfort with her presence.

He left her house that night with just a quick kiss and a longer hug. Neither of them was really in the mood for more.

Caitlin, Aaron's secretary, gave her an apologetic look when Aaron still hadn't come out after ten minutes. "Sorry, Cassie. He's running late with this meeting. It's with Bryan Tilman, one of the authors he just got a contract for. A really hot author."

"Really?" While Cassie wasn't interested in him, Aaron was gorgeous. If this new guy was cute enough to affect Caitlin, he must be really, really handsome. It made her wish she'd worn something a little nicer than a blue sleeveless top and khakis.

Her suspicion was confirmed five minutes later when Aaron opened the door. Her agent was movie-star glamorous in an elegant black suit: a classic example of tall, dark, and handsome with wavy brown hair and melting chocolate brown eyes. In contrast, the man with him reminded her of a stereotypical blond surfer, even while wearing a tan three-piece suit. That was, until he glanced over at her. His sky-blue eyes exuded intelligence and shrewdness.

"Cassie!" Aaron said when he noticed her. He strode over to her, grabbed a hand to help her to her feet, and dragged her over to his client. "Cassie, I want to introduce you to my latest contracted author, Bryan Tilman. Bryan, this is best-selling author Cassie Ellis."

Cassie could see the consideration and contemplation in Bryan's eyes. "I've heard of you," he said, taking her hand.

"It's nice to meet you," she replied, returning his firm handshake and bracing herself for his questions about the previous murders.

When no questions were forthcoming, her estimation of him went up a few notches.

Aaron put a hand on the other man's shoulder. "Bryan just moved down here from Chicago. He's made a number of changes at once. New job, new location, and now a new contract. And I have utmost confidence he'll be successful with all three changes."

Bryan smiled, showing off bleached white teeth and no doubt sending Caitlyn's heart rate up. "I hope so, Aaron." He nodded at all of them, including Caitlyn—again enhancing Cassie's opinion of him—and started to step away.

"Oh, wait."

At Aaron's exclamation, Bryan stopped and pivoted back toward them.

Aaron took Cassie by the arm. "You two might be able to help each other. Bryan mentioned that he needed a new local critique group. Cassie, you're in one, right?"

"Yes, and we'd love to get a new author and some new perspective. Especially since we need a man in the group." She knew many of the women would love having an attractive man join them. "I'm sure Cheryl, our facilitator, will be happy to have you join us. We meet every other Monday at five thirty, at the main Enoch Pratt library. You're welcome to join us next week."

She glanced back at Aaron, wondering how Bryan could help her in return.

Aaron must have noticed her curiosity. "Oh, right. I don't think I mentioned that Bryan is also a lawyer. I know you need a new legal expert, Cassie."

When she glared at him for that tactless comment, Aaron had the decency to look guilty.

"I'd be happy to help, Cassie. Feel free to call me." Bryan handed her his business card.

Cassie glanced down at, noting the card came from the U.S. Attorney General's Office located in Baltimore. "Oh, you work for the Attorney General. I'm glad to see that you're a prosecuting lawyer."

He smiled. "Yes, I'm on the side of the law. That is, whenever the law manages to stay on my side. The list of questionable police officers they published this week shows that's not always the case."

She shook her head somberly, as did Aaron. Cassie hid her eye roll; she knew Aaron didn't pay attention to the news. He had confessed his ignorance to her months ago when he didn't even recognize the current vice-president.

"Anyway, hopefully things will change for the better in Baltimore," Bryan said. "Again, it's nice meeting you, Cassie. If you have any legal questions, feel free to give me call."

"Thanks, I appreciate that. Hope to see you on Monday."

Bryan headed for the elevator, and Cassie did her best not to laugh when she noticed Caitlyn obviously checking out his butt. Checking it out herself, she had to admit it was a nice one.

She turned to follow another ass into the office after he cleared his throat. She was pissed at him for making the comment about her former legal expert, considering that person had been her friend as well as the homicide victim she'd discovered.

Aaron apologized as soon as he sat down. "I'm sorry, Cassie. That wasn't the most tactful move on my part. I'm sorry to bring back bad memories."

She shrugged and did her best to let it go. "It's okay. I appreciate you trying to connect me with Bryan. I *do* need a new legal expert, regardless of why that's the case."

Taking a seat, she noticed a stack of boxes in the office. "Are you packing?"

"I am!" he said. "That's my news. Thanks to my recent success, mostly due to your sales, I'm finally moving to New York."

"That's great for you." She meant it. She'd miss the ease of meeting with him and the fabulous view from his office. But she knew Aaron hadn't particularly liked living and working in Baltimore. Most agents were located in New York near the large publishing houses. He was working in Baltimore, his home town, just until he got his break. She'd also discovered recently that he'd been dependent on his parents' money even for his fancy car and office. "I've always wanted to live in New York."

"Me, too. I hope I can afford it, but I think it's worth the risk. It's been a great year for me and for my authors. Not just you and Bryan, but others, too. Linda's got two more titles coming out in the Penelope Blanco series," he said. Linda Kowalski was another of his clients, the author of a series featuring a psychic detective. "And I'm just about to sell a new series for her, a children's book that features a parrot detective."

Cassie laughed out loud. "A parrot detective? A psychic parrot, perchance?"

Aaron furrowed his brow in confusion. "Why would the bird be psychic? Just because Linda writes psychic mysteries?"

Obviously Aaron didn't know about the Psychic Consortium, an organization of which Linda was a member. Cassie had met the Consortium before. It consisted of Linda and her three parrots: an African Grey, a cockatoo, and a budgerigar. While the birds had been fascinating, she still wasn't convinced that they—or Linda—were psychic.

"Never mind, Aaron, I was just being silly. What type of bird is it?"

"A cockatoo. We figured that would be clever since Baretta was a detective and had a cockatoo on that seventies cop show. At least, that's what she told me. Anyway, enough about Linda. Her sales are going great, but not as good as yours. I really think you're going to make all of your advance and earn royalties on your first quarter payment. You'll be the first of my authors to do so. I even talked to DSG about pushing your release date for *Matchbox Murders* forward. They haven't made any changes yet, so right now we're still on schedule for a February 28th release date. And they're looking forward to book three. How is *Merlot Murders* going?" He leaned back in his leather chair.

She hesitated. "Um, fine. I only have about three chapters left to write."

"That didn't sound very confident, Cassie."

She sighed and slumped back in the comfortable chair. "It's not. I'm just not liking this book."

"Because of killing off Elaine?"

"Yes!" She threw her hands up in the air. "It's depressing."

"I thought it was supposed to be." He pulled out a notebook and flipped through it. "I've been explaining to DSG that since this is the final book, the tone will radically change."

"The final book?" Cassie bit her lip in dismay. "I actually had more ideas for future books."

"We don't have a contract for more." Leaning back, he looked up at the ceiling. "Although with the sales we have now for your first book, we could make a strong case for continuing the Marty McCallister series."

"So does that mean you think I should rewrite *Merlot Murders?*"

"I think you should consider it. After all, how hard would it be to just rewrite the book?"

She stared at him in disbelief at that statement.

When his lips twitched and a laugh escaped, she realized he'd been trying to tease her out of her bad mood. Even though a part of her wanted to cry at the idea of rewriting the entire novel, she gave in to his infectious laugher.

* * * * *

CASSIE LOVED MEETING WHITTAKER for lunch. Even though he'd had to reschedule a few times, they tried to meet once a week at Schwartz's, a deli near the Police Headquarters.

She enjoyed going to the deli, which was often patronized by police officers. Even more, she enjoyed watching Whittaker walk in. He was always sharply dressed, and today was no exception. Maybe she was biased, but even though he was the third well-dressed man she'd checked out that day, she thought he was the best-looking of all. She always liked it when he wore gray; it emphasized the smokiness of his eyes.

She also loved to watch the other cops watch Whittaker. Usually she noticed a certain deference and respect. It was apparent that he'd acquired a good reputation. But today was different, she saw right away. This time, the other officers watched him with suspicion and speculation.

Whittaker seemed to be oblivious to the stares, but Cassie knew he wasn't. He was very observant of his surroundings and of others' body language, so she knew he was aware of what was going on. She hoped his indifference wasn't just an act.

He bent down to drop a kiss on her head. "Did you order already? Have you been waiting long?"

"No and no," she answered. She walked with him to the counter and wasn't surprised when he insisted upon paying.

They took a seat near the back. Cassie sometimes wondered how cops managed to sit in the same restaurant together. Wouldn't they all fight for the seats that gave them a view of the door? No, not the door. She shook her head as she remembered what she'd been told. It wasn't the door they watched. Most cops chose the seat with a clear view of the cash register. That's typically where the action would be.

She gave Whittaker the seat with that view and sat with her back to the door. She figured if anything happened, she had him and a dozen other police officers to handle it.

"So how's your day going? What was Aaron's big news?" he asked as he unwrapped his ham and provolone sandwich.

"He's moving to New York, evidently."

He took a bite and shook his head while he chewed. "His overhead's going to go up then. Rent's atrocious there. Don't get why anyone would want to live in New York."

Cassie thought of New York City, with all its excitement, hustle and bustle, and constant motion. She'd love to live there, at least for a little while. Obviously, this was something she and Whittaker wouldn't agree upon. "I also got to meet Bryan Tilman, his latest client."

"Oh, another member of the Flock of Psychics?" he asked, using his newest nickname for the Psychic Consortium.

She did her best not to laugh when he started singing revised lyrics.

"And they flew, they flew so far away, they just flew—"

"James, stop that. And no, not at all. He was a handsome lawyer."

"Oh, was he?" Whittaker said quietly.

She was surprised to see him jealous of a potential rival, but before she had a chance to explore further, she saw his attention switch elsewhere. Turning around, she noticed that the other officers in the place had also seen the new arrival.

Officer Carter walked up to the counter to place his order. Since all conversation had ceased the minute he entered, Cassie was able to hear the cashier call back for "the Major's usual."

She rolled her eyes as she turned back to Whittaker. "He doesn't even pick up his own lunch? What an arrogant jerk." She took a vicious bite of her turkey sandwich. She was really starting to dislike the IID major.

"Of course the major doesn't get his own lunch, Cassie," Whittaker said in a low voice. "And don't say anything else until Carter leaves."

She kept quiet and noticed everyone else was doing the same. Instead of a gradual return to the normal hubbub of conversation, the initial hush that had descended with Officer Carter's entrance had persisted. All of the police officers in the deli were completely focused on eating; there were no side conversations.

When Carter left, carrying a rolled-up paper bag out the door, she did observe several of the cops wrinkling up their noses. One even pinched his nostrils shut as Carter walked past him.

"Oh my God," Cassie whispered, then continued in a more normal tone of voice after the door closed behind Carter and the background chatter started up again. "Did everyone just imply that Officer Carter stinks?"

Whittaker snorted. "No. They're implying that the lunch stinks. Major Bianchi's 'usual' is limburger cheese with onions. That's why most officers, if they're unfortunate enough to have to meet with IID, try to schedule their appointments in the morning."

Since she'd already taken a bite of her sandwich, her shoulders shook from the effort of holding back a laugh. She took a sip of soda to wash down the food. "Why did everyone stop talking?"

"Because everyone thinks that Carter will run back to the major with whatever he hears. There's been no proof of that since Bianchi came to town, but everyone suspects it."

"So everyone shuns him? I feel sorry for him then. He has to do all these crap jobs for Major Bianchi, and no one likes him." She picked up her napkin. "Michelle said that she's isolated as a human resources director: the employees don't talk to her since they worry a casual comment might end up with management, and the managers don't trust her since she takes care of the line employees. So she's learned to not have any work friends. I suppose that's what Officer Carter feels like. I feel bad for him."

The empathy she felt for Officer Carter led her to think about Rick, and about how miserable Patti and Chloe had been the night before. "Are you feeling better after last night?"

He shrugged. "I suppose. I'm going up to Dad's tonight to tell him how it went, but I think I'll leave out the crying parts. You need to do class planning tonight, right?"

She nodded. "I do, sorry. Tell your father hello for me."

"I will." He tapped his fingers on the table as he stared out the front window. "Dad should be fine, since he's known the score the last nine years. I just hope Mom's okay. How will she handle knowing she sacrificed everything for no reason?"

"She's strong, James. I'm sure she'll handle it." She reached over and rubbed his hand. "And she had a reason. She thought she'd made the right decision, to protect Chloe from what she thought was your father's bad influence. That took strength. You get your strength from her, I think. Your temper and honor from your father, but your strength you get from Patti."

"Maybe. Dad's strong, too, considering he survived these past years alone and managed to beat alcohol addiction." He rolled up his sandwich wrapper and threw it toward the trashcan. "So where do you get all your traits from? I can see some comparisons with your father, your hair for example. I never met your mother, so I don't know what you got from her."

"Hmm—physically, not much. I got Dad's hair color, eye color—hers were green—and his height. I did get my love of reading and my writing talent from my mother. She was an English teacher and always encouraged reading." She felt a pang of grief that could still sneak up on her, even after eighteen years.

"Where'd you get your curiosity?"

"Michelle, actually." She smiled when he laughed. "She always had to know facts and information, and that affected—or maybe infected—me after a while."

He took her trash and threw it away. "I can believe that. How long have you two known each other?"

"Since second grade. Geez, that's what—twenty years now? We've gone through everything together."

"And you tell each other everything, too."

She fought not to squirm under his stare. "I knew you figured out I'd told Michelle about your father when I went quiet on the phone the other day."

"No, I figured it out when you told me the two of you were looking up articles about the D&D scandal."

She threw up her hands in disgust. "Damn it! I didn't even realize I'd done that. Why do I bother trying to keep anything from you when you manage to figure out everything?"

"I don't know," he said. "It seems like a colossal waste of time to me."

"Are you mad that I told her?"

Shaking his head, he gave her a hand to help her up. He didn't answer until they were on the street and headed towards her car. "Not really. I trust Michelle."

"I haven't told anyone else."

"Not even your father?"

"Honestly, I haven't. I felt so guilty about Michelle, I only told my dad that we were heading up to your mother's house to tell her something important, but I didn't go into detail."

"You can tell your father. I know you also tell him everything. Well, hopefully not everything." When they reached her car, he used their linked hands to pivot her around to face him. His brows and his voice lowered. "I hope, when we can actually manage a night together, you keep certain details to yourself."

She felt a thrill go up her spine at the thought of spending the night with him. "Will there be a lot of details to keep?"

"Definitely." He began stroking her palm with his thumb, in slow, deliberate circles. "I'm extremely detail-oriented. I'm planning on taking my time on this particular project. And being very, very hands-on."

She gave him points for managing to turn her on while they were on a public street. He was barely touching her, just lightly caressing her palm. She hadn't even realized her hand *was* an erogenous zone. With that gentle brush of skin on skin, his promise-laden words, and her imagination of how he'd put said words into action, she was almost dying of anticipation and lust. "I'm..." She cleared her throat. "I'm looking forward to that."

His eyes darkened with intensity. "So am I. So, very much, am I." He lifted her hand, kissed her palm—oh yeah, was that an erogenous zone—and turned to head back to police headquarters.

Cassie fumbled with her seat belt for a full minute before giving up. Leaning her head against the steering wheel, she waited until her pulse settled down. Then she finally latched the belt and headed home, although she wasn't certain how she was going to concentrate on work now.

chapter 9

*C*ASSIE WAS FINDING IT difficult to prepare for O'Reilly's funeral.

It wasn't that she didn't know what to wear. She had her basic black dress ironed and ready.

It wasn't even that she was worried that perhaps it was inappropriate for her to attend the funeral, since she didn't really know him and didn't like what she did know.

The fact that Rick Whittaker was one of the main suspects in the killing didn't bother her either. People could think what they wanted. She figured Whittaker wouldn't be happy with her for attending the funeral, but he couldn't complain that it was dangerous. She should be safe in the huge Cathedral of Mary Our Queen, surrounded by hundreds of other mourners and onlookers.

The problem was she was dressing to attend the funeral of a police officer.

She was dating a police officer.

At times like this, she hated her vivid imagination. She could all too easily visualize herself dressing for Whittaker's funeral.

> It had been three nights. Three lonely, agonizing nights. She had answered the door, expecting it to be their daughter's best friend coming to pick up Katie to go to the mall, and instead had seen two uniformed police officers.
> She'd known instantly.
> The three days since had been filled with planning the elaborate funeral, taking condolences from friends and family, and doing what she could to comfort their children. James would have wanted her to take care of them.
> But the nights had been miserable as she curled up alone in the big bed, hugging the pillow that still smelled of him. She didn't sleep.
> That much was obvious, she thought as she looked in the mirror. The wrinkles on her face had deepened, her eyes appeared sunken into her head, and her hair, now with gray mixed in with the red, was lackluster. She had pulled it back into what she thought of as a widow's bun.
> She slid the dress over her head and smoothed down the black fabric. Twisting the wedding ring around her finger she—

Cassie shook her head to get rid of these images. She stopped rubbing her empty ring finger and wiped away her tears. Those weren't imaginary.

In general, she could handle dating a police officer. She knew it came with danger and that every day he went out on the street, there was a risk he might not come back. She knew he was careful and clever, so she did her best not to think about it. Still, she found herself monitoring the police scanner more than she used to.

Needing to clear her head of those thoughts, she forced herself to think about the funeral.

She knew, both from research and from living in Baltimore, that police funerals were huge productions. The family had to find a venue large enough to fit family, friends, fellow police officers—and the hundreds of politicians, local and state, that came out on such a solemn occasion, especially during an election year.

She wasn't even certain she'd be able to get into the church since she wasn't family, friend, or fellow officer, and she definitely wasn't a politician.

"Do you think that the murderer will be there?" she asked her cat as she changed the water in his bowl. "The crowd will be big enough to hide in, I suppose. Probably thousands of people." She reached for her purse, made certain her notebook was inside, and headed outside.

Immediately, she regretted the necessity of wearing black.

The sun was bright and burning, and the dark fabric absorbed the heat instantly. The notorious humidity pasted her hot dress to her thighs. She rolled down her car windows and prayed for the air conditioning to work fast as she planned her route.

The cathedral was located up north on Charles Street. While it wasn't the fastest or most efficient route, taking Charles Street through the city was the most interesting. It passed through so many of Baltimore's varied neighborhoods, from the poorest to the richest, from tourist traps to the real Baltimore neighborhoods.

She picked up Charles Street in her own neighborhood of Federal Hill, then followed it through the Inner Harbor with its shops and tourists.

Waiting at the traffic light, she glanced over to the National Aquarium. It would make a really interesting place for a showdown between her main character and the bad guy. How long was it since she'd visited the Aquarium, anyway? She decided to ask Whittaker or Michelle to go with her in the next week or so.

A horn honked behind her, yanking her away from her plotting to focus on the drive. She smiled when the top of Baltimore's George Washington monument came into view ahead in the Mount Vernon area. Although Baltimore had erected its Washington Monument before the one in DC, a fact she never failed to point out to guests, no one ever seemed impressed. Still, she preferred Baltimore's.

As she passed Penn Station and threaded her way through the poorer sections of town, Cassie started plotting the scene for her novel again. Taking out her recordable MP3 player, she began dictating ideas while keeping a careful eye on the slow-moving traffic.

By the time she drove through the Johns Hopkins area, she'd recorded an idea for the final showdown. It would be great for it to take place in the top level of the aquarium in the Rain Forest. Several times, her plotting was interrupted when she had to stop for the college students who were capriciously crossing the street in the middle of a block. Hadn't these kids heard of crosswalks?

Uh-oh. She was thinking of college students as kids.

Oh well, she wasn't old. Not when she still snickered as she passed by the College of Notre Dame of Maryland. Didn't they realize what that abbreviation spelled?

Five minutes later, she pulled into the already full parking lot of the cathedral. She stopped thinking of the bad guy's downfall, although she did dictate her new idea of having the final scene in the Atlantic Reef section, where Marty would trip the villain into the shark tank.

Exiting the car, she tried to calculate the best way to get into the cathedral. Perhaps she'd just wait outside and watch to see if anyone was acting suspiciously. She wiped away the sweat that dampened her face. Out of her air-conditioning less than a minute, and already she could feel it trickling down her chest and back. Okay, waiting outside was a bad idea.

She passed through the parking lot filled with blue and white police cars and was impressed with how clean all the vehicles were. They must have all been freshly washed for the occasion.

The police officers also looked freshly washed and primed. Not all of them were in uniforms. She picked out the plain-clothes detectives, who all wore their badges on the outside of their suit jackets. Even if they didn't have the badges, she felt certain she could have identified them. There was just something about a detective's bearing.

The police were all somber and serious as they filed into honor guard formation outside the building. Seeing them all standing outside, she worried that she wouldn't make it in the cathedral. If all the officers weren't getting in, how would she?

Just when she was contemplating bluffing her way inside, her salvation came from an unlikely source.

"Cassandra," an alto voice trilled.

Turning around, she was surprised to see Linda Kowalski. The older woman had her pure white hair pulled back into a braid, a style that Cassie thought was very flattering. Amused, she noted that, even for a funeral, Linda had made certain her clothing matched the plumage of one of her parrots. Linda had chosen to wear the African Grey's colors today and sported a dark gray suit with a black shirt. Cassie was thankful that Linda had selected the most subdued color of her avian friends at least, and wondered for a moment if Linda had deliberately skipped the red accent. Then she spotted the scarlet purse dangling at her side.

Fortunately, Linda hadn't brought any of her birds with her, as she often did.

Cassie rushed over and hugged her. "What are you doing here, Linda?"

"We've been doing readings for Maggie, Officer O'Reilly's mother, for years. I'm so devastated at Michael's death, although we had been getting some bad vibes recently. The birds have been saying dire quotes whenever Maggie has asked about her son. How about you? How do you know him? Through James, I assume?"

Cassie felt her face heating up. "I know *of* him through James. It's more that I felt—now that I'm dating a police officer—I should pay my respects."

"That's very nice, dear," Linda said and patted her hand. "Let's go inside. I'll tell them you're with me."

Linda gave her name to the officers at the door and they were ushered inside.

Cassie sighed in relief when they entered the cool interior. The temperature—partially due to air conditioning and partially due to the marble walls and floors—felt wonderful.

She had been to the cathedral before and always loved the gorgeous rose window above the altar as well as the beautiful stained glass windows. This time, however, it was hard to notice anything but wall-to-wall people.

There were several politicians she recognized from television, including the mayor, deputy mayors, and some state senators. She even saw one federal-level senator and the governor doing the rounds and shaking hands. Not surprisingly, every politician seemed to be wearing the "I'm concerned about this matter and will do everything to address it" "Please vote for me" face.

She saw tons of police officers, in uniform and out. Many she recognized, including Commissioner Spaulding, Major Bianchi, Officer Carter, all three lieutenants from the

Homicide Division, and one very, very annoyed Detective Whittaker sitting a few rows back.

She gave him her brightest smile and signed to him. *Hello, how are you?*

When she just got a *Why are you here?* in return, she signed back *I'm doing fine, thank you.* Then she turned back to Linda.

"So how long have you been doing readings for O'Reilly's mother?"

Linda pursed her lips in consideration. "I've been working with Maggie for at least ten years, I believe."

Now here was an interesting research opportunity Cassie hadn't thought of. "So, then, you would have been doing readings during the D&D scandal."

"Correct." Linda swiveled around on the wooden pew and faced her directly. "So you just came to pay respects, did you? No ulterior motives?"

Sometimes, Cassie forgot that behind that flighty exterior, Linda was actually quite intelligent. The knowing look in the older woman's dark green eyes told Cassie plainly that Linda had figured out her motive for being here.

"Well, I did want to try and find out more about Officer O'Reilly. I don't know if you know, but James' father was pulled in for questioning for O'Reilly's death."

Linda's eyes widened. "I hadn't known that, no. But if that's the case, I'm surprised that you came at all, and even more surprised to see James. But that explains the negative energy I've felt from some of the other police officers."

Negative energy. That was one way to describe the way that some of the officers, especially the ones up front whom Cassie assumed were from O'Reilly's unit, kept glaring at her and Whittaker.

"However, Cassie, even if that is the case, I don't feel comfortable giving you information about my client. I know psychics don't actually have client privilege, but I try to respect their confidentiality."

"But O'Reilly is dead," she protested.

"His mother is not. That's her up front, talking to—listening to, actually—Commissioner Spaulding."

Cassie craned her head to pick out the people. She couldn't quite see the mother, who was hidden by a throng of sympathy-givers, but she could see Commissioner Spaulding and the concerned expression on his face. Was that concern real, or just for show? She'd often wondered about that. At the least, the Commissioner was a skilled actor.

Cassie made herself as comfortable as she could in the wooden pew before the Mass began. Noticing the tall, pointy hat on one of the elaborately garbed priests, she realized that O'Reilly's funeral was being celebrated by Baltimore's archbishop. She wondered if the Church knew that they were going all out for a dirty cop.

* * * * *

Whittaker wanted to sign some words and phrases not appropriate to a funeral service. He wasn't sure at whom he was more angry: Cassie for being there or himself for not figuring out that she'd attend. He should have expected it. Freeman, who hadn't reacted when he saw Cassie, must have.

"You have no right to be angry, Whittaker," Freeman whispered to him. "You shouldn't be here, either."

Whittaker didn't reply. Freeman was right. The older detective had complained about that the entire drive to the cathedral. But still, Freeman had used his contacts to get them space inside. Whittaker was going to owe his partner.

He was surprised to see Linda Kowalski; he had no idea she'd known O'Reilly. Did she or any of her flock forecast his death? That was one prediction he'd have been willing to make himself. People like O'Reilly often came to a bad end.

He scanned the crowd, relieved when he didn't see his father. That was probably for the best. Richard Whittaker was currently quite unpopular in the law-enforcement community. Plus, since he was a bar owner, he probably slept in late each morning.

Whittaker went through the motions of the service: standing up, sitting down, kneeling, making the sign of the cross. He remembered most of the lines. Although he wasn't a regular churchgoer—his schedule didn't allow it—his years spent as an altar boy meant that he'd never forget the rituals.

The eulogies seemed to take forever. Politician after politician. Police official after police official.

"Are they talking about O'Reilly?" he asked Freeman during one particular praise-filled homage. "Seriously, none of that sounds anything like the O'Reilly I knew."

Freeman leaned in closer. "Maybe they got the wrong guy. You should go check the casket, make sure there wasn't a screw-up. Go ahead. Go up there, lift the lid."

Whittaker fought to hold back his laugh. He was fairly certain it was a sin to snicker in church.

* * * * *

AT THE CEMETERY, CASSIE pulled into a parking space alongside Linda, whom she'd followed in the long procession from the church. She stuck close to her friend as Linda made her way to the family of the deceased. When the older woman wrapped her arms around O'Reilly's grieving mother, however, guilty stirrings disturbed her conscience. Here was

Linda, providing comfort and support...and the main reason Cassie had come was to investigate.

And her investigation would probably result in revealing some negative information about the deceased.

So she did her best to offer condolences when Linda pulled her closer to make introductions. Remembering how awful she'd felt imagining Whittaker's death, Cassie was sincere. "I'm sorry for your loss, Mrs. O'Reilly. I know this is a difficult time for you."

"Thank you for coming," Maggie O'Reilly said. "And it looks like you and your friends were right, Linda. This is the big bad world, full of mean people, where nasty things happen."

When Linda frowned, Cassie realized that Maggie must have revealed a prediction made by one of the birds.

"Anyway," Maggie continued, after swiping at her reddened eyes with a tattered tissue, "we appreciate that so many people have come out for Michael's funeral."

Cassie's nagging sensations of guilt flared again, since her reason for attending wasn't entirely appropriate. She needed to escape. Mumbling her condolences again, she turned to flee and immediately bumped into Whittaker.

He grabbed her elbow and escorted her away at a faster pace than she'd planned. "Why the hell are you here, Cassie?"

"I could ask you the same thing, James. It's not like you wanted to pay respects to Officer O'Reilly. You didn't have any respect for him."

"When an officer dies, we *all* come out to pay our respects, regardless of what happened in the past. Especially if that officer went down in the line of duty."

"Did he?" she asked.

"Did he what?"

She looped her arm through his and headed with the rest of the crowd towards the gravesite. "Did he fall in the line of duty? He was off-duty, wasn't he?"

Whittaker shrugged. "I think they're still treating it as a service-related death. That's why he got full honors. If he was, in fact, killed with his own gun, then that points toward it being related to his work."

"Have they determined the murder weapon yet?"

"Cassie, even if I knew the answer, I can't share it. Especially not here."

"Fine. By the way, what movie is " 'This is the big bad world, full of mean people, where nasty things happen' from?"

Whittaker had been the first to tell Cassie that the predictions made by Linda's parrots were actually movie quotes. Evidently the birds—who were still incredibly clever, psychic or not—had memorized certain lines.

He gave her a lopsided smirk, revealing a dimple. *"Wait Until Dark.* 1967. You've been talking to Linda again, I assume."

She nodded. "Yes. I assume that was a prediction that the Psychic Consortium made about O'Reilly."

"They got that one right. Shit, what does he want?"

She felt him stiffen next to her as a uniformed police officer approached them.

"I didn't realize we could bring a date to the funeral," the officer said.

Cassie did a double take to make sure the man was a pasty white police officer and not Billy Dee Williams. The deep, mellow tones reminded her of the handsome Star Wars actor and Colt 45 spokesman.

"Officer Anderson." In contrast, Whittaker's voice was tight and strained.

She struggled not to react to that name. This must be one of the other officers Rick had mentioned as being involved in the D&D scandal.

The officer looked her up and down and not in a flattering way. "So, you must be the infamous Cassandra Ellis. You two met while you were a murder suspect, wasn't it? How romantic. And rather unseemly, really. Do you usually sleep with your suspects, Whittaker?"

She felt Whittaker vibrate under her hand, but he didn't give any other visual reaction. "Do you usually throw insults at a fallen officer's funeral, Anderson?"

"I think you being here is a bigger insult, Whittaker. Everyone knows your father is the one who killed him."

"No, he's not," Cassie said fiercely.

Anderson sneered at her. "What, you know more than the homicide detectives? You saying you know who the killer is?"

"I do know—"

She stopped when she realized that everyone around her had gone silent. Glancing behind her, she saw why. Major Bianchi and Officer Carter passed by. Cassie knew that Internal Investigation officers were called rats, but she couldn't believe her ears when Anderson started making squeaking noises once the IID officials were out of earshot.

Some officers around them laughed, but she just shook her head.

"You live dangerously, don't you, Officer Anderson? And I do know that the killer is *not* Richard Whittaker."

"And how do you know that?"

Whittaker spoke up. "Ask Detectives Newmann and Dirruzo. They obviously came to that conclusion, since they let him go home."

Anderson shrugged. "Just means they don't have enough evidence against him. Seems like that's happened to your father before, hasn't it?"

She tried to hold Whittaker back when he took a step closer to Anderson. She was starting to worry if she could really keep him from resorting to violence when relief came in the form of Detective Freeman.

"Officer Anderson, I understand you're needed with your squad."

Cassie always enjoyed seeing Freeman, but she *really* appreciated him this time.

"Yes, sir." Anderson exchanged one last challenging look with Whittaker before leaving.

"Let it go, Whittaker, he's not worth it." Freeman took Whittaker's other arm.

Between the two of them, they dragged Whittaker away from Anderson and the crowd.

She took another glance at the offensive officer. "He's another one from the D&D scandal, right? Another one that got off scot-free?"

"I wouldn't call it scot-free," Freeman said. "He did get busted back down to patrol and had his district changed."

"Yeah, but he got the Southeastern district, the party district. That's Fells Point and Canton," Whittaker explained to Cassie. "I'd love to have seen him get a rougher area, like Eastern or Western. Yeah, I would love to have seen him get Western midnights. And why the hell did you just stick up for IID, Cassie?"

"I didn't stick up for IID," she said hotly. "I can't stand the major. But I feel sorry for Officer Carter. I'd hate to have to work for that man."

"His choice, mostly," Freeman said. "And Anderson's an idiot. I bet you the major heard his rat noises. Bianchi's not stupid. Talking about stupid, I still think it's a dumb idea for you two to be here. Anderson was the only one to say something directly, but you're getting plenty of dirty looks. Our shift is pretty much over, Whittaker. Why don't you head back with Cassie?"

"That's probably a good idea." Cassie pulled out her cell phone. "Wow, it's after three. I didn't realize these funerals could go on so long. I need to get home and do some planning for next week. Do you want me to drive you back?"

Whittaker shoved his hands in his pocket and surveyed the crowd around them for a moment or two before answering. "Yes, I suppose that would be best. Let me know if you find out anything, Freeman."

"See you later, Freeman," Cassie said. "Let me just find Linda and say goodbye, and then we'll go."

She drove Whittaker back to the city and dropped him off at his house. Once again, they parted with just a quick kiss.

As she started home, she wondered if they'd ever find a time where the mood was more conducive to romance.

chapter 10

She needed food. Like Mother Hubbard, her cupboard was bare.

Fortunately, while she didn't have any bones for a dog, she did have food for Donner. She always made certain to keep around plenty of cat food. Since he was a kitten, Donner would let her know he was hungry by nibbling on her toes. Although most people thought her cat was named after one of Santa's reindeer, he was actually named after the ill-fated Donner party in the Sierra Nevada. She didn't relish sharing their fate.

But first, she had to check her email. Scanning the Inbox, she pounced on one from Linda. Maybe she had relented and provided information on O'Reilly.

Cassie rolled her eyes when she read the first line. *The birds are concerned*, Linda had written. *They've been saying your name since I got home from the funeral.*

That meant they were saying the name "Red", Cassie knew. When she read the quote, she was excited that she actually recognized it this time: *What we got here is a failure to communicate.*

That one was from *Cool Hand Luke*. Cassie could still remember being shocked at the ending of that movie. She watched it for the first time over thirty years after the movie had been out. She'd assumed, from the few quotes she'd heard, that it was a happy movie. But it definitely wasn't happy.

She emailed Linda back and thanked her for the heads up. She also read the email from Cheryl reminding everyone about the critique meeting tomorrow. After finding Bryan's card, she forwarded him that information as well.

Then she got her rolling cart and walked to the store to buy groceries. And some extra cat food, just in case.

On the way home, she planned the rest of the week. She'd made plans to go to the Aquarium with Michelle the day after tomorrow, so she'd have to hold off on writing the chase scene until then. Although the more she thought about it, perhaps having the villain land in the shark tank was over the top. It wasn't as if the sharks would automatically eat her anyway; sharks weren't mindless killing machines.

It would be way more fitting if the villain could be killed by poison. Maybe a pufferfish? Or one of those poisonous frogs. Cassie frowned as she pondered. Shaking her head, she made sure to clear that expression from her face. She didn't want anyone on the street to think she was crazy or psychotic.

Although she didn't have to worry. The streets around her were mostly empty. Only one old man was braving the heat as he watered the flowers on his stoop. She should do that too, although it was probably too hot. The water would just steam up and evaporate.

Speaking of steam, a pick-up truck was stopped on her side of road just ahead, its hood up, its radiator steaming.

She knew next to nothing anything about cars, but she walked over to offer help, especially when she saw an older woman underneath the hood.

"I suppose the question 'Having car trouble?' would be pretty stupid?"

When the woman straightened, Cassie felt surprise at her height. The truck's owner was at least six inches taller than she was, and Cassie considered herself rather tall.

"Definitely having car trouble." The Amazon kicked the bumper. "Just what I need on this hot day. And my cell phone won't get a signal here." She whipped out the phone and glared at it, as if it was responsible for everything up to and including the hissing radiator.

"This is pretty much a dead zone for most phone carriers. Not sure why. I had to go through three different companies before I found one that worked. Here, use my—" Cassie reached into the left front pocket of her cargo shorts and frowned when she found it empty. "Oh, shoot, it's in the house. Would you like to come over and um…" She eyed the woman, trying to decide if this was some type of scam to get into her house. But the woman seemed harmless.

"Would you feel more comfortable if I said I was a former cop?" the tall woman asked. She flashed a charming smile and held out her hand. "I'm Leslie, by the way. And if I could use your phone and maybe your bathroom, I'd really appreciate it."

"Cassie," she said, shaking the woman's hand.

Leslie nudged her sunglasses up to the bridge of her nose, leaving behind grease and dirt. Cassie suspected Leslie usually was well-groomed. The jeans and green shirt she was wearing were high quality, and it looked like she had spent time on her hair… until the heat and humidity got hold of it. She took pity on the older woman.

"Come on in," she said, leading the way. She put her groceries down and headed towards the refrigerator for some chilled water. "Why don't you use the bathroom and clean up?" She gestured to the miniature bathroom tucked beneath the staircase.

Cassie put the already beaded water bottles on the table and turned to survey her cabinets, wondering if she should offer a snack. Before she could decide, the bathroom door opened.

"Ah, so much better," sighed Leslie.

Cassie turned. "I'm sure." She was envious at the speed which the older woman had managed to put herself back together—she'd even refreshed her makeup.

"Have a seat. Oh, you're not allergic to cats, are you?" She turned around to see that Leslie had already sat down on the loveseat. Donner hadn't wasted any time and had already jumped into her lap. "I hope not."

Leslie reached up and scratched the cat's ears. "No, not allergic. Have two of my own."

"Here's the phone." Cassie passed her the cell phone and a bottle of water.

She headed back to the kitchen and grabbed her own bottle of water. Leaning against the counter, she tried hard not to listen to Leslie's phone conversation. That took some doing since her first floor had an open layout.

Leslie closed the phone and drank half of the bottle of water. "Thanks, Cassie. That was incredibly helpful, both the water and the phone." She placed the bottle against her neck.

"No problem," Cassie said, then grimaced. "I mean, you're welcome."

Leslie took another chug of water and glanced around. "So, if I may ask, are you a writer or a librarian?"

Cassie laughed. "A writer."

"This is an amazing amount of books," Leslie said, waving her hand toward the shelves. "And since they all seem to have murder as a theme, I'll assume you write mysteries." She stood up and went to the shelf with Cassie's own books. "In fact, let me guess that *you* are Cassandra Ellis."

"Guilty as charged." Cassie noticed an odd expression pass across Leslie's face. "So, you said you used to be a police officer. What did you do?"

Before Leslie could answer, there was a quick knock on her open door and Whittaker stepped in.

Cassie started over to greet him when she saw his gaze swing toward Leslie. Her motion and the words of welcome rising to her lips stopped cold at the livid expression on his face. She didn't think she'd ever seen him so angry.

"What's wrong?"

Whittaker nodded towards Leslie, eyes flashing. "Like you don't know?"

"I don't," said Cassie, confusion and distress tightening her throat. She didn't know what was going on, but the tension was palpable.

"I can't believe this," Whittaker hissed between his teeth. "You promise not to go to other's homes to interview them, so you decide it's just fine and dandy to invite them to *yours*?"

"What? I didn't do any such thing!"

"Damn it, Cassie, you're not a cop."

Her temper started firing up at his accusations. She hadn't done anything to deserve his anger. "I know that. What does that have to do with—"

"You going to try and tell me it's just coincidence that Detective Leslie Harding is in your house?"

Cassie glanced over at the blond woman. She remembered the name from the articles about the D&D scandal, but she hadn't even learned Leslie's last name. That was probably stupid of her. "Actually—"

"That's not what—" Leslie tried to explain, but Whittaker cut them both off.

"Don't even *try* to give me that bullshit about how you know how to handle yourself now that you've taken one lousy RAD class. You become a black belt, maybe then we can talk. Better yet, get a gun."

Cassie tried to get a word in. "James—"

"I can't handle it when you keep taking unnecessary risks like this, Cassandra. I don't need to worry about you doing something stupid and dangerous all the time."

"I didn't—"

"Do anything stupid?" He stalked towards her. "What the hell do you call inviting Harding into your home?"

Now *she* was mad. And since he seemed to be drawing his own conclusions about her and her actions, she decided there was no use even trying to say anything in her own defense.

Whittaker shook his head. "I can't believe you did that. I can't handle this." He pivoted on his heels and stalked out the door, slamming it behind him.

Cassie stared at the door, still vibrating in its frame. After a few minutes, she slid her eyes toward Leslie. "Well, I guess I know what you did with the police."

"Yes. I'm sorry I didn't tell you that. I didn't mean to cause any problems between you and Detective Whittaker."

"You know him?" Cassie's suspicions were raised.

"I've heard of him, yes. Saw him, too, when I was waiting for my turn to be interrogated for O'Reilly's death." She laughed, the sound unexpected and startling. "You're looking suspiciously at me now. I promise you, I didn't kill Michael O'Reilly."

"Did you take money?"

The smile dropped. "I won't answer that."

Cassie shook her head. "Never mind. I really don't care about that. I'm only concerned about O'Reilly's murder because Rick Whittaker is a suspect."

"What makes you think he didn't do it?"

"He didn't do it." Cassie scowled.

Leslie shrugged elegantly. "I don't know. Rick always struck me as a patient, thorough man. He could wait years to get his revenge."

"Then I think he would have been clever enough to get a better alibi."

Leslie inclined her head in agreement. "I can't argue with that. He's a smart man. But honestly, I can't blame him if he did do it. I've always resented that others got off scot free while we were forced to resign."

"He didn't do it."

"Are you sure?" Leslie glanced over at the closed door. "I can remember he had a temper. Looks like his son inherited it."

Cassie shook her head. "He *didn't* do it."

"If you say so. Anyway, I see the tow truck is out there. Thanks for all your help, and I really am sorry that my being here caused such problems. If you want, I can talk to him, explain why I was here."

"No. I'm not explaining anything." Cassie escorted Leslie to the door. "He's the one being stupid and making stupid assumptions."

After shutting the door, she leaned against the wall and slid down to the floor. "Stupid man. Stupid, *stupid* man."

Donner came up to her and meowed.

"What, you're on his side? You're a stupid man, too, even if I did cut your balls off." She glared at the door. "Wish I could do the same to James."

She put her head down between her knees. Then she shook her head and stood up. Snatching her keys, she headed over to see the one man who wasn't stupid.

* * * * *

"He's a jerk, Dad. A completely patronizing, pompous, male chauvinist jerk. I can't believe that he assumed I was interrogating Leslie Harding. Or assume that I was cheating on my promise by inviting people to my home." She paced around her father's living room, ignoring the fact that she had actually been tempted to do just that. The fact was, she *hadn't* done it.

"You're right, Cassie." Charles Ellis leaned back on the couch. "Can you sit down? I'm exhausted just watching you."

She sat down in the blue La-Z-Boy, but bounced back up two seconds later. "He just accused me. Stood there and actually accused me. He didn't ask, he didn't question, he just—" She broke off as she realized that history had repeated itself. "Wow, just like he did with his father. Although he didn't argue with his father."

"I was waiting for you to realize that. And like Rick Whittaker, you didn't bother to defend yourself."

"I did too, Dad! But he didn't let me finish, the jerk."

"I think we have firmly established that he's a jerk. Do you want me to go beat him up now? I'd be happy to."

Cassie flopped down in the chair again and laughed. "No, not really. I'd be happier if I went and beat him up. 'When you have a black belt, then you can come and talk to me,'" she mimicked in a sneering voice. "Jerk."

She drummed her fingers on the chair and stared at the wall. Then she got up and paced some more. "I think it's over. At least, I think *he* thinks it's over, and you know what, if he's going to be a total jerk, then *I* want it to be over, too. It's over." She was totally shocked when the tears came.

Charles stood up, bringing along a box of tissues from the side table. He gently took her in his arms and hugged her. "It doesn't have to be over, Cassie. I think you and James just need to talk about this. And you also need to work out this investigating impulse of yours. I was worried about you, too, when you decided to emulate Nancy Drew and go after the bad guy."

"Well, at least Ned Nickerson allowed Nancy to do her investigating. He didn't get his panties in a wad about it. "

"Ned wasn't a cop. And that's fiction, remember? Nancy never got hurt."

"No, because Ned always came to the damned rescue," she said bitterly. She hated that aspect of the Nancy Drew mysteries: the man always had to save the damsel in distress. Cassie didn't want that to happen to her. Not only did she not want to be saved—she didn't want to put herself in the dangerous situations that Nancy found herself in. She pulled out several tissues from the box and dried the tears, then blew her nose loudly.

She'd already realized that she needed to be careful and cautious, why couldn't Whittaker understand that? Jerk. "So what do I do now?"

"I'd suggest giving a him few days. Let him calm down and realize that he's a jerk."

"Fine," she said, then smiled in satisfaction. "And I know just what I'm going to do in the meantime."

chapter 11

<small>C</small>ASSIE STARED AT THE outside of her home and gritted her teeth. Three steps up. That was it. She could do three steps, couldn't she? Had they always been so high up?

Grimacing in pain, she gripped the wobbly railing and hauled herself up the steps. Once inside, she hobbled over to feed Donner. She shook her head at the wasted effort when she remembered the automatic feeder. Which reminded her of Whittaker. Which reminded her of why she was in pain right now.

She looked in despair at the staircase and its innumerable steps. Okay, with its fourteen steps, but they might as well have been innumerable for her today. In order to take a hot shower, she'd have to make it up those stairs. She was supposed to meet Michelle that afternoon, and it was going to take an hour or more to get ready.

She braced herself, gritted her teeth again, and attempted to walk up the steps. After the second, she gave up and crawled.

Shuffling into her bedroom, she peeled off her sweaty workout clothes and threw the damp black garments onto the bed. She considered picking them up, thought about it some more, then decided it wouldn't be worth the effort.

Getting into the clawfoot tub was another challenge. Finally, she placed her hands under her thighs and lifted her legs over the edge, first one leg and then the other. With her last remnants of strength, she yanked the shower curtain closed, adjusted the water temperature, and activated the shower.

When the spray of warm water hit her tender muscles, she almost cried. Today was only her third self defense class—she'd found an instructor on Thursday and started private lessons the same day—but she'd thrown herself into the exercises with her usual enthusiastic and obsessive fashion.

The repetitive motions and exercise were catching up with her. She'd thought she maintained a good fitness level with biking, but obviously that wasn't enough. She'd heard it from others and always dismissed it as a cliché, but she really was feeling muscles she hadn't known she possessed.

She whimpered when she raised her arms to shampoo her thick hair. Her arms hurt way more than her legs. The instructor had started her out with push-ups to build uppper body strength, and she'd never been good at them. Of course, the fact that she'd been shot in her shoulder less than two months ago wasn't helping.

If she cut her hair, it wouldn't be so heavy. No. She looked like Little Orphan Annie when it was short.

Maybe she should've waited longer after her gunshot wound before doing anything this strenuous. But every time she thought about giving up, she always heard Whittaker's sneering voice. That spurred her to ignore the pain and push harder.

She reached for the body wash, winced, and realized she didn't even have the strength to squeeze the bottle. Instead, she unscrewed the top and poured it on the nylon body scrubber. She couldn't believe how much everything hurt.

This was all Whittaker's fault.

She couldn't stop visualizing their fight, every sordid detail of it. She and Whittaker really were doing what his parents had done nine years ago. He was assuming rather than asking, and her pride was preventing her from telling him the truth.

No. No, *he* had prevented her from telling the truth. She'd tried, seriously tried, to tell Whittaker why Leslie had been there. The jerk wouldn't let her get out a full sentence.

A spluttering sound brought her back to the present. She looked down and realized she'd emptied the entire bottle of shower gel. The bathroom was now perfumed with vanilla-scented steam. Laughing, she rinsed most of it down the drain and used the rest to wash.

After her shower, she made sure to wear her loosest fitting shorts and a baggy University of Maryland T-shirt. Michelle wouldn't mind if she showed up at the aquarium dressed like a bum.

"I wish I could move that fluidly," she said to Donner as he pounced on the bed. "Trust me, you don't want to lie on those clothes. They're sweaty and gross." When Donner sniffed delicately, made his "stinky" face, and bolted out of the room, she realized the warning was unnecessary.

Checking the alarm clock, she was surprised to discover she still had a half hour before she had to leave to meet Michelle. Should she clean her house? It needed cleaning. No, that would take too much energy. Instead, she opted to work on her writing.

She headed toward her office and cursed when she realized her laptop was in the kitchen. Gingerly, she limped downstairs. Then she poured herself a glass of milk and gratefully swallowed several ibuprofen.

"Work fast, please work fast," she offered in prayer. Sliding onto the bench, she turned on her laptop.

After opening the file for her work in progress, she reviewed where she was with the storyline.

```
    "That's her! She's the one who's been
poisoning everyone!" Marty felt a huge rush
of hatred for this monstrous girl who was
responsible for more than five deaths.
    When the killer turned and bolted across
Pratt Street, Marty didn't hesitate. She gave
chase. Hopefully, the police with her would
follow.
    She leaped over or darted around the
tourists who were innocently walking around
the Inner Harbor.
    She ran past the shops and attractions,
hoping to gain on her quarry. She saw the
killer race up the escalator [Check if
escalator still serves as entrance to the
aquarium??]
```

Oh, right. Cassie remembered she needed to find the floor plan of the aquarium. She opened her internet browser, intending to check the aquarium website. Instead of entering *aqua.org*, she clicked on her email bookmark.

No, no emails from Whittaker, she noted. Maybe she should—

No. She wasn't going to email him. She crossed her arms in front of her, groaning as that pulled at her triceps.

Seeing an email from Linda, she opened it, hoping the latest prediction from the parrots would cheer her up. Her grin faded as she read. Evidently Houdini, the cockatoo, had been stating, *"The pain, I can assure you, will be exquisite."* He got that one right. Maybe those birds knew something after all.

She plugged the quote into the search bar. IMDB revealed it to be from the movie *Candyman*. "Ugh."

While she might write murder mysteries, she hated horror movies. Nightmares would haunt her for days after she watched them.

Cassie was having enough trouble sleeping already.

* * * * *

"Nope. The escalator's gone," Cassie said, looking toward the entrance of the aquarium.

Michelle turned around from her place in line. "There are still escalators in there, Cassie, only it's not the main entrance anymore. Hasn't been for years. They got rid of the seals outside, too."

"Oh right, I remember the seals. Anyway, I needed to describe the entrance for my story but couldn't remember. I went to look it up but was distracted."

"Oh, now there's a shock."

"Bite me, Michelle. You promised to be nice to me today." Cassie stuck out her lower lip in an exaggerated pout.

"No, I didn't." Michelle's violent headshake sent her ponytail flying. "I promised to kick James' butt the second you gave me permission. Although it sounds as if you're training to do that."

"Aikido's for self defense, not beating people up," Cassie said, but couldn't resist imagining such sweet satisfaction.

```
"So, James, I believe you said to come back
and talk to you after I have a black belt."
    He sneered at her. "So I did."
    She grabbed his arm and pivoted. Bending
forward, she flipped him over her hip.
    The second he landed, she straddled him
and pinned him to the ground. "Let's talk
now."
    His pupils widened in shock and desire.
"Forget talking, I have a better idea." He
```

```
threaded his hand through her curls and pulled
her down to him.
```

"Ow," she said, rubbing her arm where Michelle had hit her. "What the hell was that for?"

"You weren't just imagining kicking his butt, Cassandra." Her friend narrowed her eyes.

"What makes you say that?" she asked, but felt her face getting hot. Well, hotter, since it was miserable out in the September sunshine. She couldn't wait until they got into the cool aquarium.

"You let out some sex groans."

"I did not!" Did she?

"You're just frustrated because you never got to try James out for size," Michelle said with a wicked grin. "Anyway, we're almost to the ticket window. Are we going to the dolphin show, too, or should we only get aquarium admission?"

Hmmm...the dolphin show could work for her story's chase scene.

```
          Marty sprinted over the bridge to the
     dolphin exhibit. She ignored the many postings
     of trivia above her head as she raced across.
     Right now, she didn't care that jellyfish were
     ninety-five percent water.
          She had another focus—the lowlife who had
     poisoned Elaine.
          It felt rude to run past the ticket taker,
     but since he'd already been pushed to the
     ground by the murderer, Marty barged right
     in—she didn't have a ticket anyway.
          Searching through the crowd of parents
     and kids, visiting Mennonites, and senior
     citizens, she finally found her target racing
     toward the lowest row of the stadium seating.
     Trapped with no way out.
          Marty realized she was wrong when the
     clever girl ran up the blue stairs and dove
     into the water. Marty decided to follow suit,
     even though she didn't have a suit. Bathing
     suit, that was...
```

"Hey, wait!" Realizing that Michelle was striding away, Cassie hurried to catch up, thankful that the pills she'd taken earlier let her do so without moaning. That was the last thing she needed to do in a public place. Well, perhaps do *again* if Michelle was telling the truth. "Did you buy my ticket, too?"

Michelle rolled her eyes and handed her the tickets. "Yes. And since the dolphin show caused you to go into la-la land, I figured we'll go there so you can figure out exactly how and where Marty is going to capture the bad guy. Or, in this case, bad girl. What are you planning on doing, having them jump in the dolphin tank?"

"Maybe. It would be an exciting end to the foot chase." She stared up at the giant waterfall, listening to the sound of the rushing water. The cold splashes against her heated skin almost made it worth having to stand in yet another line. "Although tumbling, what, four floors would be pretty exciting."

"Yeah, this waterfall isn't too bad for a *temporary* exhibit."

Cassie laughed and shook her head. "I still can't believe that idiot in front of us asked if the Australia exhibit was temporary. Right. A huge glass, stone, and steel structure is temporary." She eyed the waterfall again, checking out the protruding rocks and tree trunks. Falling on that would *hurt*; hurt even more than she had earlier. "Still, I think the dolphin show might be a more interesting ending. If it's doable."

"We can find out at the next showing, that's the one I bought tickets for. And you owe me a hundred and twenty bucks."

"How much?" Cassie glanced down at the tickets. "Okay, the aquarium is expensive, but not that expensive."

The two of them avoided the photographers set up at the entrance by joining a group of German tourists who were barging past. Cassie owned enough cheesy pictures of her and Michelle together; no need for another one.

Michelle turned back with a smile as they finally reached the ticket taker. "No, but you still owe me. From Corks."

"Oh my God! From July, you mean? I never paid you? And darn it, now you've made me think about James again." Cassie handed over her main aquarium ticket and made sure to store the dolphin show pass in her back pocket so she wouldn't lose it.

"You never paid me. Hey, wait a minute."

"What do you want?" Cassie stood dumbfounded for a moment, until she realized her friend's destination was the visitor's information desk. A large poster with a cruise ship and the words "ENTER TO WIN" provided the necessary clues. She glanced heavenward and joined her Michelle at the desk. "Oh bother. Why do you always have to enter these stupid contests? You never win."

Michelle didn't look up from filling out the index card. "And you'll never win if you don't play."

Cassie couldn't disagree with that. Curious, she looked at the display. "A cruise for four to the Bahamas? That's a pretty cool prize. I've always wanted to go on a cruise. And now that they're leaving from Baltimore, it's much easier."

"You can probably afford one when you get your first royalty check."

Cassie didn't want to think about her royalty check, so she turned back to watch the people taking tickets. "Do you think it would be easy for someone to run past these guards and into the aquarium?"

Michelle dropped the card in the box. "I think it would be easy. Why, are you regretting spending so much to get in?"

"Of course not," Cassie said as they headed to the main area of the aquarium. "I want Marty to chase the bad guy in here. I doubt either of them will stop to pay."

"What are they doing in Baltimore anyway?" Michelle asked as they rode up the escalator. "I thought Marty taught at College Park." She took Cassie's arm and dragged her off before the doors had opened completely.

Cassie didn't protest Michelle's insistent lead toward the aquarium's large windows and their sweeping view of the city. "I decided to set the third book in a new location. So she's teaching a summer session at Loyola." Cassie looked out at the busy waterway. "They really have cleaned up the Inner Harbor, I'll tell you that. There's not much trash, especially considering it's right after the tourist season."

"That's for sure." She tugged on Cassie's arm again. "Let's go to the bubble tubes."

Cassie happily followed her friend. The bubble tubes weren't much to look at, just dozens of large plastic columns filled with water. But looking at them wasn't the point. She leaned her ear against the tube with the same anticipation as when she was a kid and waited anxiously for a large air bubble to rise up with its accompanying *blorpy-blurp-blurrble.*

"I swear these have been here forever," Michelle said with a giggle. "All the other exhibits come and go, but these are still here."

"How long have they been here?"

Michelle shrugged. "I don't know. Since the first time we came with our parents, and that was a long time ago."

"What, twenty years ago? God, we're getting old," she said, only half-joking. What was she saying? She shook her head. Twenty-eight was hardly old. Of course, she'd expected to be married by this point, and she couldn't even keep a boyfriend. "Ow. Darn it, Michelle, stop hitting me." She glared at her friend as she rubbed the spot Michelle had hit. Again. In the exact same place, too.

"Then stop thinking about James. We were talking about bubble tubes. Not bubble-headed detectives."

"Fine. Let's just go to the dolphin show."

"Wait, I want to hear one more bubble." Michelle leaned against the tube. When she giggled again at the noise, Cassie decided they'd never be old. Not when they could still act like eight-year-olds.

As they crossed the bridge, she was proud of herself for remembering one of the trivia statements correctly. Jellyfish are in fact, ninety-five percent water, compared to humans, who are only sixty-five percent water. The aquarium currently featured a display of jellyfish, but after one too many encounters at the beach, she hated the things and had no urge to see the exhibit.

When they reached the entrance to the dolphin show, Cassie decided it would be just as easy for Marty and her quarry to rush past this ticket taker as at the main entrance. When the real-life usher held out his hand, she panicked. She dug into her purse, searching for the dolphin show pass.

"It's in your back pocket, Cassie," Michelle reminded her.

Thank God for her best friend. She followed Michelle down to the bottom row and sat down next to her. It wasn't their usual spot, but she was more interested in figuring out her storyline than why Michelle had chosen different seats. Instead, she focused on whether Marty was a good swimmer and how the dolphins could be incorporated into the final scene. Would she need permission from the aquarium if she used them so prominently?

The dolphin show could work well as the climactic chapter of her book. The two jumbotrons on each side of the tank would add poignancy to the scene as they broadcast

Marty's victory and the bad guy's humiliation to everyone around.

She'd rather consider the ending of *The Merlot Murders* than think about *The Mystery of the Ex-Boyfriend*...or *The Mystery of the Ex-Cop*. She'd rather think of *anything* rather than Whittaker. Gah. So why was she thinking of him now?

It wasn't Whittaker, she argued with herself. She was worried about his dad. Even if she and Whittaker were no longer dating, she was concerned for Rick. He hadn't been arrested, so the police probably hadn't found any evidence against him.

She hadn't seen Rick since the day of O'Reilly's murder. Thank God he hadn't gone to the funeral. That would have been a bad scene. It was bad enough that she and Whittaker had gone. Officer Anderson probably wasn't the only one who'd objected to their presence; he'd just been the only one annoying enough to say it to them.

Cassie tried to pay attention as the announcer talked about the bottlenose dolphins and their habitat. The jumbotrons were showing how pollution damaged their ocean environment. Glancing over at her friend, she wasn't surprised to see that Michelle's eyes were damp. Most everything caused her friend's tear ducts to overflow. Sappy movies, Hallmark commercials, even the big reveal on home improvement shows. It didn't take much to set her off.

"Bottlenose dolphins are perfectly equipped for their environment," the wetsuit-clad announcer said as the dolphins performed several tricks to demonstrate their various abilities. Even with the microphone, it was hard to hear her over the crowd noise.

Cassie loved watching the dolphin streak around the clear plexiglass tank, but she felt sorry for it, too. Anything that could move that fast must hate being so limited in the tank. The pool was large and deep, but still nothing like the expansive ocean. At least here they didn't have to worry about predators.

She felt a chill go up her spine and had the oddest feeling she was being watched. Now it was easy to imagine how a prey animal felt when sensing a predator. She casually turned and glanced around the theater.

The place was packed, and everyone else seemed focused on the show. There were lots and lots of children and babies—no wonder it was so loud—staring wide-eyed at the action in the tank, squealing and applauding each time the dolphins jumped. She didn't see anyone familiar, which surprised her. Baltimore was a small town, and it was hard to go out without bumping into someone she knew.

Actually, she did recognize a face in the crowd. She sucked in a breath. That must have been who'd been staring at her, who was *still* staring at her.

Major Bianchi. She masked her surprise and met his gaze with a defiant stare. What was he doing here? The aquarium didn't seem like his scene. He broke eye contact when a sandy-haired girl next to him yanked on his suit jacket. When he frowned but leaned down to the little girl, she realized he must be there with his family. None of them looked happier than he did: both children acted sullen and the wife bored.

At least poor Officer Carter had been spared. She was surprised the major didn't make Carter take the family on an outing. The man made Carter do everything else. Probably had Carter wipe his butt for him, too, she thought with a narrow-eyed stare at the head of the Internal Investigations Division.

A huge sheet of cold water hit her back. Only then did she register the happy screams and the splashing noises coming from the tank behind her. She turned around in time for another cascade of water and saw a dolphin poised upside down in the tank, using its powerful tail to throw water on the crowd.

"Crap!" She covered her mouth at the disapproving glares from the mothers in the splash zone. This must be why Michelle had chosen a different seating location. "Michelle!"

Michelle smiled evilly as she wiped away the water from her face.

Hunching down her shoulders, her T-shirt now plastered to her chest and back, Cassie glared at her friend, ready to kill. The deluge had cooled her overheated body, yes, but *still.*

Looking up at the jumbotrons and seeing her drowned image, she realized she'd been right in her thoughts about her story, about the bad guy's humiliation. It *was* awful to be embarrassed on the large screens. Especially when the camera then panned around the audience and showed the smirk on Bianchi's face.

chapter 12

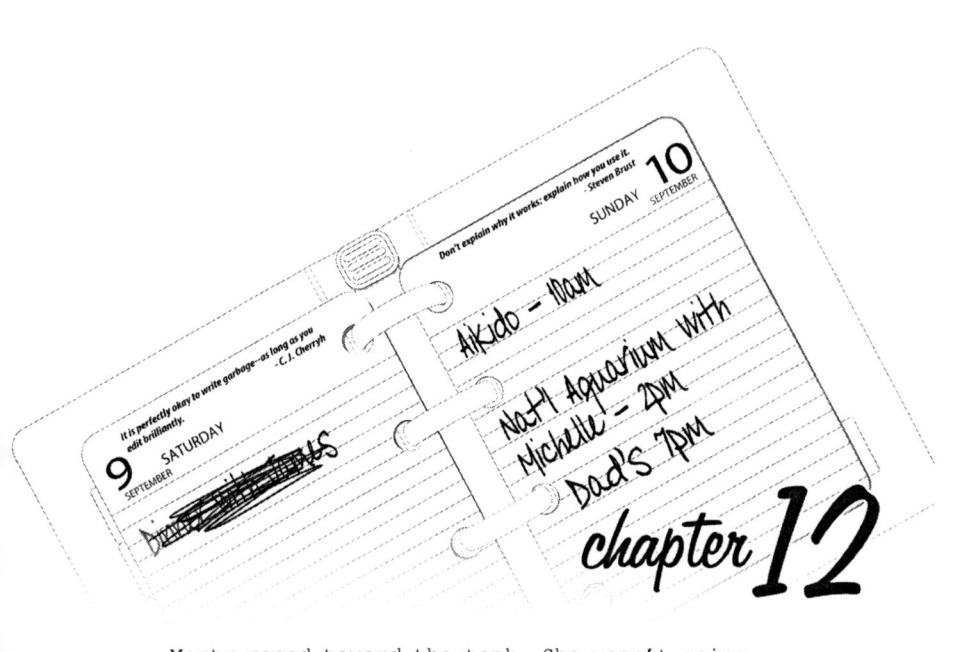

Marty raced toward the tank. She wasn't going to let this killer get away. She glanced behind her to make sure the police were also following.

She wouldn't have been surprised if they weren't, the idiots.

The police were too stupid to figure out this killer, even with the string of victims left behind her. If Marty hadn't pointed out that her friend received the wine bottle from a student, and figured out which student, they might still be standing around with their thumbs up their butts.

Not that Marty was surprised at the stupidity of the police officers. The jerks made assumptions about everything and jumped to the wrong conclusions.

And this latest homicide detective might have been cute, but he was the stupidest yet. He actually believed that—

"WHAT DID THAT COMPUTER do to you, Cassie-girl?"

Cassie lifted her fingers from her laptop. Considering her father's question and the tingling feeling in her fingertips, she must have been bashing the keys. "Oh, nothing. I'm getting a little too much into what I'm writing."

He gave her a sympathetic smile across the dining room table.

She enjoyed these evenings at her father's house. It reminded her of when she was a child and she'd do her homework while he graded papers or prepared the next day's lessons for his high school history class. Now, she wrote novels, he worked, and they enjoyed a typical quiet Sunday evening together.

Well, sort of quiet.

Cassie preferred writing with plenty of noise around her. Her father was able to ignore it after years of teaching teenagers—and being her father. So, she had her killing music playlist—she was definitely in the mood for murderous songs—and her police scanner going at the same time. She'd gotten into the habit of bringing the scanner with her to monitor police action. Before her fight with Whittaker, she'd listen in case something happened to him. That wasn't why she'd brought it tonight, of course. This time, it was only for the background noise.

It sounded like a busy night. Cassie gave the dispatcher credit for juggling the various calls.

"So what were you writing?"

She scanned the words on her screen. "Crap, honestly. I'm, um...allowing my personal life to influence my writing." She highlighted the offending text and hit the delete key. Then she stood up and stretched, raising her hands over her head. At the motion, her injured shoulder and sore muscles protested, and she winced at the knifing pain.

Her throat ached, too. She told herself it was dry and headed into the kitchen. "You want some juice, Dad?" She didn't wait for him to answer, automatically getting down two glasses and pouring ice cold juice. If only the pain in her heart was as easily relieved, she thought as she took a quick sip of hers.

She was turning to return to the table when another call on the scanner caught her attention.

"Attention any cars in the area. Reported alarm at the Canton Elementary School."

"Canton?" she repeated, turning up the volume in time to hear a silky smooth voice respond to the call.

"This is 2Baker23. I am in the vicinity and will report to the scene."

"I recognize that voice!" she said. "I do," she insisted when her father raised his eyebrows. "That voice is distinctive. It's Officer Anderson. Or else Billy Dee Williams has become a Baltimore City cop."

She sprinted to the front of the rowhouse and knelt on the couch. Pushing aside the heavy curtains, she peered into the street.

"You can't actually see the school from here, Cassie."

"No, but I should be able to see the flashing lights of the police car." She started to stand on the couch, but a quick admonishment from her father squashed that urge. A moment later, she spotted red and blue lights reflecting on the buildings up the street. "He's there."

"So I heard on the scanner. Will you get back here and write? I'm certain this Officer Anderson can handle things without your help."

Resisting the urge to stick out her tongue at her father, Cassie let go of the curtain and went back to the kitchen. "I guess so. He's supposed to be a dirty cop, but I suppose he's still an effective one."

That seemed to be the case when Officer Anderson's voice came over the scanner again. "2Baker23. It looks like a false alarm. You can cancel back-up, I've got this."

"Thank you, 2Baker23." The dispatcher sounded relieved. "Are you leaving the scene?"

"I'm just going to go on back and do a final check. I'll advise. Car 2Baker23 out."

"That's a relief," her father said as he picked up his juice. "Glad to know crime has been averted here in Canton."

"Hey, crime does happen here now, Dad. I mean, it's pretty safe, but it's definitely not the same neighborhood I grew up in." Canton used to be a blue-collar, ethnic area, but in the 90s, it was discovered by young office workers who moved there in droves. It was still a safe enough neighborhood, but it was different.

"Oh, crime happens," he agreed. "But it's normally small stuff, like break-ins, drunk and disorderlies—especially on the weekends—and people behaving stupidly."

"True." She winced when she heard car tires squealing. "And idiot drivers. But it's mostly peaceful." She took a deep breath and tried to inhale some of that peace. All she got was the lingering smell of the pepperoni pizza she and her father had shared. "Okay, let me try writing again, but this time not quite so violently."

"Good idea." Her father picked up his pen and went back to grading.

Cassie succeeded in putting aside her own thoughts and placed herself in Marty's head. Marty was already angry, since the poisoned wine had not only killed her friend, but one of Marty's favorite students as well. The girl had been innocently sharing the bottle with one of the most recent victims. So Marty was livid. The fight in the pool would be rather violent.

Perhaps a dolphin or two could break up the fight.

She snorted as she envisioned a dolphin nudging between the two grappling women, pushing them apart with his flippers, and squeaking "Break it up, break it up."

"Writing a funny scene, dear?" her father asked without looking up from his papers.

"No, just imagined something silly." She banished the thought from her head with some difficulty and started writing.

Forty minutes later, she angled her neck right and left to stretch out some kinks. "I should probably head home."

Her father glanced over to the clock in the kitchen. "Why, yes. It's almost midnight. I turn into a pumpkin at midnight. Don't forget to call me when you get home."

She kept the eye roll internal. Her father always said that. "I will, Dad." She packed her laptop and reached for her police scanner. She was about to unplug it when she heard the hail from Dispatch.

"Car 2Baker23, you never gave a final code. Are you clear?"

Cassie turned up the volume instead and waited for the answer.

"Car 2Baker23? 10-1?"

She exchanged a look with her father when no one answered.

Another voice came on the scanner, but it wasn't Officer Anderson. "This is 2Baker20. Where was 2Baker23 last?"

"He was checking on a false alarm at Canton Elementary," Dispatch answered. "He stated that everything was under control, and he was going to do a final check around back."

"Can anyone in the area swing by and check on 2Baker23?"

Cassie ran over to the window. "That's Anderson's sergeant asking for someone to swing by."

"You recognize his voice, too?" her father asked.

"No! I recognize it by his code number, that's what the 20 means. Anyway, I don't think the car is there anymore," she said to her father. "I don't see the lights. Should we go check?"

"Cassandra, I'm fairly certain that the police sergeant wasn't asking if any civilians were in the area."

"I know. But it couldn't hurt for us to take a quick walk over there, see if his car is there. Just a quick—"

Her father held up a silencing hand so they could listen to the responses on the scanner.

"See," she said, after a few patrol officers replied to the sergeant. "The closest cop is fifteen minutes out. We should walk over and make sure he's not hurt. Please, Dad?"

Her father closed his eyes and took a deep breath. When he opened them again, she saw she'd won.

"Fine. Just a quick check couldn't hurt." He got two flashlights from the hutch.

She was glad her father agreed and even gladder he'd joined her. Baltimore was spooky this close to midnight. She knew it was busier closer to O'Donnell Square and all the bars and restaurants. But since her dad lived a few streets over, there wouldn't be many people on the streets until the bars closed at two.

"His car's not there," her father said as they got closer.

"No. But he said he was going in the back, maybe he drove there?" Cassie headed around. She'd attended this school as a child, had met Michelle there. She remembered it as a place of constant excitement and commotion. But without the kids and teachers to fill it up with noise, attitude, and hopefully even some learning, the school was just an empty, desolate building.

They followed the alley to the back of the school. "Isn't that his car?" She peered into the dark. There was a car there, facing the back wall. She lifted her flashlight and aimed the beam at the car.

She dropped the flashlight. "Oh my God!" She turned to her father. "You saw it, saw him, too, didn't you?"

He swallowed hard, nodded, and lifted his own flashlight. Cassie picked hers back up and followed suit. In the glow, they could see Officer Anderson. He was completely motionless, his body plastered against the wall, his lower half pinned by the grill of the police vehicle.

Cassie fumbled out her phone as they approached the body. Her father sidled past the the car and felt for a pulse. He shook his head. She called 9-1-1, trying hard not to remember the last time she'd needed to call the emergency number.

After giving the information to the operator and promising not to leave the scene, she stared at the phone.

"He's going to kill me," she said as she dialed. "But he'll kill me more if I don't tell him first." She took a deep breath as she waited for him to answer.

"Cassie? It's rather late for a call, isn't it?"

Whittaker sounded cautious. Well, it *was* late. Maybe he wondered if she was drunk and calling to weep and apologize and beg him to forgive her. She almost wished that were the case.

Unfortunately, this was business.

"I suppose it is, *Detective* Whittaker." She firmed her voice and emphasized his rank. His quick inhalation told her he got the message loud and clear.

"What's wrong?"

"Dad and I are standing outside Canton Elementary, looking at the body of what once was Officer Anderson." Okay, technically, she wasn't looking right this second. She'd needed to stare at the sidewalk so her voice wouldn't wobble.

"I'll be right there. Have you called 9-1-1? Are you safe?"

She heard shuffling noises and assumed he was throwing on clothes.

"I have. I'm with my father."

"Don't touch anything," Whittaker ordered.

"We won't. Well, Dad checked for a pulse, to make sure. But other than that we haven't disturbed anything." She looked over at her father. He was still staring at the body in horror. She gently took him by the arm and guided him around. She closed the phone when it was clear that Whittaker had hung up.

Now all they had to do was wait.

* * * * *

Cassie wasn't surprised Whittaker arrived first; he lived only a few blocks away.

He was in pure professional mode, which she appreciated. She wasn't in the mood to rehash any of their personal problems. Not in front of her father and definitely not in front of the dead body of a dirty cop.

He glanced at the body but didn't approach it. Shoving his hands into his pockets, he faced her. "I think Wertz and Garcia are on shift and next on the roster, so they should be the ones being summoned from headquarters. I can't take it due to the connection to you."

And to his father, she knew, but he didn't want to say that. She was relieved to hear his statement on the choice of homicide detectives. Wertz and Garcia were on Whittaker's squad, so she was acquainted with them.

Several squad cars arrived with squealing tires, and Whittaker walked over to greet his fellow officers. After a few moments, he rejoined them while the uniforms secured the scene. More police cars converged on the scene from every direction—she didn't think she'd ever seen so many in one place.

She stood with her father and Whittaker in the swirling lights of the police cars and emergency vehicles, watching as the neighbors and bar crawlers came to check out what was happening.

The uniformed officers tried to keep the crowd back as paramedics worked on Officer Anderson. The police car had to be moved before they were able to extract the body.

She tried to see what they did after that, but Whittaker nudged her away.

It reminded her she was still pissed at him. She tried to maintain that anger, but when the coroner came on scene, she remembered there were some things far more important than petty fights. Officer Anderson might have been dirty and a jerk, but she'd bet he had family, friends, people who loved him. Maybe she should simply explain to Whittaker that he'd misinterpreted the situation.

Before she could speak up, Wertz and Garcia joined them.

"Investigating again, Cassie?" Garcia asked.

She clenched her teeth hard enough to cause pain. Were they talking about what happened in July or were they referring to her talking to Leslie Harding? No, it had to be the other murders. She couldn't believe Whittaker had told them he'd found her talking to the former cop.

Her father took a step forward. "We were trying to do our civic duty and check up on a police officer, Detective. I would think you would appreciate that."

Wertz pushed in front of his partner. "We do appreciate that, Mr. Ellis. Now, we'd like for you and your daughter to go with these officers to Headquarters. You'll need to go in separate vehicles."

Cassie placed a hand on her father's shoulder when she saw him tense up further. "It's routine, Dad."

Her father glanced over at Whittaker for confirmation. When he nodded, her father accompanied Wertz to the waiting police car.

Garcia walked her towards another car. "Thank God we have you as an expert to explain things to your father," he said snidely before he closed the door.

Perhaps she shouldn't have been relieved that Wertz and Garcia had caught the case.

> **9** SATURDAY SEPTEMBER
> *It is perfectly okay to write garbage—as long as you edit brilliantly.*
> —C. J. Cherryh
>
> ~~[scribbled out]~~
>
> **10** SUNDAY SEPTEMBER
> *Don't explain why it works; explain how you use it.*
> —Steven Brust
>
> Aikido - 10am
> Nat'l Aquarium with Michelle - 2pm
> Dad's 7pm
> BCPD Homicide Department????

chapter 13

*T*HIS WAS TOTALLY UNFAIR, Cassie thought for the fiftieth time as she paced around the tiny room. It wasn't even a room, it was a box. A gray, dirty, dingy box. She couldn't believe they'd placed her in one of the holding rooms while they interviewed her father.

This wasn't her first time being a witness to a murder and having to wait for the interview. Before, she'd been allowed to wait inside one of the interview rooms. They were just as small, but at least they were cleaner and less intimidating.

Garcia had deposited her in one of the holding rooms designed for suspects. She wondered if they were punishing her for the fight with Whittaker. Would he have told them about that?

Garcia had even given a glance to the manacles chained to the bench. Luckily for him, he hadn't tried to place them on her. If he had, she'd have called harassment. She was claustrophobic enough in the tiny room; she would've freaked if she'd been chained down in one place.

She couldn't even sit down. She'd toured the holding rooms before and had no desire to touch whatever body fluids, bacteria, and germs were left on surfaces from previous occupants. She was curious, though, about how the walls came to be covered with graffiti, since the police confiscated all pens, pencils, and other personal objects from any suspect they placed in the cells.

This time, they'd taken all her things, too. She couldn't even take out her notebook, as she'd done while waiting for that first interview, the one after poor Seth Montgomery had been found murdered.

The only entertainment available was the graffiti, which taught her some new anatomically creative phrases. That kept her mind occupied for only a few moments, though. She went back into worrying mode.

She hoped the detectives were treating her father better than they were treating her. It wasn't his fault that she and Whittaker were fighting, and definitely not his fault that they'd stumbled onto a dead body that night.

Feeling guilty, she tried to peek out the narrow glass rectangle in the door to see if they were done with her father. He was getting older—although he'd have been annoyed if she said that. He shouldn't be out this late, especially after the shock they'd received. Darn it, why'd she ever let him come with her to investigate the school? And what was taking them so long?

She could almost sympathize with all the criminals who'd waited in these rooms. She even felt kinship with the ones that had tried to dig their way out through the crumbling ceiling tiles above her head.

The wait gave her time to wonder about Anderson's murder... death... murder. It *had* to be murder, she couldn't see how anyone could have been crushed that badly by accident.

So since it was murder, she wondered if this was a random cop killing. If Anderson had been targeted, it didn't necessarily have to be connected to the D&D scandal and O'Reilly's murder. Anderson was a dirty cop. She was sure he had plenty of enemies.

Relief surged through her when she saw Garcia escort her father from the interview room. A few minutes later, he came for her. He ushered her into the interview room ahead of him. While this room was as tiny as her former grungy prison, at least it was cleaner.

It was hot in the room. Either the air conditioning was broken or they were deliberately adjusting the temperature in the room to make her uncomfortable.

She'd been here before, although it had been Whittaker and Freeman on the other side of the table. As always, they brought in a female officer in order to prevent any claims of sexual harassment.

Cassie wished they'd get more female homicide detectives.

The room was small enough for three people, but four was really pushing it. The female officer stood in the back corner behind the yellow plastic seat that would be her own place of honor.

Wertz was already seated, so she was careful where she placed her feet and legs when she sat down. That left Garcia to stand nearby and hover, a sneer on his face. She was glad that Wertz was taking the lead in this investigation. The blond man had always treated her with respect, unlike his partner.

Even before tonight, she'd had some issues with Garcia. Although she knew he was a good cop and had Whittaker's respect, he could be a jerk. He'd made suggestive remarks to Whittaker in front of her. She knew a part of that was due to the occasionally dark humor of police officers, but it made her uncomfortable.

"So, Ms. Ellis," Wertz began. "I have to say that this is the most unusual way I have ever seen for a woman to get back together with her boyfriend."

Okay, so she wasn't going to be comfortable with Wertz. She hid her shock that Whittaker had shared the news of their breakup and tried to sit up as best as she could in the cheap, flexible chair. "You can't be serious."

"Oh, I'm completely serious. Whittaker's a homicide detective, what better way to get his attention?" He leaned in until his face completely filled her field of view.

She'd been through this routine before and ignored the prickle of discomfort at this intrusion into her personal space. "Right. So I decided to run into a police officer with his own vehicle in a desperate attempt to get James back."

"You said it, not me," Wertz said as he leaned back in the chair and folded his arms.

"Of course. And I convinced my father to go along with this? And then somehow popped the alarm at the school, managed to convince Officer Anderson to get rid of his back-up, and asked him to stand up against the wall while I ran into him with his own car."

"How did you know about the alarm, Ms. Ellis?"

She wasn't affected by the icy look in his blue eyes. "You have my father's testimony, Detective Wertz, so stop pulling my chain. You already know we heard everything over the scanner."

"The scanner, right," he drawled. "Because most people have police scanners in their homes. They sit around the scanner and listen all night as a way of family bonding. Eating popcorn and singing Kumbayah."

Cassie glanced over when Garcia snorted at Wertz's statement. "More people than you might think have police scanners. In fact, over forty percent of people who own them aren't emergency personnel." She paused, waving the words away. "And you don't care. I don't have a scanner as entertainment. I have one as research. Listening to police calls on the radio has been a good method of learning how you talk, how you think. But in general, I have it on as background noise."

"And you take it with you everywhere?"

It was none of their business why she kept the scanner with her. "Yes. Anyway, we had the scanner on and heard Officer Anderson respond to the call."

"How did you know it was Officer Anderson? There are no names given over the radio, Ms. Ellis."

"I know that."

"Of course you do," Wertz interrupted.

She clenched her teeth, then deliberately relaxed. She was going to end up with some type of jaw disorder if she wasn't careful. Ignoring the detective's statement, she answered his first question. "I recognized his voice after meeting him on Thursday."

"At O'Reilly's funeral. Another unusual entertainment venue." Wertz made a few notations on his pad.

Cassie tried to read them, but they appeared to be in Greek. "Anyway, Officer Anderson has—had a distinctive voice. I recognized it when he came over the radio."

She went through everything with the detectives and hoped it matched what her father had said. Although, hopefully it hadn't matched too much or the detectives might think they'd rehearsed their testimony. She frowned when she realized where her thoughts were going. Yet again, she was sitting in an interview room, worried about a crime she hadn't committed.

She was fairly certain that the detectives didn't really think that she killed Officer Anderson; if they had, they'd surely have pressed harder. Wertz was probably trying to get the details from her and get in a few cheap shots against her while he did so.

"Did you touch the body once you came upon the scene?" Wertz asked.

"I did not. My father did, to check his pulse. We've both had some first aid training and would have done whatever possible to save him if he'd been alive. When it was obvious he was not, I called 9-1-1, then called Detective Whittaker."

"Why?"

She blinked at him. "Well, as you know, Detective Whittaker and I are—were—are in a relationship."

She bristled this time when Garcia snorted.

"In addition, as you also know, I had contact with him and Detective Freeman when I was a material witness for two other murders. So when I found Officer Anderson, I felt I should notify him after calling 9-1-1."

"And the fact that Rick Whittaker is Detective Whittaker's father had nothing to do with it?" Wertz asked, leaning across the table again. "The fact that Officer Anderson was known to Rick Whittaker, had worked with him in the past had nothing to do with it?"

She took a deep breath. Perhaps Wertz wanted more from her than her statement and a few cheap shots.

Wertz continued to press. "The fact that Officer Anderson would've known that Rick Whittaker was dirty—might even have evidence against him—didn't come into it?"

Cassie started to blurt out that Rick wasn't dirty, that Officer Anderson was. But she bit back the words. It wasn't her right to say the former, and she didn't have proof of the latter. She didn't have proof of anything, really. All she had was a gut feeling and her trust in Rick.

"No answer this time, Ms. Ellis? No statistics to quote or facts to spout?"

She took another calming breath to hold back any cutting remarks. "I was not concerned, at all, about whether Officer Anderson had evidence against Rick Whittaker." *There's no evidence to be had, he's innocent, you idiots.* "I will admit I was concerned about the fact that Officer Anderson knew Rick. Considering the police brought Rick in for questioning in the death of Officer O'Reilly, based on purely circumstantial evidence, I was worried that another death so soon might result in him being brought in again."

"You think it was merely circumstantial evidence, Ms. Ellis? You don't believe Rick Whittaker is guilty?"

"I believe Rick Whittaker is completely innocent," Cassie said, happy she could say what she wanted without revealing what Rick had told her. "Completely. No one would be stupid enough to kill someone—nine years later—without establishing a good alibi."

"Maybe not in your stories." Wertz tapped his finger in a repetitive beat on the table. "But it does happen in real life. People are stupid."

"Rick Whittaker is not. He's not stupid, and he's not guilty."

She and Wertz engaged in a short staring war. She lost. She blamed her defeat on his really irritating habit of finger tapping. The incessant noise was distracting.

"All right, then," he said finally. "You're free to go, Ms. Ellis. Thank you for your time. Garcia, why don't you get our next subject?"

She stood up, wincing when the back of her legs stuck to the plastic seat. "I don't have to go back to the holding room? Thank God for that."

As she stepped out of the interview area, she almost bumped into someone. Rick Whittaker.

"Cassie, darling. We really should stop meeting like this. People will talk." He glanced around. "Actually, I guess they already are."

* * * * *

WHITTAKER WAS HAVING TROUBLE concentrating on his conversation with Cassie's father. It was made even harder since the older man was basically giving him the cold shoulder. Cassie must have told him about their argument, but he couldn't blame her. After all, he'd told Freeman about the fight when the older man had pestered all the details out of him.

Telling Freeman had been a surprising relief, but maybe they should have spoken elsewhere, far from here. It wasn't hard to guess Wertz and Garcia had overheard, considering the way they were treating Cassie.

It was also an uncomfortable conversation since they were surrounded by other police officers, including IID again. He noticed Major Bianchi checking them out a number of times.

Hopefully his father was more comfortable in the holding room than he was out here.

Anger filled him that they'd brought his father in—again. His dad closed the bar at ten on Sundays, so that meant he probably didn't have an alibi for this evening either.

Whittaker hated that more suspicion was being thrown his father's way. Shaking his head, he tried to focus on Charles. The late night was obviously wearing on him; his face was pale and his blue eyes, so like Cassie's, seemed sunken in.

"How much longer do you think they'll keep her?" Charles asked. "This is ridiculous. Almost as ridiculous as your argument with Cassie." Then he shook his head. "Never mind. I'm not getting in the middle of that."

"I appreciate that, sir." He was about to say more, but broke off when the door opened. Both he and Charles stood up as Cassie walked out the door.

Hearing Charles' deep sigh of relief, Whittaker struggled to keep his own on the inside.

Charles pulled his daughter in for a hug. "You okay?"

"Fine. You?"

The older man nodded. "Tired, but okay. Are we free to leave?"

"I think so." Cassie and her father looked over at him. "Aren't we?"

"Of course," Whittaker answered. "I can drive you home if you'd like."

"No, you stay with your dad," Cassie said. "We'll get home on our own."

He should stay until his father was out of interview. But he wanted, *needed* to talk to Cassie.

She laid a hand on his arm. "Stay with your dad, James. We'll be okay, and he needs you right now. He needs people to support him." She lowered her voice and gave a pointed glance towards the IID contingent. "Too many people here who don't. Text me when he's out, please."

He nodded his agreement, then asked Officer Morris, one of the uniforms assigned to homicide, to drive them home. After they were gone, he sat back down. Freeman wandered over to join him.

"Did you get any information?"

Freeman nodded. "Some. First of all, Newmann and Dirruzo are trying to take the case. They're claiming it's connected to the O'Reilly murder."

"It's a totally different murder method," Whittaker protested.

"Yes, but they think it's connected to the D&D scandal. Our sarge is fighting to keep it in our squad, since we answered the initial call. The other interesting thing is the fact that they found keys to the car on Anderson's body."

"Does that mean that someone hot-wired a squad car? Gutsy killer."

"Not from what I heard. It looks like Anderson had a spare set of keys and left the original keys in the car. He usually did everything to get that vehicle."

Whittaker knew that plenty of cops did that. Although squad cars weren't assigned, most patrol officers did their best to get the same vehicle, especially if they managed to find one that wasn't too damaged.

The same officers sometimes made a spare set of keys for those vehicles. That helped them grab the car before others.

"Or someone had a spare set of keys," Whittaker said.

"Or that. If so, the killer was lucky as hell, managing to get Anderson to the school without any back-up on the way."

"The killer obviously was lucky, since he killed Anderson."

"Or she," Freeman said, staring across the room.

Whittaker followed his gaze and saw that Leslie Harding was being escorted inside. She went back to the interview area without glancing their way.

"Talking about Harding, did you tell Garcia and Wertz about my fight with Cassie?" Whittaker swiveled in his chair to stare at Freeman, so he caught Freeman's look of surprise.

"No. Why?"

"They're really being snide to her. If you didn't say anything, then they must have overheard when I told you."

"Maybe, or they just recognized, like I did, that you were in a really bad mood the next day and deduced Cassie was the cause."

Whittaker slouched in his chair. "I know. That's how you figured it out. But I was pissed. I still can't believe she was interrogating Harding."

"Now it looks like Wertz and Garcia will be doing that, since Rick just walked out."

Relief flooded through him at the sight of his father. "I'll take him home. You stay here and see if you can get more information."

Whittaker quickly ushered his dad to the garage.

"These murders have caused one good thing," Rick said on the drive up to his house. "I've seen more of you this month than I have in nine years."

"I'm really sorry about that. Very sorry."

His father sighed. "Don't apologize, son. It's as much my fault for not saying something when I could. In fact, I'm so used to keeping everything to myself about the D&D scandal, it was hard to actually explain when Wertz and Garcia asked about it."

"They asked?"

"They did. I was more surprised than you were just now. Wertz flat out asked if I'd been on the take. When I denied it, he asked where the extra money came from. I told him I'd been working for the Feds."

"Why the hell did you tell them that tonight, but you wouldn't tell Internal Affairs when you were originally accused?" Whittaker gripped the wheel.

His father sighed again. "Because back then, I didn't want to blow my cover. I'd naively thought I'd go home, call my contacts, and find out what to do. I thought I'd get them to explain things to the higher-ups, so I could get back to finding out what was going on. Instead someone leaked my name to the media—and you know the rest."

"Yeah, I know the rest."

chapter 14

BIKING IN BALTIMORE—IN EARLY September—was asinine. Even though it was early evening, Cassie was soaked in sweat by the time she got to her critique meeting. Too bad libraries didn't come with showers, not even one as old and elaborate as the Enoch Pratt Central Library.

Since she'd expected to be sweaty, she'd packed a clean bra and T-shirt. After freshening up in the bathroom and drinking as much as she could from the faucet, she rushed up the stairs to the Poe room for the meeting, not even taking time to admire the three-story high interior or the expansive skylight. She was already late.

This wasn't going to be her best meeting. Not after last night.

She immediately noticed her all-female critique group swarming around Bryan Tilman like sharks at a feeding frenzy. Great, she'd forgotten all about him. And here she was with a flushed face, frizzy hair—doubled in size thanks to the exercise and humidity—bike shorts, and a T-shirt. Well, at least it was a fresh T-shirt.

She shook her head and headed for the swarm at the end of the long table.

Cheryl, the facilitator of the critique group, was the first to notice her. "Cassie. It's so good to see you. And so good of you to have invited Bryan. We were all just getting to know him." She placed a proprietary hand on his shoulder.

Cassie saw a touch of panic cross his handsome face. "I'm glad you could make it, Bryan," she said. "I told you everyone would be happy to get a man in the group."

His reply was drowned by a feminine chorus of agreement.

"I'm glad you could make it, Cassie," Cheryl said with a glance at her watch. "You are one of the presenters. Did you bring enough copies for everyone? Erica didn't know that Bryan was going to be here, so she's one copy short."

"Actually, I am, too," Cassie admitted. "I, well, I forgot he was coming. I've had a lot on my mind." That was an understatement.

"Oh, I don't mind sharing with Bryan," Cheryl assured her. Once again, the other women twittered assent.

This time, Bryan's expression was resigned.

Cassie passed out her chapter and read Erica's work in progress. She marked up a few places where the point of view had switched, but didn't have many other suggestions. Erica's romance stories were always good. While everyone read her piece, she waited. Usually, she used this time to peruse the various glass cases displaying Edgar Allen Poe memorabilia. Today she relaxed and willed her body to cool. She wished she could have some water, but the library frowned on eating and drinking in the rooms.

She amused herself watching Cheryl and Susan, the poet in the group, as they read the two pieces submitted for critique. She could tell they were both appalled at having to read not only a romance story—with a sex scene; she suspected Erica had chosen that deliberately—but also her mystery complete with the action scene.

Cassie was gratified that everyone else in the group seemed to be enjoying both stories. When they read hers, people laughed and smiled at what looked to be the right places in the story.

She loved watching people read her work.

Being an author was often an isolated job. *We do our best, put our heart and soul into the stories, and send them out to the public.*

And wait.

It was the reason she was so addicted to checking Amazon for reviews. She wanted to know how people felt about her work. It was tempting to do that now while waiting for the others to finish reading. She hadn't checked last night—for obvious reasons.

Bryan, she noted, was reading her story without any facial reaction. She wasn't certain whether that meant he didn't like it, or if it was ingrained in him, as a lawyer, not to reveal his opinions.

"Is everyone finished reading the stories?" Cheryl asked when everyone put down their papers. "Good. Why don't we begin with Cassie's submission? Who would like to start?"

Even though she'd been published, Cassie was still nervous when it was her turn to receive critiques. Especially today, since she hadn't polished this chapter.

"Why don't we have our new member start?" Cheryl suggested, fluffing her sable-brown hair.

"I'd be happy to," Bryan said. "I first have to say, I'm glad to see Marty McCallister in action again. I felt she was a great, strong protagonist in *Mailbox Murders*. I know it happened in an earlier chapter, but I'm sad to know that Elaine is a victim in this book. I really liked her character."

Cassie felt an odd rush of guilt at that comment. She also liked Elaine and regretted killing her off. She'd known while writing her first book that Marty's best friend would be killed in book three, but it was hard to follow through with that idea.

"That said," he went on, "this scene doesn't really fit this novel. After Elaine's death, it's inappropriate to have this slapstick chase scene into a swimming pool. And the chapter doesn't seem to have as much polish as what I've read in the previous book."

She couldn't disagree with him on either comment. "You're right on both parts. I worried about that last night." When she couldn't sleep after arriving home, she'd used that time to write. "The lack of polish is because I wasn't focused when I wrote this. As I said before, I've had a lot on my mind lately."

"Probably due to that police officer you're dating," said Ronda, an elderly woman who was writing her second memoir. "I bet he's taking up all of your time."

"Oh, you're dating a police officer?" Bryan asked.

Was she dating a police officer? Cassie didn't actually know anymore, but she nodded.

"A homicide detective," Cheryl said. "No wonder she can write her murder stories with such accuracy."

"He doesn't help me with my writing, Cheryl," Cassie protested.

"I bet he's too busy right now, anyway," Erica said, tapping a stack of paper against her leg. "It looks like the Baltimore Police are completely flummoxed by these latest murders of police officers. You know there was another one last night."

"I hadn't heard that," Susan said. "I try not to watch or read the news. Too depressing."

"This one is actually a rather gruesome murder, too," said Marianne, the other romance writer in the group. "The poor man was run over with his own police car. It's a dangerous life."

Ronda reached over and patted Cassie's knee. "I don't know how you handle it, young lady. I'd be worried constantly if I was dating a police officer."

Bryan put down the copy of the chapter and leaned forward. "It can be dangerous. I work with the police in my line of work. I'm an assistant attorney for the U.S. Attorney's Office," he explained to the other women.

Cassie stifled a laugh, detecting a brightening of the avaricious gleams in the other women's eyes when he said "attorney". If Bryan noticed that, she didn't see any sign.

"I knew a number of cops in Chicago," he was saying. "Good cops—and bad. Some of them have gone down in the line of duty. It's a hard life."

"It can be," Cassie agreed. "Still, I don't believe we're supposed to be talking about cops, unless you want to tell me about the ones in this scene." She smiled to soften the sharpness of her tone.

Cheryl nodded. "She's right. Let's get back on track, ladies—and gentleman," she added, with a smile and eyelash flutter for Bryan.

Cassie was glad that she'd invited Bryan to the session, despite Cheryl's blatant flirting with him. He made some very good comments about her work and Erica's. She could see Erica appreciated getting a male perspective on her romance stories. Cassie was especially amused that he critiqued the sex scenes—without blushing.

"Thanks for inviting me," Bryan said as he walked with her out of the ornate building. "I had a good time."

"Despite the rather aggressive behavior of some of the ladies?"

"Despite that. I'm very happy to get out of there alive." Bryan turned around as Cheryl called out to him. "Uh-oh. Perhaps I spoke too soon."

Cheryl raced up, the sound of her needle-thin heels on the concrete like cracking knuckles. "Bryan, it is wonderful to have you with our critique group. We used to have a few other males, but they left."

"I can't imagine why."

Cassie admired Bryan's ability to keep a straight face. She faked a cough to hide her reaction to his comment.

"I thought I would take you out to dinner—to welcome you, that is." The gleam was back in Cheryl's brown eyes.

"I appreciate the offer, Cheryl, I do," Bryan said. "But actually, I just now made plans with Cassie to go to dinner. I have to thank her for connecting me with all of you wonderful writers. Plus, didn't you have some technical legal questions for me, Cassie?"

"Right. Regarding whether or not Marty's testimony will be admissible in court." She pulled that out of nowhere, despite Cheryl's glare drilling into her.

"We'll have to do a rain check then, Bryan." Cheryl pivoted and strode away, her sundress flowing around her long legs.

"Thank you, Cassie," Bryan said, wiping imaginary sweat from his brow. "I think that woman wanted to have *me* for dinner."

"Cheryl is a man-eater, so you're probably right. And you're welcome." She laughed as she bent down to unlock her bicycle.

"You biked here?" He sounded shocked.

"I did. I often bike around the city. It's easier than driving, since I can maneuver around the traffic jams."

"I can understand that. I don't miss much about Chicago, but I do miss the El. It was easier to get around the city that way. Does Baltimore even have public transportation? I mean, not counting the buses."

One passed by at that moment, belching gas and noxious fumes.

"Sort of. There's the light rail. Or the snail rail, as it's called. It doesn't go that fast and has a very limited range. There is a newer metro system. Same answer. So I bike. Plus, it gets me some exercise, which I need since I spend most of my day at a desk."

"You don't look like you spend most of your day at the desk." He looked her up and down, but managed to make it flattering and not obnoxious. "I was more surprised because it's so hot. These rainy days haven't cooled us down much. Isn't today a red day on the smog alert?"

She shrugged. "It was earlier. But it was after five when I started biking, so it was a little better."

"Right—I think it dropped at least five degrees. And maybe another five while we were in the library. So we're all the way down into the eighties now. That's too hot to bike. Why don't I give you a lift?"

Her mind and body argued over the offer. Her body, which was still hot from the ride up, thought it was a great idea. Her mind, however, kept reminding her that she should increase her fitness level so she could handle the Aikido classes. Plus, she didn't want to inconvenience Bryan or give him the wrong impression.

"Where do you live?" Cassie stuffed her bike lock in its pouch.

"Roland Park."

She wasn't surprised to hear he lived in such an affluent neighborhood. While Roland Park was her dream location for the future, it wasn't conveniently situated near her current home. "I live in Federal Hill. That would be totally out of your way."

"It wouldn't be a problem." He sighed when she put her hands on her hips. "Okay, okay, a compromise then. How about if I take you to dinner? We can throw the bike in my trunk and eat somewhere closer to the harbor. By the time we're done, it should be cooler, you'll be closer to home, and of course, we won't have lied to Cheryl."

She considered it. She was still in her T-shirt and bike shorts, and he was standing there, looking elegant in slacks, dress shirt, and tie. She suspected the suit jacket was stored in his car. Still, there were places where her casual look would be fine.

"I'll agree, as long as we split the meal." She didn't want him to think of it as a date.

"Agreed. Follow me."

She trailed him to his vehicle, a dark blue SUV. She glanced at the Illinois license plates while he loaded the bike in the car.

"I know, I haven't had a chance to go to the DMV yet," Bryan said.

"MVA," she corrected. "Maryland has to be different. It's the Motor Vehicle Administration here rather than the Department of Motor Vehicles. And I don't blame you for avoiding that, it's always a pain in the butt."

"So, where are we headed? Inner Harbor? Phillips?"

She grimaced. "Not Phillips. I'm underdressed, first of all, and second of all, it's a chain restaurant."

"I thought it was the epitome of Baltimore seafood. I haven't even had the famed Baltimore crab cake yet."

"Oh, Phillips shouldn't be your first Baltimore crab cake. Ask any Baltimorean, and you'll get a different answer for best crab cake. Faidley's, in Lexington Market, is usually high on the list, but you're a little overdressed for that. Why don't we go to *my* favorite place for crab cakes?"

"Sounds good. What's the address?" he asked with his fingers poised over the built-in nav system.

She could have given him directions, but gave him the address anyway. Men seemed to love their gadgets.

When they were seated at the patio terrace of Regi's American Bistro, she indulged her curiosity. "So, what brought you to Baltimore?" She picked up the menu, but didn't really need to read it. She went to Regi's so often she knew the menu by heart.

"I worked with some lawyers from the Maryland office on another case. We'd gotten along really well, so I used that connection to transfer to this office. I was looking for a change, anyway. I've lived in Chicago since I started undergrad, and that was fourteen years ago."

She did two quick calculations as they placed their orders for crab cake sandwiches. If undergrad was fourteen years ago, that ought to make him around thirty-two. And if he'd been in Chicago that long—"So, I know Chicago is a huge city and all, but were you familiar with Anthony Bianchi? He's the police IID major here, but I understand he—"

She stopped when Bryan grimaced. Considering that was the most emotion he'd revealed since she met him, she was guessing he was familiar with Bianchi.

"Unfortunately." Bryan sipped the beer the waitress had served him. "Not for very long, thank God, since he left for Baltimore a year or so after I started in the AG's office. But I swear the entire city drew a breath of relief when he left. He used to show up at trials where police officers would testify. The defense lawyers loved it, since the officers would be so concerned about messing up in front of him, they'd often screw up their testimony."

"No wonder. I'm sure any officer would feel nervous testifying in the same room with anyone from IAB there. Oh, is it the 'IAB' in Chicago?"

He shook his head. "IAD. Internal Affairs Division. Of course, they also have the Independent Police Review Authority, which has civilian investigators rather than police."

"Really? I bet that doesn't go over well either."

"No, not really. Still, it's better now than it was when Bianchi was chief. He was completely ineffectual. Cops were abusing their powers left and right and he didn't do a damn thing about it." He lowered his voice when the waitress came over with their crab cakes. "I almost didn't take the Baltimore position knowing that Bianchi was here. Anyway, we shouldn't dwell on him. On to happier things. Here goes my first Baltimore crab cake." He took a big bite and chewed slowly, a contemplative expression on his face. "It's good. Really good."

"They are. Regi's uses panko for their crab cakes. Some locals don't like the fact that they use something other than traditional bread crumbs, but I like the consistency. You do need to go to Faigley's, though."

"I'll make a note of it. The crab's sweet. Succulent."

"Blue crabs are the best." She took a bite of her sandwich. As she savored the taste of the Chesapeake Bay's most famous resident, she let her gaze wander around the other diners and out to the street.

Forgetting she still had a mouthful of food, she took a deep breath. What the hell was *he* doing here?

chapter 15

*G*REAT.

First the jerk breaks her heart, now he was causing her to choke to death on a crab cake.

Since she couldn't think of a less appealing way to go—what a waste of good crab—she used her remaining breath to cough hard and dislodge the blockage. She swallowed and gulped down water.

"Are you okay, Cassie?" Bryan asked, handing her a napkin.

"I'm fine, thanks."

She turned to see if Whittaker had noticed her. Of course he had, after her coughing fit. She was relieved when he went into the restaurant. The relief was short-lived, since he came back out in a few minutes carrying a take-out bag. He took a step towards them and hesitated. *Please don't make a scene*, she prayed. No, never mind, what was she thinking? Proper Detective Whittaker would never make a scene. She rolled her eyes, regretting the action instantly when he narrowed his and strode over.

She braced herself.

"Good evening, Cassie," he said, ignoring Bryan completely. "I'm glad to see murder hasn't affected your appetite."

With that, he stalked away.

Bryan swiveled around and watched him leave before turning back to her. "I don't suppose that was your cop, was it?"

"He's not *my* cop." *Especially not now,* she thought bitterly. And damn it, his comment about the murder was affecting her appetite.

"Why was he talking about murder?" Bryan leaned toward her, curiosity as apparent on his face as sympathy.

She pushed away the plate of food. "I witnessed a murder last night. Well, not directly, but I found the body."

"Officer Anderson, I assume, since miraculously that was the only murder last night. I heard about that this morning. I'm sorry, Cassie. Sorry that you had to witness it. Can't say I'm sorry about Anderson's death."

"Not very many people seem to be," Cassie said.

"Doesn't surprise me. I hate dirty cops. I can't tell you how many cases I lost because a cop planted evidence, or used excessive force, or was just careless. Anyway, I don't want to spoil dinner. Let's talk about something else."

"Like what?" Cassie pulled the plate back to her and tried to regain her appetite.

"Do you want to talk about the cop who's not your cop?"

"Something other than that. How about…what do you write?" She was shocked she hadn't asked him that already. It was usually her first question for a writer.

"Guess." He picked up a french fry.

"I know that Aaron handles genre fiction, especially mysteries, so I'll start there."

"Okay, I'll give you that it is mystery, but what subgenre?" He bit into the fry. "The fries are interesting. But did they burn them?"

"No, they're boardwalk fry style. Goes great with vinegar." She picked up the malt vinegar bottle and liberally anointed her fries.

"Vinegar?" He shook his head. "Marylanders are weird. So, guess the sub-genre."

Legal was the logical choice for a lawyer, but since he was taunting her, she went the opposite route. "Cozy mystery. Involving a little old lady, her Chihuahua, and her pet ostrich."

He snorted. "So close. Guess again."

"Okay, police procedural."

He shook his head.

"Hard-boiled."

Another head shake.

"Traditional." That was her sub-genre, since Marty was an amateur detective, not a private detective or police officer.

He drank some beer before again indicating a negative.

"Psychic. Historical. Legal. Romantic. Supernatural. Paranormal. Locked Room." She went through all the sub-genres she could name. "What, then?"

"Children's," he said with a satisfied gleam in his eyes.

"Really?" She was surprised; she wouldn't have pegged him as a children's mystery writer. She was also delighted. Cheryl was *really* going to hate reading his submissions. They hadn't had a young adult or children's book author in the group before; Cheryl and Susan always rejected them. But Cheryl wouldn't want to get rid of Bryan. "That's awesome. I love children's mysteries. It's how I got interested in the genre."

"Me, too," he said. "Obviously."

"Do you have kids?" Cassie asked.

"Nope. Four nieces and one nephew, but none of my own. I've just never grown up. I'll still reach for my Hardy Boys books when I want something to read."

She laughed again and picked up her sandwich. "I still read books from my childhood. Especially when I've got writer's block. There's nothing like Trixie Belden to inspire my creativity."

"Trixie Belden?" he asked, picking up his napkin. "Not many people know about her."

"No, most know Nancy Drew." She appreciated that Bryan knew her and Michelle's favorite book series. "I have to introduce you to Michelle, my best friend. She's a Trixie Belden fan, too."

"Uh-oh. That sounds like a set-up."

"No." She pictured Michelle and Bryan together. They'd make a really cute couple. "Maybe."

He rolled his eyes and leaned back in the chair, his hair glinting gold in the fading sunlight. "Uh-oh. I hate getting set up. It always starts out with: she's a sweetheart, has a great personality. Right?"

"Actually, she is a sweetheart and has a great personality. But here." She flipped out her phone and searched through her pictures. "Here, that's Michelle."

He looked down at the image, then back up. "Um, she's—cute. Furry, but cute."

"What?" Cassie turned the phone back to check for herself. "Oh, wait. That's Donner, my cat." She snorted as she slid her finger across the screen to find the other picture. "Here. That's Michelle."

His eyebrows shot up in appreciation. "She's cute, too. Not the same way as Donner, of course, but cute. Is she a writer?"

"No." Cassie found one of Michelle's business cards in her wallet and handed it to him. "Human resources director."

"Good." He pocketed the card. "I don't like dating other authors. There's too much competition and snarkiness. Plus, what do you do if you hate their writing?"

She started to laugh. "Hey, wait. So you weren't trying anything by inviting me to dinner?"

"No. Not after hearing you're dating someone who routinely carries a gun. I honestly was giving you a lift and thanking you for inviting me to the critique group. There are some good writers there, and good reviewers."

"Definitely. It's a good mix, too, of published and unpublished authors." She tried to decide if she was relieved or disappointed that Bryan wasn't interested in pursuing her. She finally decided it was a combination of both.

Still, it had been a good evening with Bryan. He was a great distraction from her worries: about Rick, the murders, and her personal issues with Whittaker. He also had some good suggestions as to the problems with her current work in progress. She promised to email him the entire story so far, and a copy of her second book, *Matchbox Murders*.

After saying goodbye to him, she turned on her bike lights and donned her reflective vest so that drivers could see her.

She was glad she chose to bike home rather than accept his offer of a ride. The temperature had cooled down noticeably since the sun went down. The breeze felt good as she pedaled toward her home and left the busier streets for the less traveled side roads.

She was two blocks from home, trying to figure out if she was in the mood to write, when she heard the roar of an engine. Checking the mirror on her helmet, she saw a car speeding toward her. Didn't the idiot realize he'd forgotten to turn on his headlights?

No wonder the moron didn't see her. She edged closer to the parked cars, but there wasn't much room. She put on some speed to get to the end of the block and out of the way. It didn't seem to work; the car was speeding up as well.

Cassie swallowed her panic and reminded herself that this wasn't her first encounter with an idiotic driver. She pedaled harder to get away and almost managed to get to the end of the street. The car came yet closer, that driver must be talking on a cellphone or something and still didn't see her. If she didn't do something now—

She squeezed her handbrakes tight against the handlebars. The sudden motion while trying to steer to the right caused her to go down, and go down hard.

The car cut sharply around the corner, clipping the front wheel of the bike.

"Jerk!" Carefully, she sat up. She took off her backpack and checked to make certain that her netbook and smartphone were undamaged. They were. Thank God for the protective padding.

She stood up and winced as pain shot through her leg. Why did she wear shorts today?

"Oh right, because it was hot," she said aloud, examining the road rash that extended from thigh to ankle. At least that seemed to be the worst of her injuries, she noted with gratitude.

The bike looked like it was toast, at least the front tire. She cursed again as she picked it up and started limping her way home. After four steps, she stopped short. Wait a minute. Maybe the driver wasn't just an idiot. She shivered.

Had someone tried to run her over?

She shook her head. She was reading and writing way too many mysteries. She'd been hit by a car before, although then it had only been the car's side mirror whacking her butt. Only her dignity had been bruised that time.

She dragged the bike up her steps and leaned it against the wall rather than putting it in the holder.

Her phone rang as she limped upstairs to treat her bleeding leg. The phone, of course, was still downstairs in her backpack. With another curse, she changed direction and hobbled down again to get it. Scrambling for the phone, she managed to answer before it switched to voicemail. "Hey, Michelle, how are you? Better than me, I hope."

"What's wrong with you?"

"Some idiot almost ran me and my bike over. I'm okay, but my bike is toast," she said as she climbed the stairs.

"Oh, no. Poor Cassie. No injuries?"

She grunted as she got out the hydrogen peroxide. "Scraped up, mostly."

"What were you doing biking so late? Did your critique meeting run long?" Michelle asked.

"No. Actually, I had dinner with Bryan, a new writer who's joined the group. Oh, and I gave him your business card."

"Why? Does he need a job?"

"Oh, no, he's a lawyer for the federal government. Actually, I thought the two of you should meet."

"Cassandra!" Michelle sounded annoyed. "Are you trying to set me up?"

"He's also blond, blue-eyed, tall, gorgeous—and he likes Trixie Belden," she said, knowing the latter would be what convinced her friend.

"Really?"

Cassie smiled at the sudden interest in her friend's voice. "Yup. He's a children's mystery author, in fact."

"Have you read his stuff yet? I don't want to date him if he's a bad writer."

She giggled. Michelle's words almost matched Bryan's. "No. But he gave some good critique today. What? What's so funny?"

" 'Gave some good critique' just sounds perverted. I like a man who can give good critique. Anyway, never mind, that's not why I called. Turn on the news."

Cassie snagged the remote and turned on her television. "Local or national?"

"Local."

Cassie plopped down on her bed at the sight onscreen. Suddenly, her legs wouldn't support her. The reporter was standing in front of a bar that looked distressingly familiar. Television didn't make it look any better.

"This reporter has learned from anonymous sources close to the investigation that not only is Richard Whittaker, formerly Sergeant Whittaker of the Drug Unit, Baltimore City Police, claiming innocence in the murders of Detectives Michael O'Reilly and Lawrence Anderson, but he is also claiming innocence in the Drug and Dollar scandal from the previous decade.

"Richard Whittaker retired from the force under a cloud of suspicion during the height of that scandal. However, today we have learned that Whittaker had allegedly been working for a federal agency."

That was enough. She turned off the TV and flopped back on the bed. The cat jumped up and head-butted her.

"Shit," she said into the phone as she scratched the cat's ears.

"That about sums it up."

She threw down the remote. "You know, James is probably going to blame this one on me, too, claiming I'm the one that leaked it to the press."

"I doubt he'll think that, Cassie," Michelle said gently. "But don't be surprised if you both get dragged into this. The two of you are linked to each other in the public mind after the other murders."

Cassie sighed. "Too bad we're not linked forever in James' mind."

> 7-3 shift
> After work - Freeman
>
> MONDAY 11 SEPTEMBER   14:45:06

chapter 16

"Of all the gin joints in all the towns in all the world," Whittaker muttered aloud. "She walks into mine."

"Actually you walked into hers," Freeman said. "Not that she owns it, but she was there first. And that was my fault, I'm the one that wanted crab cakes. Damn good, too." He took another bite.

Whittaker stared at his sandwich and brooded. Since they'd been in the area, he'd chosen to go to Regi's even though he knew he was taking a risk—it was one of Cassie's favorite restaurants. He'd figured she wouldn't be there, since he remembered her critique group met that night. He'd figured wrong.

"Aren't you glad we decided to come back to your place to talk about the case, at least?" Freeman said. "If not, you would have had to sit there and watch her with another guy."

Whittaker couldn't believe she was already dating someone else, but then again he couldn't believe she'd invited a suspect into her home for an interrogation. She'd twisted his words, twisted the promise she'd made just so that she could do what she wanted. That was the part that drove him crazy.

You'd think she was a lawyer instead of an author, Whittaker thought as he watched Freeman plow through the food. Sitting there playing semantics while he was trying to keep her safe. Well, forget it. If she wanted to go out there and risk her life, then she could.

"If you're going to sit there and pout, I'm going home," Freeman said, stealing one of Whittaker's fries.

"I'm not pouting. I don't pout." Whittaker pushed the remaining fries towards the older man.

"I'm the one looking at you. You're pouting because Cassie was with another man. A good-looking one."

"You looking at guys now, Freeman?"

"You wish. And no. I just know a good looking guy when I see one. And I know a pouty guy when I see one." Freeman stood up and cleared the food off the dining room table. "Anyway, why don't we talk about what we've learned today?"

"We didn't learn anything today," Whittaker said. He winced when he realized that sounded perilously close to a whine. Great, he was pouting *and* whining.

"Did. We learned that O'Reilly's neighbors thought he was an ass and abused his badge and his power."

"And again, I could have told you that before we talked to his neighbors. Which we weren't technically supposed to be doing, Freeman, as the O'Reilly case is not ours." Whittaker still felt guilty about that. He and Freeman had gone off their shift and done some investigating of their own.

"No, but I think it's possible that it links up with the Williams case." Silverware rattled as Freeman closed the dishwasher. He helped himself to a beer out of the fridge. "You want one?"

"Thank you for offering me my own beer. Yes, I definitely want one. And the Williams case, huh?" Whittaker shook his head. The Williams case was over seven months old, might have been drug-related, and all leads had fizzled within a matter of days.

Freeman wandered over and handed him the beer. "The Williams case. See, Williams was from that neighborhood, too, remember?"

"I remember," Whittaker said dryly. "Fine, so during our investigation of the Williams murder, we've discovered that it was well-known that O'Donnell was dirty and had been dirty for years. Which we knew already. We haven't learned anything that the actual investigators of this case don't already know." Whittaker flicked O'Reilly's file folder on the table, one of the duped copies that Freeman had "accidentally" picked up.

"Not yet. But we will, and we'll exonerate your father, don't you—" The older man broke off when his cell phone rang. "Freeman."

Whittaker saw Freeman's dark brown eyes widen.

"What channel?" Freeman stood and sprinted across the room. He picked up a remote and aimed it at the television.

The walls rattled as Metallica came on at full volume. The remote went flying as Freeman clamped his arms over his ears. His mouth kept moving, but Whittaker couldn't hear a word. That was probably for the best.

Whittaker scrambled into the living room, vaulted over the ottoman, and reached for the remote at the same time as Freeman bent down for it. They narrowly missed bashing heads.

Whittaker stabbed his finger on the OFF button. "Wrong remote," he said and chose the correct one. "What channel?"

Freeman gave him a look of utter disgust before telling him. As the image brightened on the big screen, Whittaker cursed. That was his father's bar. This was not good.

He grabbed an Orioles cap out of his closet and was out the door before Freeman even said a word.

* * * * *

Whittaker cursed again when he saw the television vans sitting in the bar's muddy parking lot. He parked at the gas station across the street.

He made sure to angle his head away from the cameras as he raced for the door.

The place was more packed than he'd ever seen, probably a result of the damned camera crews. Making his way through the throng and to the bar was a challenge. Since the patrons were all watching the televisions, and the televisions were all turned to the news stations, his hypothesis was confirmed.

He caught his father's eye as he nudged some people out of the way. "What the hell, Dad?"

Rick shook his head. "I don't have time for this. I have too many customers."

That he did. Whittaker had to step back as customer after customer came up to place orders. Some were actually reporters—their camera-ready makeup and hair gave it away.

He leaned across the laminate countertop. "How the hell did they find this out?"

His father shook his head again, his lips compressing into a flat line.

Whittaker watched his frantic dance for ten more minutes, until he couldn't take it anymore. He slipped behind the bar and reached for an abandoned glass on a soggy napkin. His father pivoted in surprise, hands raised in a combative stance.

"At ease, Dad," Whittaker said, tossing the napkin in a trash container and putting the glass with an army of other soiled glassware in danger of overflowing the confines of a sink.

Rick's tense position relaxed. He popped the tops off several longneck bottles and asked, "What are you doing back here?"

"I'm helping you, what do you think I'm doing?"

"Have you ever worked a bar before?" Rick slid the beers down to a burly biker guy wearing a pink hat and a turquoise nose ring and rang the money through the till.

"No, but I guess I'll learn. I don't suppose you have a price list?"

"You supposed right. Fine, you can do the easy tasks."

His father's definition of easy tasks was different than his. Whittaker had expected he'd be drawing draft beers and mixing drinks. Instead, he spent his time as a barback, hefting boxes and kegs back and forth, carrying empty stuff back to the storage room and coming back with full stuff.

"Last call!" his father finally said.

Whittaker wanted to applaud, but that would break the glasses in his hands. Those were the two sweetest words he'd heard in hours.

He swiped sweat from his brow and took a glance around the once-packed interior. Most of the crowd had left after the camera crews departed; more when the midnight hour passed. The ones who yet lingered were Rick's regulars.

Now they had more time to interact.

"So, this must be James." The white-haired man who spoke had been drinking seltzer water all night. Whittaker guessed he was probably one of his father's friends from Alcoholics Anonymous.

"You got it, Gordon." Rick passed the man another glass without being asked, then slid a non-alcoholic beer down the counter to another waiting customer.

"It's nice to meet you, Detective. Your dad talks about you all the time. You and your sister. He's damn proud of both of you."

"How is Chloe?" another man asked. "She's back at Gallaudet, right?"

"Yes, the semester started last week. She's glad to be back." Whittaker was surprised the regulars knew so much about him and his sister.

"Made Dean's List again last semester," his father bragged. "You know she gets her intelligence from me."

Gordon snorted. "Well, that explains what happened. You gave all your smarts to your daughter."

"Hey, it's a father's job to sacrifice for his kids," Rick said, scooping up money from the bar.

It was definitely an education for Whittaker, watching his father interact with the people. His father had been a quiet, solid man when he was a police officer. As a bar owner, he'd obviously learned how to be more outgoing and extroverted. But he still had a great skill for listening, something he'd first picked up in the interview room.

Last call meant a big rush on everything, but Rick made sure that they'd prepped and stocked what they'd need. They passed out O'Douls, Millers, and the Natty Bohs that Baltimore still loved, even if it was no longer brewed there.

"I'm going to have to place a rush order tomorrow." Rick slid past to make change at the register for the last straggler. "I won't have enough, especially if I'm that popular tomorrow, too. Who would have thought something positive would come out of this damned story being dragged out into the public? Don't you need to get home?"

"Not just yet."

Rick peeked out the door before closing and locking it. "I wanted to make sure there weren't any more camera crews out there. Hopefully they've moved on to some house fires or murders." He slumped into the nearest chair. "Is it bad that I'm even hoping there's another cop murder tonight? Both of us would be alibied."

Whittaker chuckled as he walked around, picking up empties. The speedwasher was already loaded so he went to the storage room to fill up the sinks.

"Fill up the middle one, too," Rick called from the front. "Then follow the instructions over the sinks."

He was learning something else new. He'd already learned how to change out a draft beer CO_2 container... with far less mess than the time he'd deployed Cassie's CO_2 wine opener. Damn it. Why'd he have to go and remind himself of her? Firmly, he redirected his thoughts to the here and now. His father's situation was more important. He'd deal with Cassie later.

When he came out to pick up more glasses, his father was reluctantly boosting himself out of the chair.

"Sit down for a while, Dad. You deserve a break."

"I suppose I do. God, I feel old."

"You didn't look that old tonight. I was impressed watching you move. You were a hell out of a lot faster than I am, and I'm twenty-five years younger."

Rick huffed out a laugh. "I've been doing this for five years now. I got good at it."

"Why'd you open a bar, Dad? Was that really the best choice for a recovering alcoholic? I'm not accusing you of anything, just asking," he rushed to add when his father scowled at him.

"Maybe not the best choice, but evidently a fairly common one, I've been told. I don't know, I guess I wanted to remind myself of what I beat. And it would remind me of what I was when I'd see the customers who were addicted to what I was pouring. I've actually helped a few of them, even if it cut into my profits. Seltzer water doesn't have as much of a mark-up as beer."

"Yeah, I noticed how many of your customers weren't drinking alcohol. Again, is coming to a bar the best idea for them?"

Rick shrugged. "In some ways, it's a temptation. But honestly, you end up missing more than the alcohol when you give it up. You miss the friends, the hanging out, the atmosphere. We've got a pretty good crowd here of friends of Bill W, so they support each other if someone is tempted. And they know I'll never serve any of them alcohol."

It made sense, Whittaker thought as he continued to pick up glasses.

"And I'll tell you what," Rick said then paused to go into the storage room. He came back with a few dishpans, passed one to Whittaker. "Here, it's easier if you stack them in here. I'll get the bar, you get the tables."

"You'll tell me what, Dad?"

"What? Oh, right. Since we've been talking about alcoholics and about two late and not lamented police officers, I was thinking about O'Reilly. He had a serious problem with alcohol when I worked with him. He wasn't a happy drunk, either. Alcohol turned him mean and loud. I doubt it got better after he got demoted back to patrol."

"Do you think that he abused drugs, too?" Whittaker hoped the answer was no. There was something wrong about a cop abusing the very thing he was trying to take off the streets.

"I don't think so. Number one, I would have recognized the signs. Number two, while drinking is something tolerated, even accepted by our superiors, using drugs isn't."

Whittaker followed his father to the storage room, wishing he could have convinced the stubborn hardhead to let him carry everything. But he knew his dad would have been insulted if he even mentioned it.

His father left him to wash the glassware, saying he was going to do up the tills.

Left to his own thoughts, he methodically washed and disinfected the glasses. He really wanted to call Cassie and tell her about the news report. Did she know that the media had broken the story about his father's innocence, or, as he'd seen on the closed caption, his father's "alleged innocence"? He gritted his teeth. Alleged. They were insinuating his dad was guilty.

Cassie would probably be just as insulted at that, but still happy that the whole world knew the truth.

"Hot damn!"

His father's shout brought Whittaker, suds and all, to see what's wrong. "What?"

"This is more money than I make in a week. I should be on the news more often." He carried the money to the storage room and dropped it in a time-lock safe next to a battered desk. He dropped down onto an equally battered desk chair.

"Does it bother you, Dad?"

"That people know the truth? I mean, the 'alleged truth'," his father said wryly. He sighed, leaned back in the chair, and stared at the ceiling. "I don't know. It's kind of a shock. It was shocking enough when you, Patti, and Chloe finally found out. I should have told you earlier."

"We've already covered that, Dad. Stop bringing it up."

"Yeah, yeah. Anyway, once you all found out, it was easier to admit the truth when Wertz and Garcia asked me. You know that's who leaked it to the media, right?" Rick asked with a shrewd look in his eyes.

"That was my theory, too. I have to assume they think the leak will somehow affect the killer."

Rick nodded as he swiveled the chair back and forth. "I hope it does. I can't stand any cop killer, even if the cops killed were dirty. But back to your original question, what sort of bothers me is that a lot of people are going to think the 'alleged innocence' is bullshit. I guess I can't blame them, they'll all wonder why, if I was innocent, I didn't come forward then."

"I know you weren't able to do that with the police since you had absolutely no evidence you were working for the Feds. But why didn't you explain it to us, Dad? I know you said that you were crushed by Mom's reactions." Whittaker sighed deeply. "By my reaction. But why not turn around and shove it in our faces that you were innocent, that we were wrong?"

"You'd already made your decision, so I thought 'Why bother'? It was stupid of me, I realize that now. But I was so angry that my family could think those things of me."

"I'm sorry, Dad. It was just...I was at the Academy and heard everyone talking about evidence, about proof, about means, motive, and opportunity. Then those same instructors were the ones I heard gossiping about you and the news reports."

"Yeah, well sometimes evidence and proof aren't what they seem. You should never go into a situation, personal or police-related, and make automatic assumptions." His father stood up and stretched. "I'll finish cleaning up out there."

Whittaker continued washing the never-ending glassware as he considered his father's words. Hadn't he said the same to Cassie when she was trying to investigate the murders of her sources, back when they first met? He felt hypocritical, since he'd done that with his father. And then, he supposed, he'd done the same with Cassie the other day. But he hadn't misread that scene. He was certain of that.

He'd have to be careful with how he was handling the O'Reilly and Anderson murders. He was going into those with assumptions, too, thinking that being dirty cops had led to their deaths.

"I suppose you're right, Dad," Whittaker said when his father returned, carrying another bin of glasses. "But sometimes assumptions are right. Sometimes, a cigar is a cigar. And how many freaking glasses do you have?"

Rick laughed. "I don't know. I've never had to use the ones from storage before. But I think there's only two more trays full left."

"Thank God. Let me help and then at least that'll be done." He grabbed a tray and followed his father into the main room.

"A cigar could be a cigar," Rick said as he cleared another table. "But again, if you go in assuming it's a cigar and it's really an explosive, it'll blow up in your—" He stopped when there was a knock on the door. "Who the hell is that this late?"

"I don't know. Check the camera." Whittaker put down the tray and placed a hand under his jacket and on his gun.

"Huh." His father stared at the security screen. "Never thought to see her again." He strode over and unlocked the door. "What brings you here, Leslie?"

Whittaker tensed up immediately when he saw the tall woman, but he lowered his hand.

"Hello, Rick," Leslie Harding gave the older man a warm smile, then jumped in surprise. "Oh, Detective Whittaker. I didn't think I'd see you here. Word on the street is that you and your father never talk."

He scowled. "Word on the street is wrong."

"So are you," she retorted.

He was confused by her simple statement. "I'm wrong? About what?"

"About your girlfriend. You shouldn't have yelled at her." Leslie slid onto a bar stool. "Can I have a soda, Rick? I won't ask for alcohol, I know it's after closing. And I know you'd never disobey laws, no matter what others thought."

His father stopped looking back and forth from Leslie to his son and walked behind the bar. Handing her a ginger ale, he turned back to Whittaker. "You yelled at Cassie? What for?"

Whittaker shoved his hands in his pockets. "Earlier this week, I stopped by at Cassie's house. She was in there interrogating Leslie. After promising me she wouldn't go interviewing suspects."

Leslie shook her head violently, but not a hair came out of place from her updo. "That's not what was happening." She glanced at the monitors behind the bar. "Take a look at the screen, tell me what you see."

Whittaker approached the bar and peered over. "A mostly empty parking lot. Except for a white pick-up. I assume that would be yours."

"That assumption is correct. Do you remember seeing it before, Detective? Perchance on the day on your previous, incorrect assumption?"

He scowled at her patronizing tone. "I don't remember every vehicle I see, Ms. Harding." He deliberately left out her former rank. "There are quite a number of them in this city."

"James," his father admonished. "Be nice."

"Can you describe the scene outside Cassie's apartment?" Leslie took a delicate sip from her ginger ale without taking her eyes off Whittaker.

He removed his hands from his pockets and threw them up in frustration. "That was days ago." He huffed out a breath. "Let's see. It was a hot day, I can remember that. I was dropping by Cassie's house, only had a few moments to spare. I parked behind a…" He darted his eyes back to the security camera. "Shit. I parked behind a white Dodge pickup with a steaming radiator. Yours?"

"Mine." She set down the drink with a snap. "It had overheated."

He felt a lump in the pit of his stomach. "It had overheated. And Cassie invited you inside."

"Yes. She was passing by, saw me in distress, and invited me in to use her phone and to get some water. She had no idea who I even was."

The abdominal distress worsened. "Oh hell. She was only trying to help you."

"Yes." Leslie nodded. "Help. Not interrogate. She was being nice. She wasn't disobeying your orders, Detective."

"It wasn't orders," Whittaker protested. "I don't give orders, or expect her to obey me. I just thought she'd broken a promise. Why didn't she defend herself?"

"You probably didn't give her a chance." His father spoke up for the first time. "I know how she feels."

Whittaker sank down in a chair. "Oh hell, I've done it again."

"What were you doing in Federal Hill anyway?" Rick asked.

"Oh. Um, I was, seeing an old friend." She rose gracefully and slid on her purse strap. "Anyway, it was great seeing you again, Rick. Hopefully next time will be under better circumstances. Same thing to you, Detective."

Rick walked her to the door, locking it behind her. "I'd say that cigar blew up in your face, James."

Whittaker leaned his head on the table in front of him. "Did it ever. I'm an idiot."

"I want to support you, son, I do. So how about if I just agree with you that you're an idiot?"

"Thanks, Dad." He lifted his head up. "What'll I do?"

"Flowers would be good. And groveling. Lots and lots of groveling." His father held out a hand to help him up.

"Should I have brought you flowers to apologize for being an idiot?"

His father laughed. "No, but some tickets to the next Orioles game would do for me."

"Actually, that might work for Cassie, too."

"The girl likes baseball? You better go after her, then. After you finish those glasses."

Whittaker eyed the sink in dismay. "Yes, sir."

chapter 17

CASSIE STARED AT THE monitor and rubbed her temple. On the way home from self defense class, she'd been hit by a brainstorm about the murders and had immediately jumped onto her computer. She hadn't even bothered changing out of the gray leggings and T-shirt she'd worn in class.

Now, three hours later, she wasn't certain what to do next.

Apparently sensing her distress—or just wanting some petting—Donner leaped onto the table and butted his head against her hand. She scratched under his chin, his favorite spot, and pondered.

The insistent, sharp rapping startled her to her feet and Donner to the floor. She almost tripped over the cat as they both raced to the front of the house. A squint through the peephole made her grab her cat. She carried him back to the kitchen and shooed him through the basement door, making sure it was closed securely before going back to admit her guests.

"Hello, Linda," Cassie said, standing aside so the psychic and her entourage could enter. "Hi, Houdini, George, and Dorian."

She wasn't surprised that the older woman had brought her birds along. Linda often traveled with her parrots. As usual, Houdini was attired in a flightsuit and leash, since the cockatoo was too large to easily transport in a cage. The bright yellow material matched his crest and Linda's skirt.

Dorian, the beautiful and intelligent African Grey, was in a mesh-screened backpack especially made for birds, while George, the tiny green and yellow budgie, was in a similar, smaller carrier, designed to wear in the front.

"Donner's been put away?" The older woman set Houdini on the arm of a ladder-back chair.

Cassie was about to respond, but an incensed yowl from the basement provided the answer.

"Everything okay?" She reached out a hand to help a distracted-looking Linda take off a carrier strap.

"The birds are saying something important. Is it okay if I let them out?"

Cassie agreed, but at the same time, she made sure she closed her laptop. The last thing she needed was a "parrot-enhanced" keyboard. Linda had been sending emails lately without using any punctuation or the letter "m" since Dorian had removed several keys.

"But I can't understand what it is," Linda said, unzipping George's carrier. "I thought if I brought them over, you might be able to interpret."

"They *are* all aflutter about something, aren't they? I've never heard them this talkative before." Cassie sat down to hear what the birds were saying. It seemed to be some type of pattern. "I think they're saying the same thing over and over. First George, then Dorian, then Houdini."

"Can you understand it, Cassandra?" Linda asked. "I've been listening to them for three hours now, and I can't tell what they're saying. They've never done anything like this before."

"Do you think it's a movie quote again?"

Linda angled her head as she stared at her flock. "I don't know. George doesn't usually do movie quotes. I've had her since she was a chick, and unlike the other two, she wasn't raised in a movie theater."

Cassie nodded. "Did you ever figure out where George got her statement last month of 'Red's friend danger'?"

Linda glared at Cassie. "You mean if you're going to discount the fact that George made an accurate prediction? Your friend *was* in danger."

Cassie ducked her head. "Other than that. I mean, how did she know the words?"

"Oh, every evening she practices the words that the boys are saying. It's cute listening to her talking to herself in the cage. I believe danger was from 'Danger, Will Robinson.' I don't know where she got the word 'friend' from. And, of course, the birds have been calling you Red since they met you. They actually said your name again before they started this incessant chanting. That's why I brought them to you. It's driving me crazy."

Cassie propped her elbows on the table and rested her chin on her fists. But when the parrots came closer, she shot up straight. Linda's birds were friendly, she knew, but she also retained many gruesome images of birds in her mind from watching Hitchcock movies.

"They won't b—oh, never mind." Linda sighed. "Can you figure out what they're saying?"

"I think George is saying 'pop' and her second word sounds like 'uh oh.' Dorian is saying—" Cassie wrinkled her nose. "Is he saying 'sex'?"

Linda giggled. "You must have sex on the brain. It's '*six*'. Like the number. And then I know Houdini says 'squish' after that."

"Squish?" Cassie was impressed how well the birds could enunciate. George was a little squeaky and quiet, but Houdini spoke clearly, and Dorian's words were almost human-like. "Okay, you're right. Is Dorian's next one 'Cicero'? Why does that sound familiar?"

"It does? Oh, thank God. I hope you can figure it out." Linda looked more hopeful as the birds went through the chant again. "I think Houdini's last word is 'lipstick' before they go back to the beginning."

Cassie repeated the pattern in her head. "Ha! No, it's not 'lipstick'." She opened her laptop, shaking with laughter. When the computer woke up, she clicked iTunes and selected her killing music playlist, scrolling through until she saw the song she wanted to play. "It's 'Cell Block Tango'."

After the first few bars of music, Linda nodded her head. "Shoot. I should have recognized that. I adore that musical and have watched it, with the birds, many times."

Cassie grinned as the parrots started dancing to the rhythmic music. Houdini was especially talented. Actually, he was better than she'd been after her night of tango lessons. Her smile died. Too bad Whittaker was a jerk; she would have loved to take more tango lessons with him. More, she wished they could have continued the dance moves back at her house that night. Now they'd never—

She jerked her head up. "Wait. Wait! The musical. It's *Chicago*."

"I know that, Cassie dear. I just said the birds and I have watched it several times."

Cassie minimized iTunes. That displayed the browser window with the article she'd been reading before Linda's arrival. She backed from the table and spun in a circle. "I'm right! I knew I was right."

"About what?" Linda moved closer to the computer. She reached into her large white purse and pulled out some reading glasses. "Why are you reading about murders in Chicago?"

"Murders of *police officers* in Chicago," Cassie clarified. "Just like we've had here."

"Well, that's not surprising, is it? Being a police officer is a dangerous occupation."

"Yes, it is. And although over fifty cops have been killed over the last five years, there are six that I'm interested in particularly."

"What six are that?" Linda asked, peering at Cassie over her glasses.

"Well, within the unsolved deaths, six of the victims had been mentioned in other articles, either for complaints lodged against them or for unseemly conduct. And these six were killed either by their own service weapon *or* by their police vehicle."

Linda wrinkled her forehead. "Like the two murders here. So you think the birds are telling you that those murders in Chicago are related to the ones here?"

Cassie bounced up and down, then switched to pacing. The birds followed her movements, walking back and forth on the table. "Yes! More importantly, they're telling me that I'm right to suspect Major Bianchi. I knew he was a jerk and a male chauvinist pig, but this morning I realized there was a pattern. Bryan had mentioned the murders when I talked to him, and had mentioned that Bianchi wasn't very well liked. So this morning, as I was driving home from class, I was thinking about who would benefit most by the deaths of dirty cops."

"You suspect the person in charge of—what is it, the Internal Investigation Division?" Linda looked far from convinced.

Great. Even the person who believed in psychic parrots didn't believe her. How was she ever going to convince the police? "Yes! Who else would benefit the most from getting rid of dirty cops? Especially ones he couldn't remove any other way. And IID just released its list of the police officers with the highest number of complaints lodged against them. And guess what? Anderson and O'Reilly were both up there."

Linda didn't say anything for a moment. She preened Houdini's head when he demanded her attention. Cassie supposed he'd gotten bored with pacing.

"But these murders took place after Major Bianchi came to Baltimore." Linda's fingers stopped moving. Houdini nudged his head under her hand again, his feathers puffed up. "I can remember that date, because Mrs. O'Reilly started coming more often for readings, hoping to find out if the new changes to the police force would affect her son."

"Well, it would be clever of Bianchi to go back to his old town and take care of the cops that pissed him off, that he hadn't been able to get to." Cassie took a satisfied breath. "It makes logical sense."

"If this were a book either of us were writing, it would be. But you're basing all of this off of the birds singing about Chicago? Does this mean you now believe they *can* predict the future?"

That stopped Cassie in her tracks. "No. I don't. I mean, I don't know." She was relieved when another knock on the door gave her an excuse not to look into Linda's smug, knowing eyes.

The relief morphed into shock, anger, and then dismay as she peered through the peephole. "What the hell is he doing here?" She paced away from the door, then stalked back and yanked it open.

"What the hell are you doing here?" she said again, this time to Whittaker, who was standing on the stoop with his hands behind his back.

"I'm here to apologize. Profusely." He stepped into her living room. "Oh, I didn't realize somebody was here. Hello, Linda," he muttered and shoved his hands in his pockets. In an explosion of crackling cellophane and bending stems, flowers went flying everywhere. "Crap, I forgot about the bouquet."

"Hello, Detective Whittaker," Linda said, smothering a laugh. "It's nice to see you, but why don't I get the birds and take off? Cassie, thank you for figuring out what they were saying. And I hope they did help."

Cassie helped Linda pack George and Dorian back in their holders as Whittaker scrambled on the floor, picking up squashed blossoms and soggy petals.

Linda lifted Houdini onto her shoulder and looped his leash around her neck. "Have a good day, children." Her laugh followed her out the door.

Whittaker handed Cassie the few surviving flowers, one with a bent stem. "Children?"

"You certainly behaved like one," Cassie said as she let Donner out of the basement. The cat prowled quickly around the room, jumped onto the table, and sniffed intently at everything. He howled once, glared at her, and ran upstairs, probably to sulk.

She placed the measly bouquet in a vase, grateful to notice none of the flowers were lilies. Lilies were poisonous to cats. "So, you said something about an apology?"

He shoved his now-empty hands into his pockets again. She half expected him to stare at the floor and scuff his feet. Instead, he looked her directly in the eyes.

"Yes. I'm sorry, Cassie. Incredibly sorry. Sorry that I yelled at you, sorry that I accused you of interrogating Leslie Harding, sorry that I once again made a stupid assumption about someone I lo—someone I care about. Sorry I didn't just ask."

Her anger might have lessened after his first "I'm sorry", her heart might have leaped at his almost-declaration, but the hurt was still there. "You really thought I'd do something like that?"

"I don't know. I mean, I couldn't believe you'd take that huge risk. But the evidence that I saw—"

"I thought you weren't supposed to make instant assumptions, Detective Whittaker." She flopped down on the couch and deliberately arched an eyebrow in an imitation of him.

He shut his eyes. "I know, I know. I was an ass, I'm sorry." He sat down next to her and ran his hands through his hair again, disheveling it.

She fought herself not to smooth it back down. "I can't argue with you there."

"Thanks. I really am sorry, Cassie. Leslie came to the bar last night and told us that her truck had overheated right outside your door."

"Correct. I was bringing home groceries and passed her by. I invited her in since it was hot and she needed to use my phone, not to interrogate her."

"I'm really sorry I was an idiot. My behavior was unforgivable—although I'm hoping you can forgive me anyway." He smiled slowly.

As always, the dimples were her downfall. "Maybe. I'll think about it."

"I'd appreciate it. And I promise not to jump to conclusions again, at least, I'll try not to. Not about you, not about my Dad—who also thought I was an idiot, by the way. I promise I'll always ask from now on. I'll even seal the promise with a kiss." He leaned toward her.

She jumped up at that moment. "I just remembered! Here, look." She ran over to the table for her computer. "Look!"

Whittaker took the laptop from her and set it on the coffee table. "You're looking at police deaths in Chicago? Why?"

"Because it's Bianchi." She waited expectantly for him to realize what she meant.

"What's Bianchi?" He glanced at the laptop again. "What, the murders?"

"Yes. There and here." She sat down next to him, tucking one leg underneath the other.

"You think that Major Bianchi is killing cops. Why? Because they're dirty?"

"Yes. See! You get it."

"Now who's making assumptions?" He shook his head. "Cassie, what makes you think that Anthony Bianchi, the major of the Internal Investigations Division, is off *killing* people?"

"*Because* he's the major of the Internal Investigations Division. He can't get rid of all the dirty cops via protocol, so he finds another way." She pointed at the computer. "Look, I found six unsolved, unwitnessed murders of police officers in Chicago over the last five years. All six of the officers show up in other articles that mentioned they were suspended previously for inappropriate behavior. And they were killed with their own gun or with their own police car."

He narrowed his eyes at her. "Cassie, he's been *here* for the past five years."

"Exactly." She stared back at him; why wasn't he getting this? "So he went back."

"And now he's killing people in Baltimore?"

"Yes. More dirty cops that he can't get to. Didn't you notice that both O'Reilly and Anderson were on the list the IID released?"

"Of course I did. Which means, if the murders are due to them being dirty, it could be anyone who read the article, Cassie. That's a lot of people."

Scowling, she took back her computer. "And this is a lot of dead cops."

"Dirty cops often meet bad ends." He sighed when she continued to glare at him. "Okay, I happen to know that the detectives for both cases are looking into the fact that the list was released and suddenly cops are dying. So you're probably correct there."

"But…" she said through gritted teeth.

"But I don't believe the major would kill his own officers. In Chicago, or here. You don't piss in your own pool."

"Maybe not. But if people are already pissing in your pool, then wouldn't you want to get them out of the pool before it contaminates the entire—okay, this is a really disgusting analogy. Can we choose another?"

Laughing, he pulled her closer. "I have a better idea." He tilted his head and came closer.

She pushed against his chest. "Oh, no. It's not going to be that easy for you. Number one, I know you're trying to distract me from my theory. Number two, while I've forgiven you, I haven't forgotten. You were a jerk, James. First you hurt me, and then insulted me last night—in front of Bryan."

"Oh, so that was Bryan," he said in a low, dangerous voice.

She pushed him again. "Now you're being a jealous jerk. Yes, that was Bryan. Who doesn't date other authors. In fact, I'm trying to set him up with Michelle."

"Michelle's a good idea."

She saw his tense face brighten for a moment before settling back into sober lines.

He stroked a finger along her cheekbone. "I'm sorry for being a jerk last night and making that statement. I was upset at the idea that you were dating somebody and was frustrated already because—"

"Because?" she asked.

"Because I'd been having a frustrating day investigating a murder with Freeman."

She narrowed her eyes. "Oh, really. Whose murder were you investigating?"

"Why do you ask that?" He laid an arm behind her on the couch.

"Because you wouldn't have paused like that if you'd been investigating a regular case. You're investigating O'Reilly's and Anderson's murders, aren't you?" When he opened his mouth, she cut him off. "And don't tell me I'm jumping to conclusions, I *know* I'm right."

"Fine," he admitted. "Yes, we're investigating the murders. I want to clear my dad's name."

"I know." She gave into temptation and smoothed down his hair. "I want to, too. I'm impressed to see you going outside of regulation to do so." This time, she closed the distance and kissed him.

Whittaker moved his hand from the back of the couch and pulled her close, changing what was supposed to be a light kiss into instant heat. She thought about protesting again, but hey, this was one way to make up after a fight, wasn't it? Releasing those pent up emotions in a healthy, enjoyable way. A very enjoyable way.

It took a moment for her eyes to focus when he broke off the kiss. She blinked rapidly, realizing this felt exactly like the transition she made from her imagination to the real world. Fanning herself with her hand, she decided that his kiss was much better than anything her imagination ever created.

"Sorry," Whittaker said as he leaned his head back on the couch and tried to catch his breath.

"You've apologized a number of times today, James. I don't think you need to apologize for kissing me."

He smiled and shook his head. "No, not for that. I'm apologizing for starting something I can't finish. I'm on my lunch break, so I need to go back to the office. Can I come over after my shift?"

She glanced at the clock and saw that it was almost one. "Yes, but I'm meeting Mark at five."

"Oh." He flicked his wrist to check the time. "I need to help my dad unload a rush order anyway, so maybe I can come over around nine or so. I assume you caught the coverage yesterday."

"I did." She placed her hand on his forearm. "How do you feel about it?"

"I don't know. Honestly, it doesn't change anything. The media still had to say 'allegedly innocent', so people are going to believe what they want anyway. Dad can't prove he was working for the Feds."

"Still, at least you know and believe him. That has to make him feel better, at least."

"I hope so." He stood, pulling her up with him. "I'm glad he was able to forgive me for assuming he was guilty. And thank you for forgiving me for assuming you were guilty."

"Just don't do it again," she warned.

"I won't. At least, I'll try not to. So we'll have a nice, fresh start and I'll try to ask you what's going on instead of just assuming."

"Sounds good." She got up on her tiptoes and kissed him. "Now, about Bianchi."

"Oh, not that again. There's no way he's killing his own people."

She thought about bringing up her proof from Linda's Psychic Consortium but decided against it. "Why not? Again, it's a way to get rid of dirty cops."

"Cassie. He's in a powerful position. If he wanted to get rid of these cops, he could transfer them to some horrible position. Or if he did have some type of illegal intent, he could set them up with false evidence. But again, he's IID, he's even more of a stickler than I am about following the rules."

"Worse than you?" She gave a mock shudder. "What a horrible idea."

"Ha ha." He kissed her nose. "Now, I really have to go."

She followed him to the door. "Why don't you suggest this to Wertz and Garcia? Or to—um, the detectives on the O'Reilly case."

"Newmann and Dirruzo," he said. "But I'm not sure accusing the head of IID is a good idea, Cass."

"He'd have access to the patrol car keys," she pointed out, grateful when that gave him pause. "And he'd have been able to get O'Reilly's gun from him by asking him to surrender his weapon. Tell him he'd been suspended or something."

He shook his head. "No. If someone from IID tells you you're suspended, they'd have to do it in a formal setting, with your supervisor there and probably your union rep as well. He couldn't just demand your service piece and badge in a dark alley."

"Not even Bianchi?" she asked stubbornly.

"Not even Bianchi. No way would O'Reilly have surrendered anything to IID without proper representation. Anyway, I gotta go. Bye." He kissed her one last time.

That threw a major hitch in her theory, she reflected, closing the door after him. She'd have to come up with a new reason why O'Reilly would surrender his gun.

Luckily, she knew just who to ask.

chapter 18

"Mark, I have a question."

"Color me amazed." Mark Griffin, Cassie's gun expert, loaded rounds into the cylinder of the revolver.

She decided against sticking her tongue out at him. Not only was it immature, but she felt it was unpatriotic to do that to a retired Marine. Not even his casual attire of jeans and T-shirt could disguise his military bearing.

"You're funny. Seriously, I have an important question."

"Go ahead and ask, Cassie. I can hear you with these ear protectors, remember?"

She remembered. His electronic ear protectors were cool, in her opinion, letting low decibel sounds through, but muffling loud noises. Which was good, since they were shooting a Model 29 Smith & Wesson, and it was loud. Very loud. In general, she preferred semi-automatic pistols, but she did like shooting the big .44 Magnum.

This was the weapon that Clint Eastwood called the most powerful handgun in the world. She always felt like

Dirty Harry when she fired it, adding "Do you feel lucky, punk" under her breath as she squeezed the trigger.

Mark picked up the gun and shot in a quick succession.

Cassie couldn't help but count the blasts. "I don't see the big deal. It's easy to tell if you shot six times or five. I don't know why the punk didn't know if Dirty Harry had any bullets left."

"This from the girl that charged toward a loaded weapon?" Mark laid the gun on the shelf.

"It was supposed to misfire," Cassie protested. "And you were in danger."

"Yes. And in a dangerous situation like that, you have other things to worry about rather than counting shots."

She decided to change the subject rather than argue. "You heard about the murder of Officer O'Reilly, right?"

He nodded as they traded places. "Yes. Pretty nasty business, getting killed with your own weapon."

"Oh, was that finally confirmed?" She scowled. She should have asked Whittaker that question, but she'd been… distracted.

"According to the news today, yes." Mark clipped on a new target for her and punched the button to send it back twenty-five feet.

She took careful aim while thinking *do you feel lucky, punk?* and fired six times. Squinting at the target, she thought she'd done pretty well.

"So, the question is, how did the killer manage to get the gun from Officer O'Reilly?"

"Why would I know that?"

She scowled at him. "Well, how would someone get your gun from you?"

"Out of my cold, dead hands."

She grinned, even though she knew Mark had been completely serious. They changed places again. She stepped back and leaned against the end of the partition between the shooting lanes. When he nailed the center ring with each shot, she admired his marksmanship, as always. She was getting better, but she wasn't that good.

She was glad that she hadn't developed a phobia about guns after getting shot. Mark had dragged her to the firing range almost as soon as they were discharged from the hospital.

"How about if he had you at gunpoint?" she asked when it was her turn to shoot.

"I'd pretend to cooperate, carefully take my gun out...and then shoot him with it. I believe most police officers would do the same, rather than surrender their weapon. Once they do that, they'd be completely at the mercy of their foe."

After her turn, she carefully placed the revolver on the shelf, making certain to point the muzzle downrange. "Okay, I get that. What if..." she paused. "What if you were ordered to by a superior officer?"

"Then I'd surrender my weapon." He bent over to get more ammunition, then froze. He turned shocked blue eyes toward her. "You think another police officer killed him? A ranking officer?"

She shrugged. Mark looked as dubious as Whittaker had been. Somehow, she doubted he'd be very impressed that Linda's parrots had corroborated her theory. "It's an idea."

He put down everything and turned around. "I would surrender the weapon, because I'm a Marine and would obey my commanding officer without hesitation. However, these are police officers. He wouldn't surrender his weapon unless there was a solid, valid reason to do so."

"Like being suspended?"

His nostrils flared as he took a deep breath. "You really do suspect a superior officer."

Shrugging again, she moved over to allow three men into the next stall. She glanced over, and decided from their posture, demeanor, and short hair cuts that they were soldiers from the nearby base. "Like I said, it's an idea. When an officer is suspended, he's required to give up his badge and service piece."

"That's correct. However, that's in an official surrounding. Not in a dark alley where Officer O'Reilly's murder took place. And there'd be others around to document it. Everything would be official with reams and reams of paperwork."

She wanted to pout. "Never mind, then."

He picked up the .44, loaded it, and took some shots before turning around slowly. "Actually, I can think of one circumstance where someone might have given up his weapon without resistance."

"Really? What?"

"If he was inebriated. If someone noticed that the officer had too much to drink, perhaps if he was being belligerent and irrational, then that person might state that they should surrender their weapon until they were sober and more themselves."

"Like turning over car keys?" she asked, reaching for the revolver.

He blocked her. "Yes. And by the way, I told you it's not that easy to count shots when you're distracted." He turned, picked up the gun one-handed, and fired the sixth round directly in the center ring. "Punk."

* * * * *

WHITTAKER LOOKED UP FROM the report he was writing. Freeman was talking to their sergeant about one of his open cases, and McMillan and Peters were off that day. It was the perfect time to talk to Wertz and Garcia.

He stood, stretched, and went to join them at the coffee maker. Passing by the white board, he couldn't stop himself from reading the victim's names. Anderson and O'Reilly were written in the red marker that denoted an open case.

"You two have a minute?" he asked.

"We've got a couple of them," Wertz answered with a sideways glance at his partner.

Whittaker nodded towards the interview area. They followed him into the hallway, ignoring the NO WEAPON EVER IN INTERVIEW ROOM sign posted on the door. Since no one was being interrogated at the moment, it wasn't an issue.

"What's up?" Wertz asked as soon as the door closed.

Whittaker figured the man already knew he was going to ask about the Anderson case, since it was Wertz leading the questions, and he was primary. Wertz might be blond, but he wasn't dumb.

"You guys leak the news about my father?"

Again Wertz was the one who spoke. "You mean about him being innocent of the D&D scandal?"

" 'Allegedly innocent', you mean," Whittaker sneered.

"Innocent," Garcia corrected. "And yeah, we did. With approval from the higher-ups."

That surprised Whittaker. "Really? Why?"

"Why'd we leak it?" Wertz asked. "Number of reasons. First of all, it's a strategy. We want everyone to know we're no longer looking at Rick Whittaker, for the D&D scandal or for the murders. We're hoping that'll make this cop killer nervous and cause him or her to make a mistake."

Whittaker nodded. That was a tried and true reason for leaking information to the media.

"We want the public to know we're not looking at your father. He's had enough false accusations for one cop, in my opinion."

"Thanks." Whittaker was pleased and surprised at that information. "Does that mean you believe him?"

Wertz shrugged. "He has no way of proving it, obviously. But honestly, it's easier to believe Rick Whittaker was working for the Feds than it ever was to believe he was skimming drug money. No way a guy with your ethics came from someone willing to do that."

"Thank you again." Whittaker was overwhelmed enough to lean against the wall.

"Man, you don't want to do that," Garcia said.

"What? Oh, right." He walked over to the dispenser and squirted out some antibacterial lotion. "Don't want to touch anything in here. Why did you guys ask my father if he'd been on the take in the first place?"

Wertz slid another glance towards his partner. "Honestly? It was something Cassie said."

Whittaker sucked in a breath, ready to get mad.

Luckily, Wertz was quick to clear up his statement. "Not directly. I asked her if she thought that your father was guilty of the murders, and she answered that she thought he was completely innocent. The way she said it made me think she wasn't only talking about the murders. So I asked your father when it was his turn in the box."

Whittaker couldn't feel upset at Cassie for that. Knowing her, she thought she was being clever. And she was, but Wertz was smart enough to figure out her double meaning.

The blond man cleared his throat. "There's one final reason we put that info out, Whittaker. It looks like we have someone going around killing dirty cops. Now, it might be related to the D&D scandal, it might be related to that list that IID just released. Regardless, if there's someone killing dirty cops, we figured it was best if that person knew that Sergeant Whittaker wasn't dirty."

Whittaker took a deep breath. His father had brought up that possibility before. He was glad to see the detectives taking that into account. "I owe you guys."

"It's no problem," Wertz said.

"Yeah, no problem. Talking about problems, it looks like you've made up with your sexy, redheaded problem," Garcia said with a grin.

Whittaker snorted. "What makes you think that?"

"You weren't such a jerk when you came in," Garcia explained.

He shook his head. "Yeah, I suppose I've been a jerk for the past few days."

"Longer than that." Wertz grinned. "Actually, we're all waiting for the day you come in *real* happy."

Whittaker snorted again. "Me, too."

"We've got a pool going, actually. So if you could wait maybe two more weeks, I'd appreciate it." Garcia grunted when Wertz hit him across the chest. "You're just mad that you picked last week."

"Yeah." Wertz grinned. "I probably would have won if you hadn't called him up the night before his off day."

Whittaker shook his head. "Can we stop talking about my sex life and talk about the Anderson case instead, please?"

Garcia laughed one more time before sobering up. "We can't reveal everything, you know."

"I know. But I'm wondering what tack you're taking. I see you put together the possible connection to the IID list." He debated passing on Cassie's hint about the major, but he was certain the two detectives would find it as insane a concept as he did.

"We are. The timing is too perfect. I know both victims were part of the D&D scandal, but they were mentioned in the article, as well. Maybe somebody read the article and decided they needed killing." Wertz stuck his hands in his pockets and rocked on his heels.

"Which, of course, gives you a whole pool of suspects," Whittaker pointed out.

Garcia and Wertz nodded glumly.

"Have you...have you thought maybe it's another police officer?" He caught himself about to lean against the wall again and straightened just in time.

"Another police officer?" Wertz asked.

"God, I hope not." Garcia stroked his goatee. "But it would explain how the person had an extra key to Anderson's police car. We figured Anderson had two copies of the keys."

"Anderson was well known for taking that particular patrol car out," Wertz added. "He'd gotten in fights with others who tried to take it."

"Yet another thing he got away with," Garcia said disgustedly.

No one said anything for a moment. Finally, Wertz broke the silence. "It's an idea. We'll run it by Newmann and Dirruzo, too." He yawned.

Whittaker realized they were both exhausted. "Have you guys been on since the murder?"

"Pretty much," Wertz said. "I'm not sure Newmann or Dirruzo have gotten any rest either."

"Are they still trying to take the Anderson case from you?"

"Nah," Wertz said. "We're cooperating with them. Oh, you need to tell your girlfriend that's why I was such a hardass with her in interview. I was already worried they'd try and take Anderson's case away from us due to our connection to you and therefore your father. I didn't want them to say we were too soft with Cassie. So I took a real hard line with her. You let her know that's why, so she doesn't hate me."

"I'll let her know." He decided to tell the truth. "It was her idea, by the way, that it was another cop."

Garcia's eyebrows shot up, making a single hairy line on his forehead. "Really?"

"She'd even thought it was someone from IID, going after the cops they couldn't get formally."

Both men broke into laughter. Whittaker started to laugh with them, but it felt like he was betraying Cassie. He'd already had to grovel once with her; he didn't want to do it again.

"Oh, I love the idea of a vigilante IID officer, Whittaker. You tell Cassie that when you see her, and also why I was so hard in interview," Wertz said.

"I'll make sure to tell her."

Wertz pushed open the door, glancing back at him. "Make sure to tell Detective Cassie that we've taken her theory into account and will immediately pursue her suspect."

Wertz stopped in his tracks so suddenly Whittaker almost bumped into him. He quickly realized why Wertz had stopped. Major Bianchi and Officer Carter were waiting outside the door.

Bianchi raised an eyebrow. "I don't believe weapons are supposed to be worn in the interview area, gentleman."

"They're not, sir," Wertz began. "But there was no one—"

"That's not the rule, Detective," Bianchi stated. "However, I am not here to remind you of regulations, I am here for a status update on the Anderson case."

"Yes, sir."

Whittaker didn't envy them the upcoming briefing with Bianchi.

* * * * *

WHILE SHE ENJOYED DINNER at Gianni's Pizza, Cassie was cranky. "I still can't believe I didn't notice he only fired five times," she grumbled to herself as she threw away their trash.

Mark held the glass door for her, and they were immediately assaulted by the humid darkness. She took one step off the curb. "Thank you for—"

The car roared down the street, aiming right for her. She had a split second to comprehend what was happening before she was yanked backwards and onto the sidewalk. Or rather, Mark landed on the sidewalk, she landed on top of him.

The front tires of the car came up on the curb and almost grazed their feet. Then the driver peeled away, tires squealing as he headed for the highway. The squealing brakes, heavy thunks, and sounds of crushing metal told her the maniac had taken off in complete disregard for the traffic. "Did you get the license plate number?" she asked when she got her breath back.

"It didn't have any plates," Mark said tersely. He sat up, his arm still wrapped around her shoulders. "Are you okay?"

"Thanks to you, I am." She stood up and gingerly wiped dirt off her pants. At least for this dive onto concrete, she was wearing jeans and not biking shorts. "I guess we're even. I saved your life once, now you've saved mine."

"Good. I hate owing favors." He stared out to the road at the carnage left behind. "What the hell was that?"

"I don't know. An idiot driver? I didn't get a good look, did you?"

"No." Mark shook his head. "That wasn't an idiot driver, Cassie. He was aiming for you. Any idea why?"

"Maybe he likes running people over." Her stomach clenched as the words sank in. "Oh, shit. He likes running people over. Like Officer Anderson."

"You think O'Reilly and Anderson's murderer is going after you?"

"I don't know. I don't see why, I'm not a dirty cop." She headed toward her car after carefully looking both ways.

"No, but it sounds like you're trying to catch one if you're right and the killer is a cop." He walked her to her car. "Are you sure you're okay?"

"Yes."

"Then why are you limping?" He stared down at her. With that piercing glare, she was certain he'd been an effective Marine drill instructor.

"Oh, I reinjured the leg I messed up after falling off my bicycle." Her stomach spasmed again. "A car tried to run me over then, too. Oh no, he *is* after me."

"When was this?" Mark demanded.

"Yesterday. I thought it was a careless driver. But now I don't know." She pondered for a moment and decided to lighten the mood. "Although I might also be limping because I'm sore from the Aikido classes."

He raised both eyebrows and looked impressed. "Aikido, huh? Is that because you're concerned someone is after you?"

"No, it's for…personal reasons." She put her key in the car door. Before she could turn it, Mark clamped his hand around her wrist.

"You aren't going anywhere alone right now, young lady. You need to call Detective Whittaker and let him know what's going on."

Pulling out her phone, she checked the time. "He's supposed to meet me later tonight."

"Then I'll follow you home and we'll wait until he comes over. I'm not leaving you alone, Cassie. I almost think I should drive you, but unless this guy is an idiot, he won't try anything in traffic." He didn't let go of her wrist until she nodded.

* * * * *

CASSIE HAD BEEN TENSE the entire way home, hands gripped on the steering wheel. Mark's presence in the car behind her had been reassuring, but she didn't relax until she pulled up to her curb. As she waited for Mark to join her, she felt arms wrapping around her shoulders.

She leaned forward to prevent the attacker from getting a grip around her body. Then she reached between her legs, grabbed his calf, and broke his balance. The person fell to the ground with a loud *oof.*

Before she could make her next move, she recognized both the *oof* and the leg. She spun around. "James! Oh my God. Are you okay?" She kneeled next to him. "I'm sorry."

He stared at her in surprise as he sat up. "I'm fine. But remind me not to try and surprise you again. What the hell was that? That wasn't RAD training."

"No." Mark stood over them, his hands in his pockets. "That was Aikido. Well, something that vaguely resembles it."

Cassie scowled up at him. "And where the hell was my backup, Mark? Couldn't you have told me that it was James?"

Mark shrugged. "You figured it out soon enough."

"I'm just glad I didn't go for a groin shot or head butt."

Whittaker grimaced at that idea. "Me, too. Since when are you taking Aikido?"

She stood and reached down to give him a hand up. "I'm sorry, I can't talk to you about that yet. You told me I couldn't talk to you until I got a black belt."

He flinched at that statement. "Why do you need backup? What are you doing here, Mark?"

She exchanged a glance with the older man.

He shook his head. "I'll let Cassie explain that one. I trust she'll be in good hands with you, Detective Whittaker, so I'm heading home. Have a good night." He pivoted and marched back to his car.

"What happened, Cassie?" Whittaker demanded as he followed her into the house.

"Let's just say you're not the only one who had a hard meeting with the sidewalk tonight," she admitted as she leaned down to pet Donner.

"Again, what happened?"

She told him about the near accident by the shooting range and the biking accident the day before.

"Remind me to thank Mark later. Damn it, Cassie. I wish you would have told me about all of this earlier."

She folded her arms, ready to get angry at him, but realized he looked more worried than upset. "I didn't think until this evening that it was deliberate. Yesterday, I figured it was an idiot driver."

Whittaker threaded his hands through his hair before dropping his arms to his sides. "Understood." He glanced around her house. "Number one, I'm staying with you until this killer is caught. Any problems with that?"

"Of course not."

"Number two, I really don't like your house—"

"Hey!"

"No." He reached out and rubbed her shoulder. "That's not what I meant. I love your house; you've done a great job with it. But it's too accessible. Too many entrances. And your back door leads to a yard and then a secluded alley, right?"

"Yard" might have been an exaggeration considering the miniscule back area, but she nodded.

"Way too accessible," he said. "How about if you stay with me?"

She looked at the cat, who was rubbing against her leg. "I'm not leaving Donner. I don't want him hurt if someone breaks in here to harm me."

"No problem on my part, as long as you can provide kitty litter and other cat stuff. My house isn't feline-ready."

She retrieved a box of litter and a spare litter pan from the coat closet. "That's easy. Can you get his automatic feeder and his food? It's under the counter. I'll go up and pack."

"Why don't I go with you?" He followed her upstairs.

She said a quick prayer of thanks that she'd made her bed that morning. Well, that afternoon.

"How much stuff should I bring?"

"Meaning how many days worth?" Whittaker shrugged. "I wish I could tell you that we'll catch the killer in 'x' number of days. But I don't know, really. Why don't you pack for three days and if it's longer than that, we'll come back."

She went to get the suitcase from the guest room closet. She scowled at it; she'd hoped to be done traveling after coming back from her book tours. At least staying with Whittaker should be more pleasant. She shivered, wondering how pleasant it would be.

It felt awkward to pack clothes and personal items while he watched. She was especially uncomfortable when she got out the bras and underwear, although she still chose her sexiest ones. She also made a note to buy some sexy sleepwear. She usually slept in boxer shorts and tees, but she now that she was in a relationship, she should upgrade.

Whittaker made an impatient noise. She grabbed up the bag that was already packed with travel-sized toiletry items rather than heading to the bathroom. She threw the toiletry bag on top of her clothes. There was barely enough time to zip it before he grabbed it off the bed.

"Why don't you take the suitcase to the car and come back in," she suggested. "Our next move will require two people."

When he came back, she was already in position. "Okay, now you can get the cat carrier out of the closet."

Donner took one look at the carrier and tried to bolt up the stairs, where she was waiting. She snagged the cat, unhooked his claws from her shirt, and after several tries, stuffed him into the carrier.

Whittaker followed her as she drove across town. She really wished she'd thought to bring ear plugs. Donner hated traveling. His yowls echoed through the car the entire way.

chapter 19

CASSIE BLINKED AWAKE, CONFUSED to be in an unfamiliar room.

"Oh, right, I'm in James' room. In his bed," she said to the cat who was sitting on her chest. "Too bad he isn't."

She scratched Donner behind his ears. "But I'm glad to see you this morning." Last night, the poor kitty had hidden under Whittaker's leather couch when she'd released him from the cat carrier. He must have ventured out some time after she and Whittaker had gone to bed. Or, rather, beds.

He'd chosen to stay in the guest room. As in her house, the guest room was at the top of the stairs and therefore the most accessible if someone broke in.

She pushed the cat off her chest. Turning on her side, she stroked the empty expanse of cotton next to her. He'd been tempted last night, that much had been obvious. She also knew that he was more worried about protecting her than…seducing her. Not that it would take much seduction.

She wouldn't mind at all if their relationship progressed while she was staying at his house. She'd forgiven him for jumping to conclusions. Any residual anger had evaporated when she managed to drop his assuming butt on the sidewalk. "Black belt? I don't need no stinkin' black belt." She went into the upstairs bathroom, brushed her teeth, and washed her face.

She checked her smartphone for the weather forecast and sighed at the prediction of hot and humid. After changing into blue capris and a sleeveless white shirt, she shoved her hair into a ponytail. She could hear Whittaker rattling about in the kitchen.

The enticing scent of coffee reached her when she was halfway down the stairs. She took a deep breath and appreciated the aroma. Normally, she preferred tea, but today was going to be a coffee day.

"Good morning, honey." He leaned in and kissed her. "I have coffee, or do you want tea?"

"Coffee sounds perfect." She let him get the coffee cup for her. While she'd been in his place before, she didn't know where everything was yet and didn't feel comfortable rummaging about his cabinets. She couldn't wait for an opportunity to explore the ultra modern layout to her heart's content.

"Have you eaten breakfast?" she asked.

He lifted up his cup of coffee, saluting her with it. "Right here."

She shook her head. "That's not breakfast. How about if I cook?"

"Um, sure. If you can find anything."

"So I can look around?"

"Feel free. You're staying here now. You can do whatever you want."

She opened the refrigerator door to hide her wicked grin. What she wanted to do could wait until after breakfast. If there was breakfast to be had. "Okay, you weren't kidding."

The interior of the stainless steel fridge was spotless—and empty. There was a bottle of ketchup, one jar of mayonnaise, and three beers. For the hell of it, she opened the freezer.

"A bottle of vodka," she said and rolled her eyes. "Do you have a pantry?"

He pointed towards a tall cabinet. Opening it, she stared inside at her dream pantry: each shelf was on rollers and could be pulled out for easy access to all of the items within the space. Since there was only a single box of strawberry Pop-Tarts, she decided the designer details were wasted on Whittaker.

Shaking her head, she took out two packages of pastries. "Where's your toaster?"

"I don't have one. Pop-Tarts are fine as is."

"You're such a bachelor. If you're off today, we should go grocery shopping."

It was his turn to roll his eyes as he ripped open the foil packaging. "I hate grocery shopping. I don't cook anyway."

"I do, James. So we'll go shopping after 'breakfast'." She used her fingers to make quote marks in the air.

"Do we have to?"

"Yes. I'll cook for you, you'll like it." She put the box back in the pantry and realized she'd been wrong. There was one more thing in there. "Why do you have dog treats?"

He grinned. "Long story." He closed his eyes when his cell phone started ringing. "But it'll unfortunately have to wait. What's up, Freeman?"

She nibbled her Pop-Tart while she listened to his part of the conversation.

"No. You're kidding. Really?" He shoved in the rest of the pastry while he listened to Freeman. "Hell, yeah, I want in."

He closed the phone. "That was Freeman."

"I gathered that. I'm clever that way. Even managed to figure out you need to go. What's up?"

"Freeman got some intel on the Williams case. The case had gone cold, hell, months ago. But it was our cover for why we were canvassing O'Reilly's neighborhood. Amazingly enough, it actually led to a possible lead. I'd rather have gotten a lead on the O'Reilly murder, but I'll take what I can."

She followed him upstairs and toward his bedroom. He paused at the threshold. "Sorry, I have to change."

"That's okay...I could help."

"Not this time, unfortunately. Then I'd never get to the scene." After one intense look, he closed the door behind him.

"Well, I guess I wouldn't want you to start something you couldn't finish anyway," she muttered under her breath. She leaned against the wall opposite the door. "So, you're not going to, like, expect me to stay stuck in here while you go out and get the bad guy, are you?"

"If I said yes, would you listen?"

"I don't want to be held hostage by this jerk, James."

He came out, knotting a turquoise tie that complemented his dark suit. "He's not only a jerk, Cassie. He's a killer. One who has killed twice—"

"At the minimum. I still say he's killed before, in Chicago. I don't see why you don't believe me that it's Bianchi."

Whittaker sighed. "Whoever he is, he's killed at least twice and tried for you twice. So while I understand you don't want to go into hiding, I think it might be safer if you stayed here." He kissed her on the forehead and headed downstairs.

"But all his actions have been at night. O'Reilly, Anderson, the bike incident, and the attempt yesterday were in the evening. Shouldn't I be safe during the day? After all, he's probably at work." At IID, she thought to herself.

He looked up from tying his shoes. "Is there some place you need to go?"

"Aikido class for one."

"I didn't see you pack a uniform."

"They didn't have one in my size. They're letting me wear gym clothes while it's on order. I have a clean set of clothes and tennis shoes in a bag in my car."

"Fine. Just be careful. I'll call you when I'm free. Keep an eye out to see if you're being followed."

She kept watch to and from Aikido but didn't notice any obvious tail. To be certain, she drove around Canton for a while before returning to Whittaker's home.

Showering at his house felt odd. It was titillating to be naked in the same place he always got naked.

After changing back into her original outfit, she gave in to temptation and wandered into his guest room. It was painfully neat, from the bed with its hospital corners to the organized desk. Too neat. It didn't look like he used anything in the room, although she knew he did.

The only things that marred all that order were the cat curled up on the bed and two file folders on the desk chair. She raised her brows at the names on the tabs.

"The O'Reilly and D&D cases," she said to Donner. "How'd he get these files?"

She stared at the folders, fighting the temptation to open them.

* * * * *

"I DON'T LIKE LEAVING Cassie alone for long," Whittaker said.

"I don't blame you," Freeman said as he flipped on a turn signal. "Although I still don't know if those events you told me were really attempts on her life."

"I'd rather err on the side of caution. So, did you really get a lead on the Williams case?"

"I did, believe it or not. Evidently someone must have seen us in the neighborhood and called in an anonymous tip."

"That's shocking for that neighborhood; they don't usually bother."

"Agreed. At a guess, I'm wondering if the caller had been tempted to say something before, saw that we were back asking questions, and that changed her mind."

Whittaker shrugged. He scanned the run-down vehicles and homes of the squalid neighborhoods they were entering. He wished they had enough manpower to re-canvass the area months after murders took place, but there were other cases to pursue.

Baltimore had an entire squad of cold-case detectives, and occasionally they were able to find new leads or evidence and close older cases. They should have notified the cold-case squad, but since Freeman had caught the lead and used it to get a warrant, it would be his collar.

Freeman double parked next to a rusted Pontiac Bonneville with a cracked, tinted windshield.

"Congrats on being right," Whittaker said as pulled out his gun, performed a quick chamber check, and slid it back in the holster. "You called it months ago as the brother of the vic's girlfriend. Good job on convincing Judge Thomas on the warrant."

"The source was very specific on location and gave info on another murder in that area that had used the same firearm. I checked with the lab, they'd never gotten around to telling us there'd been a match. You ready?"

"Always."

* * * * *

THE SOURCE HAD BEEN spot on with the information. Freeman found the correct caliber firearm—ballistics would have to confirm it was the same weapon—exactly where the anonymous caller had stated.

Or perhaps not so anonymous. Whittaker noticed the suspect's sister, who held a crying toddler, looked both devastated and satisfied as they led her brother away in handcuffs.

That must have made a hard choice for her. He nodded at her in thanks. She ducked her head into her child's neck and began to weep.

With a satisfied look on his face, Freeman stuffed the protesting youth into the back of the patrol car. "That feels like a job well done. And you can get back to your woman after we're done with booking. We haven't been gone too long, she should be safe. Although I'm still not sure the two incidents weren't a coincidence."

Whittaker was about to disagree when the phone in his pocket started vibrating. "Excuse me a minute." He stepped away from Freeman. "Hi, Cassie. All done with your class?"

"I am, and as always, I'm sore."

"If you've been taking it every day, no wonder. You know you're supposed to take a day off, right?"

"Yeah, but I was trying to learn it as quickly as possible."

He was going to live to regret his statement. "Yeah, since you wanted to shove it back in my face. Again, I'm sorry."

"Your apology was already accepted. Anyway, two things. Number one, I was thinking of going to Fell's Point."

He was instantly suspicious. "Why?"

"Honestly, because I want to ask some questions about O'Reilly."

"Cassandra. What part of staying safe don't you understand?"

A snort came from Freeman's direction. He turned around and indicated one more minute.

"I'll be in public, it's during the day, and I'll be careful," she protested.

He turned around and headed back the car. "Jesus, Cassie. Fine, okay, just be freaking careful."

"Good. And may I use your printer?"

"No problem. Like I said, you can do whatever you want with what's in the house." *Including me*, he thought before hanging up.

* * * * *

CASSIE FELT OFFICIAL AS she printed out pictures of O'Reilly, Anderson, some of the other police officers from the D&D scandal, and the major. Then she printed out images of people who looked like them for a photo line-up. According to her research, she was supposed to have no fewer than six photos of different people for each person.

She enjoyed choosing images from different sites. Several of the lookalikes were minor actors, which amused her. She barely resisted printing out a picture of Billy Dee Williams for Officer Anderson. Of course, Anderson didn't *look* anything like Billy Dee Williams, but he sure sounded like him. "That might skew the results a little."

She didn't think anyone followed her on the way to Fells Point. Wandering around the area, she reminded herself several times why she was there. It was too easy to get sidetracked into shopping in the eclectic antique stores and other businesses.

She showed the pictures to the shop owners, taking the opportunity to imagine herself as a real detective. Several people recognized O'Reilly, but unfortunately no one pointed at Major Bianchi and declared him the killer.

Not that anyone she asked had a high opinion of Officer O'Reilly. "Oh, him," said the owner of Maggie Moo's Ice

Cream. "He's always coming in here after shift and trying to get free ice cream. Then he heads out to get drunk. I believe he's a regular...well, was a regular, at the Black Raven Pub."

Cassie made her way down the street to the Black Raven Pub, continuing to make her inquiries. A few more recognized O'Reilly and pointed her towards the pub.

She was standing right outside the door when Whittaker called. "Hello, James."

"Hi, honey. You okay?"

"I'm *fine*, James. I told you it was safe during the day."

"Well, it's getting late, so can I meet you? Where are you?"

She stared at the sign for the Black Raven Pub and decided to go for the more generic answer. "Thames Street." She pronounced it the Baltimore way with a soft "th".

She heard him sigh.

"You're still investigating then?"

"Last stop. Do you want to get dinner at Slainte Pub?"

He agreed to meet her in fifteen minutes. She took a deep breath and stepped inside the pub. Hopefully, someone here would be able to tell her who killed O'Reilly.

She rehearsed what she was going to say to the bartender. She already knew, from other's statements, that O'Reilly had been a regular here.

Should she start with the set of pictures that included O'Reilly and his look-a-likes? Presumably, the bartender would know O'Reilly. But would that make him more or less interested in helping?

She decided to toss away the mental script and play it by ear. She approached the tall man behind the taps. His glossy skin was as dark as the wooden counter and he was almost as wide as the glass front refrigerator behind him.

Suddenly nervous, she tried a smile. "May I have a ginger ale?" She'd already learned it was much easier to get information as a paying customer than as a nosy outsider. Maybe if she had a badge she wouldn't have to buy anything, but this technique worked for her. So far, it had netted her not only information, but also a tasty sandwich and ice cream cone, three used books, a birthday present for her father, and an antique vase for her dining room.

She spent the first ten minutes chit-chatting and getting to know Jackson, the muscular bartender. She learned about his failed attempt to make the Baltimore Ravens, compared stories on pets, and discovered the house specialty was her new favorite mixed drink.

Finally, she brought up her real reason for being here. She pulled out the printouts from her bag and smiled at her new friend. "Jackson, can I ask you an odd question or two?"

"I often get odd questions, Cassie. Fire away."

She opted to go straight for O'Reilly and spread the six pictures on the counter. "Do you recognize any of these men?"

He stopped polishing the glassware and spent some time reviewing the pictures. Cassie had once read that no one knew faces like police and bartenders. She hoped that would be true here.

She saw his reaction when he reached Officer O'Reilly's picture. He raised an eyebrow at her. "So what are you, a private investigator or something? You ain't a cop."

"No, I'm not a cop. Not a private investigator either. I'm more a something." She gave him what she hoped was a charming smile.

He snorted and jabbed a beefy finger at the fifth picture. "Well, this is Mike O'Reilly, but you know that already. He's a cop, but you knew that as well, right?"

She nodded.

"I've told three sets of cops now all I know about O'Reilly. Why should I tell you?"

She almost missed his question as it registered that he'd said there were three sets of cops. Whittaker and Freeman must have been here, too. She wondered if they'd gotten any good information.

"Cassie?" Jackson interrupted her thoughts.

"Oh, sorry. Why should you tell me? I guess because whatever you say can't hurt Officer O'Reilly...and it could help some people that are close to me."

He twirled the picture as he stared at her. "I suppose you're right; it can't hurt Mike. So what do you want to know?"

"Well, I've been told that he came here often, is that true?"

"Definitely. He came here all the time." He glanced around the empty pub. "Too often, really. I try not to judge my customers, but I think O'Reilly had a problem with alcohol."

That gave her a boost. Mark had theorized that if O'Reilly had been drinking too much, that might have been why he turned his sidearm over to someone else.

"How about the night he was killed?"

"Yeah, he'd been here. And had drunk too much, as usual. Had been in a bad mood that night, and got as angry as an intercepted quarterback when I had to cut him off that night."

"You cut him off?"

"It's the rules. If a customer has too much to drink, we stop serving them alcohol. O'Reilly didn't like it, though, started to pick a fight with me, and thought better of it."

Cassie could understand that. She doubted many people decided to fight with Jackson. "Did anyone stop him that night? Or approach him?"

The big man shook his head. "No. He left alone."

239

"Have you ever seen him with any of these men?" she asked, putting the images of Anderson and similar looking men on the bar.

He carefully looked through them and stopped on the one of Anderson. "This is the other officer that was killed, right?"

"Yes."

"I've never seen him. But…" He held up one of the pictures. "I think I saw this guy on this movie I was watching last night."

Cassie tried not to show any reaction, but she could feel her cheeks heating up. Perhaps she shouldn't have used minor actors for the images. "Oh, well, never mind, then. How about any of these?"

Next, just to be thorough, she pulled out pictures of Leslie Harding and her doppelgangers. The image of Leslie was nine years old, from the time of the scandal, but the older woman still looked the same. *She must be fighting against aging with every weapon she has.*

Cassie waited for Jackson to flip through those, planning to show him the ones of Major Bianchi next. Nerves flitted through her stomach as she wondered if Jackson would be able to identify the major and prove her theory correct.

"I know her."

Her head whipped up. "Who?" She wondered if he'd identified another actor.

"Her. The blonde." His finger rested on top of the printout of Leslie Harding. "She started coming here the past couple of weeks. Occasionally stopped and talked to O'Reilly. There never seemed to be any friction between them, so I didn't even mention it to the police. Let me see the next batch of photos."

"Really? Leslie was here?" She passed him the printouts as she realized Leslie could be, *should* be a suspect. The ex-cop had as good a motive as anyone. Her life had been ruined by the D&D scandal, while O'Reilly and Anderson had skated by. Could it have been—

"This guy," he said, pointing at a picture. "I've seen him here a few times. O'Reilly always got annoyed whenever he noticed him."

Cassie's heart stopped when she realized Jackson had paused on the picture of the major. It was a still shot from one of his press conferences. She was right, after all.

"Was he here the same night O'Reilly was killed?"

"Not inside. But I think I saw him once when the door was opened."

"Really? That's..." she squelched her excitement and tried for professional. "That's interesting. But you definitely have seen this man here?" She pointed at Bianchi.

"No."

"But you said—"

"Not him," Jackson said and moved her hand off the photo. "Him." He pointed again.

She looked back down at the picture and saw he was pointing at the man standing behind Bianchi.

Officer Carter.

chapter 20

Cassie was still reeling when she stepped outside the pub. Could Officer Carter really be the killer? She was so certain it had been Major Bianchi. Perhaps it still was. Maybe Bianchi was giving the orders.

Why would Carter kill anyone in Chicago, after all?

Her phone rang while she made her way to her rendezvous with Whittaker. She didn't recognize the number, but answered anyway.

"Cassie? It's Bryan."

"Oh, hi." She shook off her thoughts and tried to concentrate on her fellow author. "What's up?"

"I just wanted to tell you about a brainstorm I had about your work in progress after reading the chapters you sent me."

Cassie struggled to think about fictional murders. She sat down on a bench. "Oh, what is it?"

"I hope you don't mind suggestions, I know some authors do. But I was thinking how Elaine's murder really dragged down the story and affected Marty's personality."

"Yeah, I know." She sighed. "It also makes it really hard to include any humor. It feels inappropriate. And parts of it are too close to something I actually lived through."

"Oh, I'm sorry." He honestly sounded sympathetic. "So—Here's what I was thinking. Perhaps instead of Elaine being killed, maybe it could be that other professor. I know you wanted him as a suspect, but I think he'd make a better victim. Then Elaine can be a suspect instead, which would still give Marty a reason to investigate."

She considered. "That's a good solution, and it lets Elaine live. Hey, maybe he was having an affair with the killer."

"Good idea. That way you're killing off a letch and an adulterer, rather than killing off Elaine. I'm sorry to cause you so much work when you've only been nice to me. I called your friend Michelle. We're going out to dinner on Friday."

She smiled and stood up again. "That's great."

"So I wanted to use my inside contact and ask about her favorite flowers."

Cassie was touched that he was asking. "Believe it or not, it's carnations. Any color."

"Really? That's easy enough. Anyway, is everything okay? You sound distracted."

She figured Bryan must be an ace lawyer if he could pick that up on a phone call. "I am. You know we were talking about Major Bianchi before, right?"

"Right. You had asked about my experiences with him in Chicago."

"Yes. Have you met his driver here?"

"Officer Carter? I haven't seen him in Baltimore, no. But I saw him a few times in Chicago."

Cassie almost dropped the phone. "He was in Chicago?"

"Yeah. Bianchi brought him with him when he moved to Baltimore. Why?"

She looked up to see Whittaker closing the distance between them with long, angry strides. "Oh, nothing. Never mind. Talk to you later."

"Were you at the Black Raven Pub?" Whittaker asked in lieu of a greeting.

"I was. Why?"

"How'd you know that's where O'Reilly was last seen, Cassie? Did you—" He stopped abruptly, and Cassie watched him rein in his temper. "Wait. I'm not going to assume this time. I will ask. Cassie, did you look at the files I had at the house?"

She was proud of him for asking this time. It made her feel much better that she, in fact, *hadn't* looked at the files. "I did not."

He blinked. "Really? But you saw them?"

"I did. And I can't say I wasn't tempted. I was. But I didn't want you to get into trouble if I read information I shouldn't have."

His tense anger gave way to a smile. He kissed her. "I'm impressed by your willpower."

"You should be. It was difficult."

"So how'd you figure out the Black Raven?"

"I showed his picture around here and lots of people recognized him." She pulled out the photos from her briefcase.

Whittaker snorted as he took them. "You printed out a photo lineup? Now I'm even more impressed."

"You'll be even more impressed when I tell you I've identified the killer."

"I thought you knew it was Bianchi."

"Actually, it's Officer Carter," she said, sure he was going to dismiss her idea.

"What?" He furrowed his brow. "His driver? Why do you think that?"

She pointed at the incriminating picture. "This was the photo I showed Jackson to see if he could identify Bianchi. He didn't know—"

"Jackson? Jackson the bartender?" Whittaker interrupted.

She nodded. "He didn't recognize Bianchi, but he saw Carter in the background of this picture and said not only had Carter been at the Black Raven before, on the same nights as O'Reilly, but he saw Carter outside the bar on the night of the murder."

She was glad when he didn't dismiss her idea outright, so she pressed on. "O'Reilly was drunk that night."

"I know that, Cassie. That was in the files."

She took his hand and started toward the restaurant. "I didn't read the files, remember? But the point is he was drunk, and Jackson said he was incensed and belligerent—well, not in those words. So if Carter was waiting outside, he could have insisted that O'Reilly hand over his weapon since he was intoxicated."

To her satisfaction, Whittaker nodded at her statement. "So you think Carter did those murders in Chicago, too?"

She shook her hand free, put both hands on her hips, and turned to face him. "You knew he'd been Bianchi's driver that long? Why didn't you tell me?"

He pulled her toward the outside wall of the restaurant. "I didn't realize he was a suspect, Cassie. And I didn't believe Bianchi was one."

"So you believe me about Carter?"

He stared in the direction of the Black Raven Pub and flipped his phone open. "Enough to run it by Wertz and Garcia."

She kept silent while he relayed the news to the detectives. After a few moments, she rooted through her purse for her notebook. He was laying out the evidence in such a concise manner, she wanted to capture his words for future stories. Whittaker shook his head when he hung up and saw what she was doing.

"I better get some royalties if you use my words. Anyway, Wertz said they'd bring Carter in for questioning."

"So they agree that he's guilty?" When he just shook his head, she sighed. "Right, right. You don't go into interview with assumptions."

"Try not to, at least. But I have to admit, I can see Carter as a killer."

"Me, too. He's that type. You know, the one that the neighbors then say 'I can't believe it. He was so quiet'."

Whittaker grinned. "Don't forget 'He always kept to himself.' Me, I don't trust anyone like that. So, while we let the detectives do their job, shall we get some dinner?"

She stopped when she heard the chiming from a nearby church. It was soon echoed by her cell phone alarm. "Uh-oh. It's five o'clock."

"That's bad?" Whittaker asked, holding the door open for her.

"Not in itself. But, um, we need to go back to my house."

He released the door. "Why?"

She fought the flush rising to her cheeks. "I forgot something. Can we go before we get dinner?"

"Now? Why?"

"It's something I need to get." She bit her bottom lip. "And yes, now."

Whittaker shook his head, but headed to his car.

* * * * *

IT DIDN'T FEEL RIGHT, Whittaker thought as he parked outside of Cassie's house. "Do we really need to go inside? Can't you just wait for whatever it is you need?"

"No. I need it now."

He noticed she was blushing again. "Is it, like, some feminine item or something? Can't we go to some store and get it?" Not that *he* would actually go inside and get it.

"It's not that, James." She rolled her eyes. "And I can't just go into a store and get it."

"Because—"

Her blush spread to the tips of her ears. "I need my birth control pills."

He cleared his throat. "Okay, you need them. Why didn't you get them last night?"

"You were rushing me. And I usually have them in my purse, but I'd taken them out before I went shooting. What's the problem anyway? You don't want to go in?"

He frowned at her rowhouse. Again, something didn't feel right. "I don't. It's just a feeling."

She rested her head against the back of her seat. "You can go get them and I'll stay in the car, then. They're in the master bathroom."

"No. I don't want to leave you either." He considered his options. He'd have to keep her with him as he checked out the house, but it was definitely not ideal to clear a house with only one armed person. He could call Wertz or another officer, but he didn't have any hard proof that Cassie was in danger. Even Freeman hadn't been completely convinced.

"Can you call Freeman?" Cassie asked, apparently reading his mind.

"I could, but I know he's at his daughter's flute recital. I'm not sure I want to interrupt that for a bad feeling." He made a decision. "Okay, here's what we're going to do. We're going inside. You're staying behind me the entire time, understood?" He waited until she nodded. "Your basement door has a lock on it, right?"

"Yes, although I never knew why."

"We'll go in the first floor, make certain that no one is on the first floor and lock the basement door, in case there's someone down there. Then we go upstairs, again, stay behind me."

She looked nervous, but nodded before getting out.

He took her keys and unlocked the door. He removed his gun from his holster before entering the house, making certain that his body blocked Cassie's.

"Nothing looks out of place," she whispered.

Still, he carefully cleared the first floor, arms raised in a double grip on his pistol. He checked the coat closet and the small bathroom located beneath the stairs. In the kitchen, he quickly slid the lock into place to close off the basement. The back entrance didn't look like it had been tampered with, nor had the front door. That gave him some relief, but he didn't let down his guard.

They crept up the stairs. Cassie was doing a very good job of sticking close behind him. Straight up the stairs was the bedroom she used as an office, so he planned on clearing that room first. The guest bathroom was next door. He was glad she usually kept the kitty litter in that room, since it meant the door would be open. Down the hall was her master bedroom, which he'd need to clear before they finally reached the master bathroom and their main objective.

Once up the stairs, he started to step into the guest room, and quickly realized his error. Carter was a police officer and knew their procedures.

He felt the yank on his arms, then nothing.

* * * * *

CASSIE SCREAMED.

Carter took Whittaker's dropped gun and stepped over his prone body. He tucked the gun he'd used to hit Whittaker into the small of his back and pointed Whittaker's gun at her. She stared at his fingers over the trigger, distracted by the unnaturally smooth, pale skin of his hands. Oh. He was wearing latex gloves. She noted he also had a watch cap on his head.

"Hands up." He gestured with the gun for her to back away.

She followed his orders, wishing desperately that she'd learned how to disarm an assailant.

What would Marty do? Her main character would stall by talking to the bad guy until help arrived. Of course, considering that the only person who knew where they were was unconscious on the floor, perhaps stalling wouldn't help. Still, it was worth a shot.

"Why are you doing this, Carter? I get why you killed O'Reilly and Anderson." And all the others in Chicago, she thought, but didn't say. "But we're not dirty cops."

"No, but I have to protect myself, too," he said in a quiet, low voice.

Cassie realized this was the first time she'd heard him speak. "By killing innocent people?"

"I'll regret it, but yes. I don't want to stop my mission. Dirty cops have gotten too brash, too bold. They know we can't get rid of them legally, so I found another way."

"Two wrongs don't make a right, Officer Carter." She scanned the hallway for something she could use as a weapon.

"Maybe not, Ms. Ellis. But I'm getting rid of police officers that have no right to their badge."

"But Whittaker's a good cop. And I'm a civilian; I'm not a cop." If Whittaker had been conscious, she knew he'd have been happy to hear her admit the latter.

"No, but you've gotten too close. I heard you talking at O'Reilly's funeral when you said you knew who the killer was. So I started following you and saw you having dinner with Bryan Tilman. That's when I realized you were on to me. I knew him from Chicago."

Cassie decided not to mention that it was coincidental she was having dinner with Bryan. "So that's when you tried to run me over."

He nodded and glanced behind to make certain that Whittaker was still unconscious. "I tried to kill you then, and last night, too. Didn't succeed then, but will now. Everyone in the department knows that you and Detective Whittaker had a fight. So you'll argue, he'll kill you with his service weapon, and sadly take his own life afterward."

"Do you really think people will believe that? There's already been so many policeman killed; they won't think it's just a coincidence."

He inclined his head in acknowledgement. "I'll have to stop my mission for a while. I don't usually remove another dirty cop so soon after the first, but I heard Anderson squeaking at me and the Major, calling us rats. I hate it when people disrespect Internal Investigations," he said through gritted teeth.

"I can understand that, Officer Carter." She made sure to use his rank. "I definitely respect all police officers, including IID. And like you, I hate dirty cops."

He shook his head. "You're trying to suggest working together? I don't think so. You're trying to delay me now."

She noticed a movement behind him. "Actually, I'm trying to distract you."

"Distract me from—"

Whittaker came diving out of the guest room and tackled Carter.

Cassie screamed as the two men tumbled down the stairs.

"Oh, my God!" She raced down, praying that Whittaker would be okay. She took a few precious seconds to pick up the pistols from the stair risers.

Both men were sprawled on the floor. Carter appeared unconscious, so she stepped over him to Whittaker.

"James!" She knelt next to him and tried to waken him without moving him. If he was injured, she didn't want to worsen it.

He groaned. When he started to sit up, she held him down. "Don't move."

"Carter?"

"He's unconscious. Or dead, I'm not sure."

"Take my cuffs." Whittaker gestured gingerly toward his back.

She managed to slip them from under his body, then scooted over to Carter. She checked for a pulse and wasn't certain if she was relieved or disappointed that she found one. After confirming he was alive, she handcuffed his arms in front of him so that she didn't have to roll him over.

"Damn it, James. I said don't move," she cried out when she glanced back and saw him sitting up.

"I'm not paralyzed," he said with a grimace. "I think I broke some ribs in the fall, but not my spine." He reached toward his suit pocket and winced. "And maybe my elbow. Why don't you call 9-1-1?"

epilogue

CASSIE FELT A SENSE of déjà vu as everyone gathered around a hospital bed. At least this time, it was Whittaker's turn to be laid up.

Her father was there again, but this time they were joined by Rick, Patti, and Chloe. This was an interesting way to have her father meet Whittaker's family.

She was glad to see that Rick and Patti weren't too awkward around each other. If she were writing the ending to their story, Whittaker's parents would get back together. Unfortunately, this was the real world and that probably wouldn't happen.

She wasn't the only one happy to see them getting along. Chloe kept glancing over at her parents and smiling, although most of her time was spent fussing over her brother.

Stop it, Whittaker signed to his sister. *I'm fine.*

He wasn't quite fine, Cassie thought. Three broken ribs and a broken elbow. Luckily, that was all. His body had taken the brunt of the damage in the fall, since Carter hadn't broken anything.

Once Carter regained consciousness and was checked out at the emergency room, he'd been arrested and charged with murder. He was currently under medical guard a few doors over.

She smiled when Whittaker swatted at his sister with his good arm. She suspected he was going to be a horrible patient as he recuperated from his injuries.

"Lying down on the job again, Whittaker?" Freeman stepped into the room, carrying a gift bag.

She couldn't wait to hear what he had to say. He probably had all the details about Carter's arrest.

"Okay, now that I see you're not dying, shall I tell you what I've heard?" Freeman glanced over at Chloe and put his hand over his mouth. "Or is that not appropriate in mixed company?"

Is he talking about me? Chloe signed. *I want to know it, too.*

Cassie said the same to Freeman. Whittaker's sister was a good lip reader, but Cassie still interpreted Freeman's news to make sure she understood completely.

"The good news is that Carter has confessed to all the killings, including the ones in Chicago," Freeman explained. "He already knew Cassie could testify to O'Reilly's and Anderson's murders, and he decided to admit it all. I think he considers himself a hero for taking care of dirty cops."

Whittaker shook his head at that statement. When he hissed through his teeth, Chloe came over and fluffed his pillows.

"What would make someone start on this path?" Whittaker's mother asked from the other side of the bed.

Freeman took a deep breath. "Evidently it was because of something that happened when he and Major Bianchi left

Chicago. There was a going-away party for Bianchi. The same cops they'd been pursuing for violations of policy, the same ones they'd been trying to get kicked out of the department, came up to Major Bianchi, shook his hand, and declared how sad they were that Bianchi was leaving town. That pissed off Carter, and to add insult to injury, those same officers gave him the cold shoulder completely."

"So he went back to Chicago and killed them?" Rick asked.

"Yes." Freeman helped himself to some of Whittaker's water on the hospital tray. "He said he did it carefully, spacing out the deaths."

Cassie nodded. "He mentioned to me that he usually waited longer between homicides, but he moved up the murder when Anderson squeaked at him at O'Reilly's funeral. Oh, talking about that, what did Carter mean when he told me that I said that I'd known the killer? I never said that."

"I'm not sure," Freeman said with a shrug. "He said that again in interview, stating he heard you tell Anderson that you knew who the killer was."

Whittaker's head fell back on the pillow. "I know what happened. Anderson had asked you if you knew who the killer was. You then said 'I know' but stopped talking when Carter and Bianchi walked by. He must have thought that you were going to name the killer."

"What did you mean to say?"

Cassie turned to answer her father. "What I started to say was that I knew Rick Whittaker wasn't guilty."

Rick looked pleasantly surprised. "Thank you, Cassie."

"So he thought that meant I suspected him. He also said that seeing me with Bryan Tilman caused him to think I was after him," Cassie said.

"Yup," Freeman said. "It didn't help that Cassie discovered Anderson's body so quickly after his death. And evidently Wertz came out from talking to Whittaker and said that Detective Cassie had a suspect that they'd pursue right away."

"Shit," Whittaker said. Cassie didn't translate that.

You suspected Carter? Chloe signed to her.

Cassie hunched her shoulders as Whittaker grinned at her. "No, I suspected Major Bianchi."

"You did?" Freeman snorted. "That would have been rich. Oh, talking about IID, open your present, Whittaker."

Whittaker searched through the tissue paper and pulled out the present with a roll of his eyes. A stuffed rat. "Real cute, Freeman."

"Anyway, the murders were all Carter's idea," Freeman continued after he stopped laughing. "He took care of the ones that he detested in Chicago, then decided to start here in Baltimore, thanks to his success there and thanks to the IID list that had been released. Bianchi didn't know anything about it. He came in while Carter was being interrogated, blustering that the detectives must have been mistaken. Even when he was told that Carter had confessed to the murders, he tried to deny it."

"This is going to look really bad for him," Rick said. "He'll probably resign in shame. Oh well, I lived through it. He'll survive."

Cassie felt uncomfortable as the room went quiet.

And just like Dad, it's not Bianchi's fault, Chloe signed, spelling out the major's name.

"I agree, Chloe," Patti said. "Hopefully Bianchi can be as strong as Rick was in handling all of this."

Rick's eyes sparkled as he turned to his ex-wife with an appreciative smile.

"Talking about strength," Freeman said. "How long before you're back to full-strength, Whittaker?"

"Over six weeks," he moaned. "They'll put me on desk duty somewhere. I hate desk duty. What the hell am I going to do for six weeks?"

"I know what I'll be doing," Cassie said. "I'll be rewriting *Merlot Murders.*" Then she jumped when her phone vibrated in her pocket. She took it out and read a text from Michelle. "You've got to be kidding. Michelle actually won?"

"Won what?" her father asked. "What, she won one of those contests she's always entering?"

"Yes!" She grinned at Whittaker. "I know what you can be doing for one of those weeks. How's a cruise sound to you?"

The End

About

Cathy Wiley, Author

CATHY WILEY IS HAPPIEST when plotting stories in her head or on the computer, or when she's delving into research.

She draws upon her experience in the hospitality business to show the lighter, quirkier side of people and upon her own morbid mind to show the darker side.

In her free time, she enjoys scuba diving, dancing, wine, food, and reading. She lives outside of Baltimore, Maryland, with two very spoiled cats.

Visit her website at www.cathywiley.com. She would greatly enjoy getting e-mail from her fans. She can be reached at cathy_wiley@zapstone.com

You can also visit her website at:

www.cathywiley.com
or follow her on Facebook and Twitter.

Zapstone Productions LLC

Publishers of unique, quality voices in fiction

A small independent publisher with offices in Minnesota and Maryland. Visit www.zapstone.com for more information, sneak previews, and upcoming titles.

More Cassandra Ellis...

Dead to Writes
Cassandra Ellis is a soon-to-be published author, days away from achieving her lifetime goal. But before she can celebrate, before she can even have her first book signing, she's brought in to Baltimore City Police Headquarters for questioning in connection to a real-life murder. She was the last person to see the victim alive, and her day planner was found next to the body. Cassie must use all the skills she developed as a mystery writer—plus the help of a hot homicide detective and a team of psychic parrots—to crack the case.

Two Wrongs Don't Make a Write
Author Cassie Ellis just wants to meet his father, even though her boyfriend, Detective James Whittaker, thinks it's a really bad idea. Cassie knows that Whittaker has avoided talking to, even seeing his father, ever since the elder Whittaker was discovered taking bribes and retired from the police force in shame. But now Whittaker's father is accused of murdering the individuals that had exposed his past crimes. Cassie must take action, not only to clear the already tarnished reputation of the father of the man she loves, but to mend the void between them.

Write of Passage
Author Cassie Ellis thought she'd enjoy a nice relaxing cruise with her friends and take a break from writing. Her boyfriend, Detective James Whittaker, was hoping for a little romance. But after Cassie finds a dead body on the balcony and it seems like everyone they meet on the ship had a motive to kill the victim, their cruise starts to feel more like *Murder on the Orient Express* than *The Love Boat*. (Release date TBA)

CPSIA information can be obtained at www.ICGtesting.com
Printed in the USA
LVOW050053180612

286535LV00001B/92/P